Jeanine Englert's love affair with mysteries and romance began with Nancy Drew and her grandmother's bookshelves of romance novels. When she isn't wrangling with her characters, she can be found trying to convince her husband to watch her latest Masterpiece/BBC show obsession. She loves to talk about writing, her beloved rescue pups, and mysteries and romance with readers. Visit her website at jeaninewrites.com.

Also by Jeanine Englert

The Highlander's Secret Son

Falling for a Stewart miniseries

Eloping with the Laird
The Lost Laird from Her Past
Conveniently Wed to the Laird

Secrets of Clan Cameron miniseries

A Laird without a Past
The Lady's Proposal for the Laird
A Laird to Protect Her

Discover more at millsandboon.co.uk.

CINDERELLA'S CHARADE WITH THE DUKE

Jeanine Englert

MILLS & BOON

First published in Great Britain 2025
by Mills & Boon, an imprint of HarperCollins*Publishers* Ltd,
1 London Bridge Street, London, SE1 9GF

www.harpercollins.co.uk

HarperCollins*Publishers*, Macken House, 39/40 Mayor Street Upper,
Dublin 1, D01 C9W8, Ireland

ISBN: 978-0-263-34539-1

10/25

FSC
www.fsc.org
MIX
Paper | Supporting responsible forestry
FSC™ C007454

This book contains FSC™ certified paper
and other controlled sources to ensure responsible forest management.

For more information visit www.harpercollins.co.uk/green.

Printed and Bound in the UK using 100% Renewable Electricity
at CPI Group (UK) Ltd, Croydon, CR0 4YY

To My G-400 Sisters.

Thank you for being my 'family' and home away from home when we were all college freshmen longer ago than I'd like to admit. It is such a gift to still have so many of you in my life. Even if we go years without seeing each other, we fall back into each other's lives easily like lost pieces of a puzzle.

Hattie's purple beaded friendship bracelet is a tribute and hug to all of you. I wouldn't have made it through those years without you.

Chapter One

April 1814—Blithe Manor, outside London, England

All William Sutherland, Duke of Wimberley, wanted was peace.

His daughter, Millie, shifted in his lap, having fallen asleep as he read her a story on the sofa in front of the burning fire, which kept the damp spring chill from the air. Her head shifted, her small warm hand sliding from his untied cravat to his waistcoat. Her fingers splayed instinctively over his heart. He couldn't help but smile and cover her hand with his own. *This*, the hours between dusk and when Millie was put to bed, was his favourite time of day, and truly the only time that mattered to him any more. It was just the two of them protected by the quiet of the setting sun. He ran a hand down her smooth dark curls and rubbed her back in small circles with his palm.

His gaze flicked up to the portrait of his late wife,

Cecily. The sorrow he should feel over her death never came. In truth, her passing was well…a relief. For the lovely, sweet woman he believed her to be when he made his vows and promises to her was not the woman she was. The only blessing in her early death from a carriage accident was that little Millie didn't have to see what her mother truly was: a woman who enjoyed wasting money and taking a flourish with any man who would have her, married or not.

She had died in the throes of a tryst with such a man in a carriage accident over a year ago. Evidently, the late Marchioness had enjoyed the confines of a carriage for her pleasures, as did the lord she was with. The man's widow had grieved publicly over the death of her husband just as he had grieved Cecily's, but William often wondered if in private she felt the same relief he did. Of course, he'd never dare ask.

Truth was not celebrated in the *ton*.

Gossip and intrigue were.

A soft knock sounded on the door of his study. William glanced up and smiled at the sight of Mrs Chisholm hovering at the open door.

'Anything else I can get you, Your Grace?'

'No, Mrs Chisholm. Thank you.'

She nodded, but didn't move. 'Did you see Mr Simmons left you the tray?'

William frowned, sliding his gaze to the overflowing smattering of envelopes with wax seals and calling cards on the silver salver brought to him earlier in the evening in the hope that he might look through them.

He hadn't.

'I did,' William replied.

She still didn't move, waiting for more from him. 'Are there any you wish for him to send an acceptance or decline to, Your Grace?'

He sighed, unable to mask his impatience. 'I have not looked through them thoroughly. Nor do I wish to.'

'May I speak freely?' she asked, edging the toe of her shoe into the room.

He couldn't help but smile. 'Of course, Mrs Chisholm.' The old woman had known him since he was a boy. In many ways, she had become a mother to him after his own had passed almost a decade ago. His household did not stand on rigid formality like others of such lineage in the *ton*. They had become family, especially now that he and Millie were almost all that remained of his own. Such informality had been one of the contentions between him and Cecily in the early days of their courting. He should have seen it as a warning.

Unfortunately, he hadn't.

William shook off his malaise as Mrs Chisholm scurried before him, her petite plump frame the same as it always had been. 'There are rumours,' she began in hushed tones and settled in next to him on the sofa.

'Of?' he asked with a furrowed brow.

'Of you being a recluse…and full of melancholy.'

'And?' He didn't understand why this would be a problem. If anything, he was quite pleased to hear it. Perhaps people would start leaving him be. Since his father had passed two months ago, he had been inundated with correspondence, visits and well wishes for his upcoming succession as the newly minted Duke of Wimberley.

But all he wanted was to be left alone.

'You must think of her,' she said, nodding to Millie. 'She needs a mother and to be accepted by society, Liam,' she said softly, using her nickname for him from when he was but a boy. It tugged on his heartstrings.

'I am. I just have no wish to see anyone,' he replied. 'I have lost my wife and father all in one year and Millie…' He did not say the rest aloud for he couldn't bear to. His daughter had not spoken since the day of her mother's death, as if the horror of losing a parent had locked her voice away.

The ache of missing her sweet cherub voice and lilting laugh was immeasurable. The anger he felt over her grief was unspeakable and he blamed his wife and her proclivities for his daughter's suffering. He dared not seek out another wife and mother to Millie if the woman wasn't damned near perfect.

'If you have a betrothed, the fortune hunters and their well-intended mothers will cease their attentions and perhaps some of the…' She paused as if searching for the right words. 'Some of the unkind talk of the past might cease,' she rushed out.

He cut a knowing glance to her. He knew 'unkind talk' was a mere substitute for scandal. Since Cecily's death there had been a great deal of such unkind talk. 'You think it will all cease with such an announcement?' he challenged.

She shrugged. 'Perhaps not cease, but it would at least lessen.'

He allowed his head to loll back against the sofa. 'I cannot bear another disappointment. Or another fortune hunter. Or another…' He didn't continue. He didn't wish to say it aloud.

She placed a hand along his forearm and squeezed it gently. After a moment, he lifted his head and met her gaze. 'I know I cannot understand your…disappointment,' she began. 'Not truly, anyway, but I wish the best for you and for your future happiness. We all do and Lady Buchanan and I have an idea to end your worries about such a future match.' Her eyes twinkled.

He groaned. 'I am terrified to ask what you and my cousin have been plotting.'

She pulled a piece of folded parchment from her apron pocket. 'All you must do is select one from this list. Lady Buchanan has vetted each of them as being suitable as a wife for you and mother to Millie. And you know she knows everyone.'

He accepted the list and scanned the names with hesitation. At the end, he frowned and handed it back to her. 'None of these will do.'

'Why not?'

'Because they are all members of the *ton*. I will trust none of them with my daughter.'

'Will you consider inviting some of them to the ball celebrating your succession, Your Grace? That will end some of the rumours.' Her return to formal address saddened him. He preferred being Liam to Your Grace, but his life was long past such simplicities.

Millie's day nurse came in to put his daughter to bed. He kissed Millie's forehead and relinquished her begrudgingly. She was transferred easily to Miss Bellows's arms as Millie was still asleep. He watched them until they exited the study. Then he returned his gaze to Mrs Chisholm.

'I promise I will have a woman at my side at the ball to celebrate my succession as the Duke of Wimberley. You have my word. Will that do?'

'For now,' she said; her cheeks were pink, no doubt pleased from the progress of their conversation. He couldn't begrudge her for looking out for him, even when he did not wish to look after himself.

'And where will you find a presentable lady who is not of the *ton* in less than a fortnight?'

He sighed. Evidently, she was feeling emboldened by her success and pushed a bit further. He wished she had stopped while she had gained ground.

'I have no idea as of yet, Mrs Chisholm.' He was desperate to end this line of questioning. The idea of having another wife turned his stomach. 'My focus must be on Millie for now. Speaking of which, when is the new governess due to arrive? I thought we sent for her already.'

He was eager to see if someone else, and in this case a woman far removed from the *ton* and the likes of Society as he knew it, might be able to unlock the hidden words within his daughter and provide her the kindness she'd deserved from the mother now gone from her life.

'Later this week, Your Grace, if the weather allows. Stow is quite a distance and I am sure the recent rains have not aided their travel.'

He nodded, knowing such a distance was intentional. He wanted a kind, country woman to nurture his daughter, not someone who knew the vultures of London. 'Pleased to hear it.' Some of the pressure lifted from his chest. At least that was settled. Getting a wife would have to wait.

And, for once, the *ton* would have to wait its turn, too.

'A ticket to London, please, Mr Sneed.'

Miss Hattie Potts rubbed the two coins in her reticule together and prayed it would be enough for a seat on the next stagecoach to her new employer located just outside London. She'd never taken a public stagecoach with strangers such a distance before, but at least she wouldn't have to travel alone. Gaining confidence, she smiled and set the coins on the counter as Mr Sneed shuffled through some papers and then glanced back at her.

'No need, Miss Potts,' he answered behind the counter. Without looking at her, he pushed the coins back towards her.

'Is it not enough?' she stammered in lowered tones, her cheeks heating. She could hardly begin her new employment if she couldn't get there.

'Your transport has already been paid for,' Mr Sneed answered, leaning closer with a wry smile. 'No stagecoach for you,' he replied with a wink. 'A carriage has been sent for you from His Grace and it arrived last night. Exciting opportunity for you, Miss.' He pointed behind her.

She turned to look at the most glorious, glistening black carriage she'd ever seen. The large emblazoned gold crest reflected in the morning sunlight. Two chestnut-brown horses were already bridled and ready, nibbling on the patchy green tufts of grass beneath them. A driver dressed in a pristine black uniform sat on the box seat with his hat resting beside him as he held the reins loosely in one hand and ate a red apple with the other.

'Driver named Eddie asked me to send you on to him when you arrived,' Mr Sneed added. 'Enjoy your trip, Miss, and good luck.' He gave her a final wink.

Hattie's mind couldn't catch up with the man's words. *A private carriage for her? Paid for?*

'Next!' Mr Sneed bellowed and glanced behind her at the line of waiting travellers.

Stunned, Hattie dropped her coins back in her reticule and stepped aside. She wandered back to where her friends, Ophelia Granger and Gertrude Hastings, waited with her meagre luggage near the cluster of stagecoaches being readied for travel. Hattie stopped in front of them without a word.

There had to be a mistake. She stared at the carriage off in the distance. That could not possibly be for her. Could it?

'Hattie? What is it?' Ophelia asked, touching her forearm. 'You are absolutely ashen. If you need more money, I have some. So does Trudy. We can pool what we have. Surely that will cover your fare.' Then she gasped and gripped one of Hattie's gloved hands before turning it over within her own. Ophelia's long blonde curls flipped in the air dramatically. 'And you *must* take my gloves. Yours are unseemly,' she muttered, beginning to tug off her own gloves to exchange them. 'You simply *cannot* begin your new employ with a duke with gloves stained such as these.'

Hattie stood in a silent fog. Her new employer, William Sutherland, the Duke of Wimberley, had sent his carriage to fetch her. She had never travelled by private carriage. She didn't even know anyone who had. Her stomach lurched with nerves.

'What has you so confounded, bewattled, Hat?' Gertrude asked, her voice tinged with its usual low-grade irritation.

'I cannot go by stagecoach,' she replied. 'His Grace sent his carriage to collect me.' She nodded towards the carriage. The driver hopped down from his box seat and gave what remained of his apple to one of the horses before rubbing its sleek chestnut-covered nose. The other whinnied an objection to being left out and he whispered something to it.

Gertrude followed the direction of Hattie's gaze. For once, her friend had no retort. Ophelia prattled on and finished pulling off both of Hattie's gloves before swapping them with her own. She rolled her eyes at their stunned silence. 'What has got into both of you? Truly, I—' Ophelia's words died on her tongue as Gertrude grasped her hand and pointed.

'His Grace sent a carriage.'

'What?' Ophelia asked, joining in their shock.

After another minute of silence, Gertrude shook her head. 'What did I say about so few details, Hat? What employer sends his private carriage for a governess to ensure her comfort?' she asked, lifting a single, dark, judgemental eyebrow at them both. She dropped her voice. 'How do you know this is not something unseemly?'

The options for unseemly were vast, but Hattie batted the suggestion aside.

'Perhaps he is simply very kind and generous?' Hattie replied, putting on Ophelia's pristine white gloves.

Ophelia bit her lip and shifted on her feet. 'While you know I usually do not agree with Trudy, I think she may be right this time. It seems rather…suspicious.'

Gertrude's brow lifted even higher, threatening to disappear entirely into her dark, widow's peak hairline. 'What if this is some sort of an academy or accommodation house he is running?'

Ophelia gasped and covered her mouth at the reference to a brothel, but then nodded. Her agreement with Trudy felt like a betrayal. Hattie fought the urge to stomp her feet. She hated it when they aligned against her as much now as she had when they were children. Once united in thought, it was hard to not be persuaded by them.

But today, she would not yield.

'I am going,' Hattie said, lifting her chin in defiance.

'And if you are murdered?' Gertrude retorted, crossing her arms against her chest. A frown darkened her usually demure features, making her look like an old matron they'd once had at the orphanage.

Hattie thought for a moment and then smiled triumphantly. 'At least I will die having seen the outskirts of London and having had an adventure,' she replied.

Ophelia laughed and then tried to cover her smile. 'She has a point. None of us have ever been anywhere far outside Stow. Perhaps it is worth the risk to have an adventure, even if she might become a canary bird.'

Hattie batted her arm at her friend's unseemly reference to how they had all come into this world: daughters of unmarried women without fathers to claim them. She had vowed to never be a man's mistress, no matter how charming or wealthy the man might be, for that had been her mother's lot in life, which had landed Hattie an orphan.

While they all joked about it, as it softened the pain behind their childhoods, they each knew the sorrow resting behind such a fate, for they had lived it. Mistresses were used and discarded, and their children often suffered the same fate when the money ran out.

Ophelia smiled wide and her eyes brightened. '*Or* she might meet some lovely man and fall in love.' She clasped her hands together and gave them a dreamy smile. 'What a delicious story that will be.'

Hattie chuckled. She had long abandoned her childhood dream of a family with a loving husband and children despite her love of stories with such happy endings. Such stories weren't meant for her. It was easier to accept that than be held captive in the disappointment of longing for such an outcome and never having it.

'Please do not leave me with her,' Gertrude replied, looking up to the heavens. 'I simply cannot bear it.'

Hattie laughed and pressed a kiss to Ophelia's cheek. She adored her friend's optimistic, if not a bit overly innocent and romanticised nature. Hattie would miss her and Gertrude deeply. She pulled them both into a hug.

'I shall write to you as often as I can,' Hattie said, fighting the emotion bubbling up in her. They were her family and this was the first time she would be separated from them in years.

'And Trudy will write to you for us,' Ophelia replied sweetly. She had struggled with reading and writing as long as Hattie had known her, but she was as brilliant and fanciful as Gertrude was sensible and exacting. They were a beautiful and unlikely trio thrust together by childhood misfortune. Hattie knew how lucky she was to have them.

After leaving the orphanage, they'd found and let joint rooms from the nearby boarding house run by Mrs Kipp, so they could live together, and found work to pool their funds to pay their bills each month. She and Ophelia worked as shop girls at the general store in town and Trudy sold her needlework, as she had a keen penchant for precision. Together they had weathered everything.

Hattie worried her lip. Could she weather this without them?

Momentary doubt snaked through her before she tamped it down with force. She could. She had to. *This* was her chance to make something of herself and she had to seize it. If she did well during this two-week trial as governess for the Duke of Wimberley and his daughter, she might even be asked to stay on permanently. Then she could earn and save enough money to help them all leave this place and start a new life elsewhere. She wanted to give that to Trudy and Ophelia more than anything. She longed for their happiness almost more than she did her own.

With one last, warm embrace, savouring the comfort of them and storing the memory in her mind so she could access it later if she needed it, Hattie said goodbye and extricated herself from them. 'I adore you both,' she said, gripping their arms for a final goodbye, her eyes welling.

'No tears,' Gertrude reminded her, squeezing her forearm.

'I know,' Hattie replied with a smile. 'Sisters for ever, tears never,' she said in unison with them both before waving goodbye.

She clutched her reticule and walked towards the beautiful black carriage that shimmered in the morning glow like the iridescent dark wings of a crow, holding her single portmanteau and small travel trunk that contained most of the possessions she had in the world. Everything within her shook with terror, but she lifted her head high and took one careful step after another, closing the distance between her and the Duke of Wimberley's carriage. The unknown had never led to anything good in the past, but she prayed this time would be different. It had to be. She stopped in front of the carriage, released a steadying breath, turned to give a final wave to her friends and introduced herself to the driver.

'Good day. Mr Sneed said you were waiting for me,' she began with confidence. 'I am Miss Hattie Potts, His Grace's new governess.'

'Aye, Miss,' the driver replied with a rolling Scottish

burr. 'My name is Eddie. Let me take yer bag. Then we shall be on our way.'

'Nice to meet you, Mr...er, Eddie,' she replied before handing off her bag.

'Eddie will do, Miss Potts,' he replied with a wink. 'No formalities needed with me.'

She chuckled, appreciating that he was attempting to put her at ease.

'Journey should take two to three days and His Grace has made arrangements for stops at inns along our journey, so ye can rest and the horses recover.'

She thought of the two lone coins in her reticule. Her cheeks warmed. 'I do not know if I have the funds for such arrangements,' she replied, clutching her reticule tightly.

'Already paid for, Miss Potts. Ye need not worry.'

She nodded and released a chuckle of relief. 'Thank you. I appreciate His Grace's generosity.'

'Aye. That he is. I'll take this, Miss,' Eddie replied with a smile. He gathered her portmanteau and small trunk under one arm and secured them in the bridle box on the back of the carriage.

She wanted to ask him if her employer was also a kind man, but pressed her lips together instead. Surely a question would be impertinent to ask. The man wouldn't dare say anything cross about his employer in front of her anyway and, if His Grace was a difficult man, it wouldn't surprise her. Not really. Weren't most wealthy people?

Did it matter? She set aside her worry for now. She would simply enjoy the beautiful journey along the countryside, watch the scenery, nap and, if possible, enjoy the three volumes of the book she had brought along with her. They were used copies of the romantic novel titled *Pride and Prejudice*, a gift from Gertrude and Ophelia. They had saved up to purchase it for her to enjoy along her journey.

Eddie returned and tipped his hat to her with a nod. 'There is a blanket on the side of the seat in case ye get chilled, Miss Potts. If ye have need of anything else as we travel, just give a couple of solid taps to the roof.' He opened the carriage door for her and offered his hand to help her inside. She scanned the lush crimson interior. It was simply the most beautiful carriage she had ever seen. She accepted his hand, stepped up and settled into the soft, velvet-burgundy squabs. The door closed gently behind her and she sighed, dashing aside all worries from her mind. With a light snap of the reins, the horses lurched forward and they were off.

This was finally her chance for an adventure.

Chapter Two

William paced along the rug that lined the far wall of his study and scrubbed a hand down his freshly shaven face. Mrs Chisholm's visit to share with him the 'latest developments' as she called them, regarding the up-coming ball he was hosting, had only heightened his nerves about the event. He stopped cold and cursed.

What was he to do now? The truth of it was he could do absolutely nothing. The invitations for the ball at Blithe Manor had been sent out without a single decline. He smirked. But in all fairness, who would dare reject the new Duke's invitation to celebrate his succession?

Ironically, he would if he could.

But he *was* the Duke to celebrate, so there was no way through it but forward. At least that was not his immediate concern. He had almost a fortnight before that horrid event would come to pass. He resumed his pacing. Today was the day the new governess was set to arrive and he couldn't help but be nervous about that event as well. What if she was horrid and cold? Or overbearing without a hint of joy within her?

Millie deserved a warm, gentle creature to nurture her in contrast to the rather cool, distant mother Cecily had been. Like their marriage, Cecily had appeared to be the perfect mother, full of beauty and grace to others, but at home she rarely sought out their daughter for walks, cuddles or games. After Millie was born, Cecily couldn't wait to deposit her with the wet nurse and be on with her 'other affairs' as she called them.

Little did he know she had meant it—quite literally, in fact.

Cecily had been the equivalent of a fine bauble in a shop, for she was quite glorious to look upon through a window and could enamour anyone from afar. It was only up close when one attempted to uncover all her secrets and know the truth of her that her coldness, cruelty and imperfections were revealed. If he hadn't been so smitten and rushed along their engagement, he would have discovered it, so he had only himself to blame.

The familiar sadness, anger and regret washed over him. How he wished he had taken his time before marrying and had had a different life. He smiled. But with a different life, he wouldn't have had Millie and he wouldn't change having his beautiful daughter for the world. She kept him tethered to what was important and what mattered.

He released a slow, steady breath as he remembered that. Perhaps they could build a different life if he garnered some patience and courage. He hoped this new governess was the first step to a new beginning for them all.

He closed his eyes and prayed the woman arriving today would be kind, young and accepting of his daughter. He had intentionally placed a generic advertisement in several of the news sheets outside London for a governess for a two-week trial to test the woman's compatibility with Millie…and to make sure he didn't rush into another hasty commitment.

He had omitted any information about the position being for the new Duke of Wimberley to avoid any ladies who merely wished notoriety. Those who answered the advertisement were asked to then write about why they wished to be a governess for his daughter. Miss Potts's answer had been the most intriguing of the bunch and thus her invitation for employment.

Once she had accepted the terms of her trial employment, the date had been set for her arrival and William had sent his driver Eddie to chariot her to Blithe Manor, not only for her protection but to ensure privacy. One couldn't gossip of an upcoming position as governess to a new duke alone in his private carriage, but one could in a stagecoach. Travelling by private coach was a way to ensure the news of her arrival was minimised and not more public fodder to be digested by the *ton*. Once she arrived, she would serve as governess for two weeks. Then he could commit to a longer contract or simply end her employment without issue. Either way he was spared.

If she ever arrived.

William pulled out his father's old, burnished silver pocket watch. It was already almost noon. He muttered under his breath and tucked the watch back in his lucky navy waistcoat pocket. Eddie and his charge were late, no doubt still hampered by the wet spring roads. William returned to pacing, now understanding full well why his father had worn a similar path in this very rug. On days such as this he missed his father more than ever.

Millie burst into the room through the open study door and crashed into his legs, hugging his knee. Miss Bellows reached the doorway moments later, her face flushed and out of breath.

'Apologies, Your Grace. She wished to see you,' she rushed out. 'I believe she might be a bit nervous about today,' she added.

He nodded and ran a hand over Millie's dark hair.

'Please do take a break, Miss Bellows. I will sit with Millie for a while until our new governess arrives.'

'Thank you, Your Grace,' she replied and left the room.

Millie tightened her hold on his leg and looked up at him, her eyes wide and uncertain.

William smiled at her reaction, for Millie was as shy of strangers as he was about the prospect of having a future bride. She was her father's daughter, and he would never begrudge her for it. 'It is time, my sweet. And think of her as a new friend to learn from and explore with. I believe you will like her if her letter is any indication of her kindness. Shall I read it to you?'

Millie nodded.

He clutched her hand, grabbed the letter from his desk and they walked over to his large, oversized chair. She clambered up his leg and settled in his lap. He cleared his throat and began reading aloud.

Dear Sir,

I am eager for an opportunity to serve as your new governess for your daughter, even if it is only a trial. In response to your enquiry, I would teach your daughter as I have learned about the world as an orphan. I would help her learn not only through books, but through experiences, for what better way is there to understand the world than to immerse yourself in its mysteries from whatever perspective you are given?

Growing up in the country with such humble means without formal schooling has allowed me the opportunity to explore history and nature by wandering through it to find those things that interest me. I then find books to learn more about those subjects. While I cannot often afford to purchase those books on my own, I have found others kind enough to loan me books on topics that interest me, which has led me to have a vast and perhaps unusual education.

Thank you for considering me for the position and for the opportunity to serve as governess for your daughter.

Kindly,
Miss Hattie Potts

The woman hadn't known he was a duke when she'd written her simple, honest reply and it was her short, direct answer that had moved him. Compared to the other letters full of boastful experiences with past employers or self-assured confidence in their qualifications to serve in such a position, Miss Potts's subtle uncertainty and openness of her past as an orphan had intrigued him.

He believed she would understand Millie and her

difficulties around losing Cecily since Miss Potts had lived through such a childhood and he hoped he was right. Millie sat quietly in his lap after he finished reading her the letter. She toyed with his loosened cravat.

'I know it has been just us for a while. Let us give her a chance, shall we?'

She studied him for a minute and then gave him a small nod before cuddling into his side. He hugged her tightly, closed his eyes and prayed Miss Potts wouldn't be yet another disappointment for his daughter to heal from.

William had all but given up on the arrival of Miss Potts when he heard the familiar sound of horses' hooves clip-clopping on the drive hours later as he worked in his study on settling this month's accounts. He glanced up to see the familiar black carriage turning into the long drive leading up to Blithe Manor. *Finally.* He exhaled in relief, shrugged on his jacket and sighed.

His pulse quickened and his gut churned with unease. He hoped he'd made the right decision. *Everything would be fine.* He almost snorted at his attempt at self-deception. Very little in his life had worked out anything close to *fine* as of late.

Anticipation along with a bit of dread greeted him at the thought of meeting her.

He exited his study and moved with purpose down the grand staircase, letting his hand slide down the smooth, polished rail before stepping into a glistening marble hall. His housekeeper, Mrs Chisholm, sent the staff scurrying to their places and his butler, Mr Simmons, sniffed and sent one last disapproving glance William's way. The older man had served under his father and was less than pleased with the selection for governess William had made. Mr Simmons wished for William to have selected a woman with more formal schooling and standing. A stranger from Stow was not his idea of a role model for 'Lady Millie' as he now called her. He was loath to remember Millie was only five years old and far from being a lady expected to know the ins and outs of being the daughter of a duke.

'Your Grace,' Mr Simmons said as he opened the door for William.

'Simmons,' William replied as he adjusted his jacket, hoping the old man wasn't right and that William hadn't blundered yet another aspect of being a father.

He walked down the large cascading stone steps to the gravel drive, his heart thundering in his chest. *Please let her look the part of a governess and, above all else, please let Millie love her.*

The mud-splattered carriage came to a rocking halt, the wheels caked heavily in muck. Just as William had expected, the weather must have hampered their journey. Eddie jumped down from his driver's box to settle the horses as a young footman rushed forward to open the carriage door. William held his breath, his chest tightening in anticipation as the door eased open.

He could have sworn the whole household took a collective breath.

The first thing he saw was a worn, mud-splattered boot. Then, an askew bonnet as the woman leaned forward to monitor the ground before her. She appeared to be a rather plain-looking young woman dressed entirely in…brown. The young woman secured her footing on the drive, lifted her head and stood staring out blankly towards him. She started at the sight of the entire household before her.

He wasn't sure how this young woman with her rather dated and forgettable ensemble and slightly rolled-in shoulders was the same person from her letter. She looked more like a baby wren having fallen out of its nest than a governess. She was a bit bedraggled and wide-eyed…and looked, well, a touch…frightened. But it was also far too late for him to rally any other options and first impressions could be deceptive as he well knew.

Best get on with it.

William sucked in a steadying breath and approached the petite, timid creature. Time was wasting as it was and this was the path he had chosen. He would give her a chance and try to trust his decision despite how uncertain he was now.

'Miss Potts?' he said as he settled in front of her.

She stilled and studied him, her brown eyes widening. 'Your Grace? Duke of Wimberley?' she replied in the form of a question followed by a staggering curtsy.

'Yes,' he answered simply, tucking a hand in his trouser pocket. 'I hope you had a safe journey,' he enquired, sticking to generalities for now.

'Indeed,' she said and flashed him an unexpectedly brilliant smile that showcased a dimple in her left cheek.

There was something. She had a lovely smile. He felt her joy in that smile. He almost sighed aloud in relief as some of his worry loosened in his chest. Not all was lost yet. She appeared to be the warm, kind woman he had hoped for.

'Then I am glad for it, Miss Potts. This is Mrs Chisholm, my housekeeper, as well as our butler, Mr Simmons,' he said, introducing those most essential to helping her in getting settled in the coming days. 'Ask them for anything you require.'

He glanced over to the carriage. Eddie removed the smallest travelling trunk William had ever set eyes on along with a rather battered portmanteau. Surely this was not all she had. 'Is your larger trunk being sent on later, Miss Potts?'

'This is all I brought along with me, Your Grace. Thank you again for your kindness and generosity in sending your own carriage for my comfort. I have never travelled in anything other than a stagecoach before.'

Her large brown eyes settled upon him. They were wide, soft and, well, a bit charmingly innocent. He shifted on his feet, disarmed by her trust and belief in him and undone by her gratitude. It had been some time since anyone had thanked him for his kindness and looked at him with such belief and trust.

He wasn't sure he deserved it.

'I am pleased to hear it,' he replied and cleared his throat, uneasy with her appreciation and uncertain what to do with it. 'You must be tired. Please come in and, when you are ready, we can meet to discuss your role here as governess at Blithe Manor in the coming weeks. I can also introduce you to Miss Bellows, Millie's day nurse, and of course my daughter, Millie.'

'Thank you, Your Grace.' She flushed, brushing at her skirts. 'I shall freshen up. I apologise for my appearance. I did not expect you to greet me upon my arrival. It was kind of you to make the time to do so.' She again bobbed her body up and down in an attempt at a curtsy, then scurried up the stairs behind Mrs Chisholm before he could utter a reply.

Simmons edged over to him, dropping his voice low. 'It is not too late to send her on her way home without harm, Your Grace. She does not look the sort to be a governess to a family of your standing.'

William was tempted, but then remembered her smile. There was something there in that smile and he had to believe and trust in his choice and at least try.

'Let us not give up just yet,' William replied. 'There may be a hidden gem within all those shades of brown. We must have the patience to uncover it.'

The lie sounded fine upon his lips. Now he merely needed to believe it to be the truth.

Chapter Three

Hattie wasn't sure she was even walking. Her limbs tingled at the opulence and luxury surrounding her. Was this even real? The soft pastels of the hallways and the glimpses into lush, wallpapered sitting and reading rooms with their fine pillows and sofas as she walked past reflected the kind of wealth she had only heard of in tales told or those fantastical stories she read about in books.

Her skirts made a delightful swish on the polished, dark-wooden floors as she moved, and gentle light cascaded through the numerous windows. Family portraits and tasteful landscapes hung in graceful and precise intervals along the corridors as Hattie followed the housekeeper, whose name she had already forgotten, to wherever it was she was taking her

Drat. Why had she not paid better attention?

When she was nervous it was hard to hold anything in her head. At least she had not forgotten His

Grace's name or to curtsy. Ophelia would be proud of her. Hattie pulled back her shoulders and smiled. She was proud of herself, too. She had travelled from Stow alone, except for the kind driver, Eddie, and now she was beginning her new post as a governess for a duke. It was a long way from her humble beginnings in the orphanage.

A door squeaked open as she walked past and Hattie turned back, catching a glimpse of a little girl who looked to be about five or six years old with a sweet cherub face, dark ringlets and wide blue eyes. The moment the little girl realised Hattie had seen her, she jumped back into her room and shut the door.

Hattie smiled and felt a flutter of excitement. That must be her new charge. She could hardly wait to meet her. While Hattie might not be the most attuned to the ways of proper Society and the people within it, she knew and understood children, especially nervous or scared ones. She'd been one most of her life.

The housekeeper stopped suddenly and Hattie nearly ran into her back. Hattie recovered and chuckled when the woman studied her with a curious glance. 'Apologies,' Hattie muttered, clutching her reticule. 'It is absolutely beautiful here. I have never seen such finery. I was distracted.'

The woman smiled and winked at her. 'Wait until you see your chambers, Miss Potts.' She opened the door wide and Hattie's mouth gaped open. She sighed aloud.

'This is where you will be staying while you are here, so you will be close to Lady Millie if she needs you,' the housekeeper explained.

'Here?' Hattie asked, taking in the soft gold, white and buttercream surroundings. 'Isn't that quite unusual? I had expected to stay below stairs in the servants' quarters.' She couldn't hide her confusion.

The housekeeper smiled. 'You will find that we are a rather unorthodox household, Miss. His Grace encourages a more informal exchange between his servants, although we always respect his standing, of course. Such ease has long been the way with the Sutherland family. With the Marchioness's passing last year, His Grace has encouraged it even more in hopes of creating a more loving and warmer atmosphere for Lady Millie as she grieves the loss of her mother and grandfather. We are more like family than servants here at Blithe Manor, Miss Potts.'

'Oh my,' Hattie continued, uncertain what to say. She stared into the room again. She couldn't believe she would be staying here. 'I may never wish to leave, then.' The room reminded her of daffodils blooming in spring. It was simply the most glorious room she had ever seen.

'It is beautiful, isn't it? It was the late Duchess's, the

current Duke's mother,' she explained, beaming with pride. 'She made it her haven and decorated it herself many years ago. It has been almost ten years since she passed, but we keep this room up just the same. His Grace hoped you would enjoy the room. Said it was time to make use of it again and he wanted you to be nearby Millie, too.'

'That is very kind. Thank you.'

'I wish the late Duchess could have known her granddaughter. They would have adored one another.' There was a sadness in the woman's voice that Hattie understood immediately: grief.

Hattie's smile evaporated. 'I am so sorry,' she replied. 'You must still miss her.'

A flicker of surprise passed through the older woman's features and her pale grey eyes softened. 'Very much so,' she said.

'I find the time that has passed since they've gone doesn't always matter, does it? You miss them all the same.'

The housekeeper studied her another moment before nodding. 'Yes, Miss Potts. I agree.' She walked further into the chamber and Hattie followed.

The room was larger than the living space she, Ophelia and Trudy had shared for most of their childhood in the orphanage. Hattie wished her dear friends were here. Ophelia would swoon at the glorious furnishings and Trudy would plant herself in one of those sitting rooms and read for days. Hattie could hardly believe this opportunity was hers. She bit her bottom lip, so she didn't squeal aloud in delight.

Even if this was only for a fortnight and His Grace decided not to keep her on, she would savour every moment of it and excel in every task so she could at least earn a recommendation to provide her the opportunity for a more permanent placement elsewhere. Then perhaps this could be the future they all led far away from Stow. Finally, they could become the people they were meant to be, not the unfortunate orphans everyone saw them as.

Hattie looked up at the housekeeper, who stared at her in expectation.

Dash it all. She had been woolgathering again. 'Yes?' Hattie asked, reminding herself not to fidget and pretending she had not missed the housekeeper's enquiry entirely.

'Is there anything else I should have sent up for you?'

'No. Everything is quite lovely. Thank you,' said Hattie.

'There is a small basin and cloth in the bathroom,' Mrs Chisholm added, pointing to a small door off to the left of the chambers they stood in. 'We can also arrange a bath for you this eve if you wish.'

My own bath? Hattie pinched her wrist and the sting reminded her she wasn't dreaming.

'Once you have had a moment, please join His Grace in his study, which is back downstairs and to your left. We are happy to have you here, Miss Potts.'

Hattie nodded, wishing she could have remembered the woman's name. *You must pay better attention, Hattie.* She could hear Ophelia's voice in her head.

She would. As soon as the door closed, Hattie rushed over to the bed, sprawled out on it and squealed into a pillow. After she shrieked once more in delight, she flipped over on her back and lay still, marvelling over the lush comfort of the bed and the beauty of the ceilings and ornately carved moulding. Then she realised she was still wearing her dirty travelling clothes and jumped off immediately. She had no wish to stain the floral bedcover.

She also needed to make herself presentable. There was the Duke of Wimberley to meet with after all.

Unfortunately, there wasn't much to be done in the way of refreshing, as the stains from her travels were many, but Hattie touched up her dress, hair, and face as best she could. She didn't wish to change and waste a clean dress to meet His Grace again, especially when he had already seen her in her less-than-pristine gown upon her arrival and only a handful of hours remained in the day. She'd brought only two other gowns in her small trunk and she needed to save them.

Who knew how long it would take for her to scrub down this dress, so it could be worn again in a few days' time? But she had washed her face, brushed out her hair after removing her bonnet and smoothed it into a stylish chignon at the nape of her neck with a few draping curls that fell around her face. While she wasn't skilled enough to weave the silk bandeau Ophelia had gifted her back into place on her own, Hattie was proud of her efforts.

Walking down the gentle, curving stairs, she soaked in the full opulence of Blithe Manor as she looked out of the large, numerous windows. While it was not within the city of London, the estate was on its outskirts and incredibly beautiful with its lush, colourful gardens, emerald lawns, nearby lake and long winding drive. The house itself was also remarkable. It was clear that His Grace and those before him maintained it with great care and his servants seemed devoted to the family they served if the housekeeper was any indication.

She reached the hall and turned to the left, slowing her pace. She came to a halt as she realised how long the hallway was and how many rooms there were. How would she know which one was His Grace's study? Some of the doors to the rooms were open while other rooms were closed. This was a problem. One she never would have anticipated until this very moment. She peered around the first open door frame. It looked to be a receiving room with its sofas and chairs all around a central table and rolling fire. No one was inside. She released a sigh and kept going.

The room across the hall was very masculine and had bookcases that went from the floor to the ceiling. *Lord above.* Poor Trudy would have fainted straight away and then immediately righted herself to begin perusing the books of this library. Evidently, the reading room Hattie had spied upstairs was only a glimpse of the enormous number of books housed at the Manor. There was even a ladder one could use to reach the books on the higher shelves. She almost squealed. Who could have ever imagined such luxury?

'Do you enjoy reading?'

Hattie froze and cringed before turning and fixing a smile upon her face. 'Yes, Your Grace. My apologies. I was distracted in my travels to see you. I have never seen such an expansive library.'

'It was my father's greatest pride and joy,' he replied. Hattie noted the tinge of sadness in his voice.

He must still miss him. His Grace had not been in his position for long from what she'd learned from the papers. 'Then it is kind of you to have the door open, so everyone can view what he built over the years.'

His Grace crinkled his brow and considered what she had said. She couldn't tell if he agreed with her words or not. 'Shall we talk about your position here?' he said, dropping their previous thread of conversation entirely. Had she offended him?

She didn't even have a chance to reply before he turned and waited for her at the doorway to exit the room.

Drat. She'd already said and done the wrong thing. She nodded to him and stepped out into the hallway, unsure of where to even go but forward. He fell in step next to her. 'My study is just here, Miss Potts,' he said as she walked past an open door. She stopped, closed her eyes and reminded herself she was doing all right and not to panic. Not yet anyway.

She walked into the study and was surprised by the warmth of it. It wasn't the typical dark wood, heavy furniture, masculine sanctuary she'd expected from the novels she'd read about such men of means possessing, but a mixture of what one might expect of such a study and...a nursery.

There was a large desk covered with a stack of what appeared to be open ledgers, several ink pots and quills, and an overflowing silver salver with unopened correspondence and calling cards. Next to it was an oversized reading chair and matching sofa in front of the fire. Each held a collection of rumpled blankets and a handful of dolls and teddy bears. She smiled at the sight of it. His daughter must be important to him. Her presence was everywhere.

He followed her gaze and at first attempted to straighten it and then stopped. 'My daughter's…' he began and smiled, leaving the items where they were. It was the first smile that seemed natural and reached his eyes, which softened all his features and made him far less imposing and very…handsome. She decided she preferred viewing him as a father rather than His Grace.

She smiled in reply.

'Please sit,' he said, gesturing to the small pair of wooden chairs opposite his desk. To her surprise, he sat in the opposite chair closest to her rather than behind the desk where she'd expected. His proximity unnerved her, and she tucked her legs to the side and halfway under the chair to create as much distance between them as possible.

As much as she was loath to admit it, he frightened her, but most men did. She just wasn't comfortable being around them. She'd had little practice and he was, well…a duke. And an unseemly young and attractive one at that. She had thought he might be old, grey, and bristly before she'd arrived. This man seemed on the younger side of thirty, quite handsome, and well…kind. He'd sent a carriage for her comfort and greeted her upon her arrival. She didn't know what to make of him.

He studied her in silence. His blue eyes reminded her of his daughter as she'd peeked out of her chamber earlier when Hattie had passed and her dark-brown hair also seemed the same chestnut shade as his own, but without the curls. His face was far different, though. He had a strong nose and brow line and his chin was sharp, almost severe in its angle, offsetting his tall, lean frame. Her gaze caught sight of the portrait of a beautiful woman above the flickering hearth behind him.

'Millie's mother?' Hattie asked, nodding to the painting behind him. 'She is beautiful. Her heart-shaped face looks just like your daughter's. I saw a glimpse of her when she peeked out of her bedchamber earlier.'

His features tightened and a muscle worked in his jaw. 'Yes, that is the late Marchioness,' he replied coolly, not even turning to glance at the painting.

Hattie pressed her lips together. *Blast.* Somehow, she'd blundered again. Perhaps her death was still too painful for him to speak of. She dared not say another word, so she sat frozen, waiting for him to continue.

He cleared his throat and pressed on, lifting his leg to rest on his knee. He appeared as uncomfortable as she felt, but why? He was a duke. Meeting with a governess to discuss the care of his daughter had to be one of the most trivial matters of his daily life.

'I must confess that I have brought you here under rather dubious circumstances,' he began.

Her stomach dropped, and she clutched her hands together tightly in her lap. Trudy and Ophelia were right. She was going to be forced into promiscuity. Her eyes widened. 'I have no interest in being a…a…' She finally sputtered out the word in lowered tones, 'Trollop, Your Grace.'

He blanched. 'Ah, no, no,' he replied, uncrossing his legs and holding up a hand. 'That is not at all what I was about to propose, Miss Potts. I would never…' he said and then stopped, colour rising in his cheeks. He ran a hand through his hair and released a chuckle. 'If only you knew how far from the truth such a request would be from me.'

She nodded, released a shaky breath and replied in a rush. 'I am relieved to hear it.'

'What I meant to say is my daughter needs perhaps more care than you might expect.' He looked at her and paused. 'And, well, I do not know your experience or if you are up to the task. I should have said more about the level of care she will require.'

She leaned forward. 'What do you mean? She seemed healthy and happy from what I saw of her. Is she ill?'

'Physically, no, but emotionally…' He paused and stood before walking quietly over to the mantel. He was moving far from her, making his discomfort even more obvious. Hattie's pulse increased. What could be wrong with the sweet girl?

Hattie clutched her skirts as she waited for his reply.

'She has not spoken since the day her mother died.'

Hattie released her grip on her gown and relaxed against the chair back. It was not nearly as dire as she had feared. 'And how long ago was that?'

'A little over a year ago. I thought she would heal and recover, but she hasn't. She has seen the best doctors and nurses and teachers, but nothing. She remains silent.' He turned to face her. The agony in his features tugged at her sympathies. She knew what feeling helpless felt like. She wouldn't wish such miseries on anyone.

'I am so sorry, Your Grace.'

'After my father passed, we moved here in hopes that the quiet and space away from the enquiring reporters, watchful gazes of the *ton* and noise of London might help her heal—help *us* heal—but even after being here two months, nothing has changed.'

'It sounds as if she needs a specialist, or at least someone far more experienced than I. Why did you offer me the position, then?' she asked, insecure and puzzled by his invitation for employment now that she knew of Millie's plight.

He hesitated and watched her for a moment before continuing. 'When you mentioned your past as an orphan… I thought you might understand Millie's loss and how not having a mother might impact her in a way another wouldn't. And how you described your learning was…inspired.' He shrugged. 'I picked you on instinct.'

It was rare Hattie was struck dumb, but it seemed the man had a penchant for it. She didn't know whether to feel embarrassed or complimented. She stared up at him and then dropped her gaze to her lap. How she managed his words was her choice. So, what would she choose? It was not too late to refuse. She had only just arrived. Then she thought of the small girl with her wide blue eyes and cherub face peeking out the door at her earlier that afternoon. Hattie understood that look and the fear of uncertainty accompanying it. The girl deserved Hattie to at least try.

She lifted her head and matched the Duke of Wimberley's gaze. 'Then I shall try to live up to your expectations, Your Grace.'

He sighed and his shoulders dropped. 'Thank you, Miss Potts. That is all I require.' His relief was evident and she knew she'd made the right decision.

Just then, his daughter came rushing into the study

and raised her open arms to him. He smiled and picked her up with ease. She pressed a kiss to his cheek and wrapped her arms around his neck.

'Well timed, my sweet,' he cooed to his little girl as they touched noses. 'This is my daughter, Millie, Miss Potts. And, Millie, this is Miss Potts…your new governess. You will have many adventures together.'

Hattie smiled at the little girl who watched her with hesitation, but said nothing. She pressed her lips together and clutched her father more tightly. The girl's fear and silence pained Hattie more than she wished to admit, but she held her smile. 'It's very good to meet you, Lady Millie,' she offered.

A young nurse came to the doorway out of breath. 'My apologies, Your Grace. She wished to see you and I could not catch her in time.'

'No apology needed, Miss Bellows. I know how fleet of foot she can be. Now run along, my girl, I must finish speaking with Miss Potts.' He pressed a kiss to her cheek, set her down and the girl ran obediently to Miss Bellows.

The girl's quietness reminded Hattie of herself when she had first arrived at the orphanage and a knot formed in Hattie's stomach. Looking at the young girl who had lost her mother so young was like looking at herself somehow. It affected her more than she expected and the knot in her stomach grew until she feared she might be ill right there on His Grace's lovely and quite expensive-looking rugs.

Once the nurse and her charge were out of earshot, His Grace approached Hattie, sat in the chair opposite her once more and leaned forward, his voice sincere and a pitch lower, and threaded with what sounded like desperation. 'I am grateful for you being willing to try,' he said. 'In a fortnight, we will meet again to discuss the next steps, whether they are continued future employment here or travel plans back to Stow. Before then, I will expect a daily summary of your interactions with her and any updates on her progress.'

She nodded.

'I can only imagine your fatigue from your journey. Please rest this afternoon and get settled in. Your time with Millie can begin in the morning. She usually rises at half past seven. Do you have any questions?'

Hattie had so many questions she didn't know where to begin, but she swallowed them down along with her aching memories of her own childhood and shook her head. She set a protective smile on her face as she'd learned to do a thousand times before and replied, 'Not at present, Your Grace.'

'Then, it is settled. I will see you in the morning, Miss Potts.' He stared at her and she realised this was her cue to leave. She stood, gave a slight bow and left, her stomach still churning. She exited the room and headed out of the Manor. Fresh air would settle her as it always did. No doubt, little Millie was probably the same.

Hattie sucked in one deep breath after another and lifted her face to the warm sun as the gravel crunched under her feet and she made her way to the lawn that led to the beautiful gardens and lake beyond it. Her pulse settled and the knot in her stomach loosened its hold. Just when she thought she'd left the memories of the past behind her, they had rushed to the surface and caught her off guard.

She released a shuddering breath. The Duke of Wimberley was right about one thing: she understood Millie and how she felt about losing her mother. Hattie lifted her skirts and walked through a patch of thick grass, feeling more anchored and settled than she had in the opulence of Blithe Manor now that she had her feet planted firmly on the ground and fresh air rushed through her lungs. The irony was not lost on her. She smiled. She knew what she and Millie would do tomorrow morning that would set both their hearts and minds at ease at their first real meeting with one another.

Chapter Four

Despite the arrival of the governess yesterday, William's sleep hadn't improved. He'd slept fitfully and wrestled down a mere three to four hours of rest at most. He had finally succumbed to the day and risen at five in the morning after tossing and turning for over two hours. He'd added to his own melancholy by sifting through the still-teetering pile of correspondence he had put off day after day. Now, the sun was rising almost two hours later and the soft faint rays of dawn streamed through his study window, shedding light on his progress.

He stared at the piles he now had before him to attend to: decline, accept, reply and pay. At least he had sorted the mess and the silver salver was almost empty, so he commended himself for his work. There was little else to celebrate. Being Duke was bloody hard work. He glanced to his father's portrait and smiled.

'How did you make it look so easy, Father?' he asked out loud.

'He asked for help, Your Grace,' Simmons replied from the doorway before he entered carrying the tea William desperately needed, but hadn't thought to ask for hours ago.

He couldn't help but chuckle good-naturedly at Simmons for his timing and the truth in what he'd said. The man knew him well. Perhaps better than William knew himself.

'That is not one of my strengths, Simmons, as you well know.'

His loyal butler handed William the warm cup of tea and replied. 'Which is why I am reminding you.' There was a small quirk to his mouth before he clasped his hands behind his back and waited for William's orders.

He sipped from the tea and let the warmth settle through him before he replied. 'If you can send out this current pile of declines,' he said, pointing to the much larger stack of invitations, pausing before then placing his hand on a much smaller, thinner pile, 'and then these acceptances, I will pay the bills and draft my correspondence to my cousin.'

'Lady Buchanan?'

'Yes,' William replied with a sigh and took another sip of his tea. 'She is quite persistent about my need to ask *specific* ladies to dance at the upcoming ball.

I fear if I do not reply to her soon, she will have me placed in an uncompromising position to hasten along a betrothal.'

'Perhaps,' Simmons replied with a smirk before regaining his generally dour expression. 'I will set to sending out your acceptances and declines immediately, Your Grace, so you can attend to your correspondence. I can then have one of the footmen gather it from you mid-morning and send out all of the correspondence at once. If that pleases you, of course.'

'A fine idea. The sooner she receives a reply the better, for all of us.' He stood and stretched, groaning from the pull of the tight muscles in his back and neck after sitting and bending over reading by candlelight for so long. 'But I will have a walk, break my fast and then begin.'

Who knew what he might reply to his cousin without some food in his stomach?

'I will see to it then, Your Grace,' Simmons replied. He gathered up the piles of opened correspondence and headed off, leaving William to enjoy his tea. He walked over to the window and stared out, watching the brilliant green edges and soft pastels of the early spring morning yawn in the soft golden glow of dawn.

How many mornings would he have alone like this? The thought dropped his stomach. As much as he hated to admit it to anyone, especially himself, he was dreadfully lonely. Even thinking it made him feel like a weak cad. He was a duke. He had a lovely daughter. He had family, small as it might be, with his servants and a cousin nearby. But his friends had slipped away after his parents and Cecily had died, as if perhaps they felt such losses were contagious. He also had been rather dreary to be around. He tucked his hands in his trouser pockets and frowned.

He couldn't remember why they had all lost touch. There was no specific moment they fell out. It was as if they had no more stories to tell or drinks to share. He rumpled his hair and shook his head. It was an odd thing to even wonder over.

He cast such ridiculousness aside. He would worry about his loneliness another time. He simply didn't have the time to mull over such things. A walk and food would do him good.

Perhaps today would be the first day of a new start for them all.

Heaven knew he couldn't bear another disappointment.

Chapter Five

Hattie woke feeling rested, joyful and eager to start her first day of real employ as governess at Blithe Manor. She squealed with glee and almost jumped out of the most comfortable bed she'd ever slept in, keen to embrace the possibilities of the day. The sun rested above the horizon, preparing for its daily climb, which was exactly how Hattie felt. *This* was her favourite part of the day, when the world and her life were full of possibilities.

While she knew she was *supposed* to ring the bell for assistance with getting dressed and fashioning her hair if she needed it, she resisted the extravagance of it, wanting to simply enjoy and explore the beauty of her chamber alone. The opulence of the fine details of the carved inlay front of the wardrobe that held her meagre clothes and even the small feminine brass pulls on her nightstand captivated her. It was no wonder His Grace's late mother loved the room so. It was simply gorgeous in every detail and Hattie decided to openly revel in it for as long as she was allowed to stay here.

She completed her ablutions and stared out the large expansive window. Morning fog and mist hovered over the serene lake at the back of the estate and the green grass glimmered as the first rays of light caught the fresh dew. For a moment, she believed she was either back in Stow or in a beautiful daydream, living like a princess. Or in this case like a governess with the chance of a lifetime. A chance she would seize and make the most of.

She smiled and slipped on her now-glistening boots that she'd arrived wearing yesterday, covered in mud. When had the maid returned them to her? She didn't even know they had come and gone from her room. She would have to ask Mrs Chisholm to thank them for restoring her shoes to such a state. She'd never expected such care and kindness from the other servants and was grateful for it.

Hattie gathered a light shawl and wrapped it around her second-best gown as she was saving her best one for later and cracked open her chamber door slowly. While she could hear the faint murmurings of servants working in other areas of the house, she knew it was still early enough for her to slip out of the room sight unseen and explore the lake and the beautiful grounds all on her own. She smiled and felt giddy with excitement.

The first breath of cool fresh air filled her with joy and relaxation. Finally, she was alone and able to collect her thoughts in one of her favourite places in the world: the outdoors. The birds sang sweetly as if welcoming her and she began a soft hum in reply. She plucked a sweet sprig of wild violet and twirled its light lavender petals against her fingertips.

Hearing a soft desperate quack in the distance, she stilled and listened. Carefully she followed its plaintive cry and soon came across the smallest little duckling she had ever seen. She bent down and the tiny yellow-tufted creature eyed her suspiciously, so Hattie stilled her advance and they stared at each other, sizing up one another's intentions.

Hattie was relieved to see the young duckling unharmed, but it was still distressed. No doubt it wanted its mother and siblings. Hattie scanned the area around the lake, but didn't immediately see either.

She smiled down at the little duckling. 'Do not fret, sweet girl, I will find your mother.' And she would. She stood slowly so as not to startle the tiny creature and began her search for the mother duckling in earnest in the opposite direction. The sunrise was cresting slowly and she lifted her skirts, taking great care with each step to ensure she didn't crush some other fragile creature hidden in the lush brush and foliage surrounding the lake. After reaching halfway around the pond, she finally spied a mother duck sitting upon a nest surrounded by her ducklings.

Excited by her find, she had not heard the approach of the Duke and his daughter until they were but a short distance away. She stilled and set her features to appear as calm and confident as she could despite the quaking she felt in her legs. She wasn't sure if she was even allowed to be out here or if she should have sought out little Millie before she went outside for her own exercise.

'Good morning, Miss Potts,' His Grace began as they approached. His daughter Millie edged closer to him, clasping his hand tightly and eventually pressing her entire body against his leg when they stopped before her.

'Good morning, Your Grace. It is a beautiful day, is it not? The grounds are quite impressive.' She smiled and scanned the area, still entranced by the beauty of it. She would act as if what she was doing was acceptable and perhaps it would be.

His gaze set out around the lake, examining it as if for the first time. 'Yes. It is.' He smiled. 'Millie and I come out every morning for a walk to see the ducklings,' he said, gesturing behind Hattie. 'I see you have found them as well.'

'They are adorable,' she agreed.

'Millie, this is Miss Potts whom you met last night. Do you remember?'

Millie's eyes widened, but she nodded before pressing her lips together and wrapping her arm protectively around her father's knee.

Hattie stooped down to speak with her. 'So nice to meet you again this morning, Lady Millie. I am so happy to spend some time with you. Perhaps you can teach me all there is to know about your home and the grounds? I love the outdoors. Do you as well?'

Millie studied her for a moment, then nodded with the hint of a smile.

Hattie smiled fully, encouraged by the simple acceptance. 'Perhaps you and your father could also help me this morning. When I came out, I heard a little duckling quacking. She is all alone on the other side of the pond, which is why I was in search of her mother on this side. I need to reunite them, but I do not wish to scare her. Perhaps she knows you both well enough to allow you to move her without injury and bring her back over here with her mother and siblings?'

The little girl's eyes widened with excitement and she tugged on her father's hand, urging him to follow. His Grace smiled. 'Of course, Miss Potts. Show us where the tiny creature is.'

Hattie nodded. 'Follow me, then.' She rose and began the trek back to the other side of the pond.

Soon they had reached the site where the small duckling continued to quack and shiver, cold and scared from being alone for so long in the cool, wet grass. 'I do not know how to move her,' Hattie said.

'When I was a boy, we used to scoop them up in our coats and hold them close to our chest, which of course made our mother livid. They are not the cleanest of creatures.'

'Oh? I will try that, then.' Hattie removed her wrap and gently scooped up the duckling, humming to it as she slowly nestled it to her chest. Its tiny orange-webbed feet pushed against her chest with an urgent flutter until it decided to trust her and settled, releasing one final plaintive squeak. The poor thing didn't know what she was about. Millie let go of her father's leg and approached Hattie. Gently, she ran her hand over the tiny duckling who chirped at the girl's touch. Millie laughed with glee and Hattie did, too.

She glanced up to find His Grace frowning at her, so she flattened her smile. 'Let us bring her back to her mother. Will you lead the way, Lady Millie?'

The girl nodded, ran back to clasp her father's hand and His Grace reset his features to a smile as if his daughter's touch had yanked him back to the present far from his thoughts, wherever they had been. Hattie walked slowly behind them. Why had he frowned at her so? All she was doing was saving a little helpless duckling. Just when she thought she might be beginning to understand him, she was thrust back into confusion. Perhaps he was simply not a morning person as she was. She shrugged and focused on murmuring to the wee duckling to keep it from jumping out of her arms and injuring itself.

After they reached the mother and her brood, Hattie slowly set down the duckling, which scurried back to its mother and siblings. A flourish of what Hattie assumed were happy greetings between them sounded, filling the area with quacks. She smiled and Millie squealed in delight.

'I do not know much about ducks, but they seem happy now,' Hattie said. 'Where is the father? Out gathering food for the brood?' She looked around the lake in concern. 'Or did something happen to him?' she added, dropping her voice low, so Millie might not hear.

'No,' His Grace replied. 'Drakes, the male ducks, don't stay after the ducklings are born. They leave. No doubt the father is long gone and on the hunt for another hen.'

For some reason, Miss Potts's upbeat demeanour fell at the mention of drakes and a flush coloured her neck.

She had asked *him* the question. All he had done was simply answer. The three of them stood watching the happy reunion until Miss Potts fractured the simple revelry and fell into an awkward silence. He tucked his hands in his trouser pockets and tried to piece together what exactly he'd said to offend her and ruin her fine mood.

'I think I shall return, Your Grace,' Miss Potts said, rubbing her arms. 'I am chilled. But thank you and Millie kindly for your help in reuniting that little duckling with its family.' She looked everywhere but his face. What had he said?

'Would you like my jacket to warm yourself?' he offered without thinking, shrugging off his coat and holding it out to place about her shoulders.

'No, thank you,' she replied, shifting away from him. She wrapped her arms around her middle, avoiding his gaze. 'I will be indoors soon enough.' A soft blush filled her cheeks, making her look quite… enchanting. He frowned and looked away. He had no need to notice anything about her. The fact that he did was rather irritating. What had begun as a joyful morning walk was turning into something rather odd. He had no idea what to make of it.

'I hope you and Millie enjoy the rest of your walk. Thank you again for your help, Lady Millie,' she said to his daughter and smiled before nodding to him and heading back to the Manor alone. He watched her disappear over the small bank and soon she was far off in the distance and their morning duckling rescue was over. Millie tugged his hand and pointed back to the Manor.

'Hungry?' he asked.

She smiled and nodded.

'What shall we have this morning?' he mused as they walked hand in hand, beginning the fun game of guessing what Millie wished for today.

'Cooked oats?' he offered.

His daughter scrunched up her face and he chuckled.

'I thought not. Sausages and blood pudding?' he asked, knowing full well her answer.

Her eyes widened and she shook her head.

'Of course not. Perhaps some scones and jam?' he asked.

She smiled and nodded.

'Then, scones and jam it is.'

Far too soon, they were indoors and entered the drawing room. They ate their first meal of the day far earlier than most in the *ton*, as William preferred dining earlier rather than later. The sideboard was filled to the brim with its usual grand fare before half past eight. Mrs Chisholm had the cook prepare the usual feast his parents had always enjoyed. She refused to prepare less despite his objections. Like most housekeepers, she believed food would heal their grief faster. He smiled at her efforts, despite knowing food had provided no healing power for him and little Millie just yet.

The sound of Miss Potts's footsteps at the other end of the hallway towards the door to the servants' entrance reminded him he had forgotten to invite her to dine with him and Millie. No doubt she had planned to eat below stairs. He called out to her, 'Miss Potts, please do join us.' He needed to smooth over whatever had upset her and he also needed her to spend more time with Millie. Them dining together would serve both purposes well.

She stopped and turned. A slight blush still warmed her cheeks. She walked over to him with a timid smile. 'My apologies, Your Grace. I did not think dining with you would be…'

'Appropriate?' he offered, nesting his hands in his trouser pockets. 'No doubt it isn't in Society, but you may have noticed our household here is a bit more… unconventional. If you would consider joining us for our meals, I think it would help Millie get to know you and feel more comfortable sooner. Would you have any objection?' He shifted on his feet. He had no idea what he would do if she refused.

To his relief, she nodded. 'I had not thought of that. Of course, Your Grace.' Her gaze drifted past his shoulder to the drawing room and she lowered her voice. 'I want to do everything I can to help her.'

And the way she said the words made him believe her down to his bones. It was a feeling he had not had in some time: trust mixed with hope. The woman made him hopeful. Unable to say anything else, he nodded and gestured for her to go through to join his daughter in breaking their fast.

He followed her in and began filling his plate, while Miss Potts stood holding an empty dish, studying her options.

He crinkled his brow. 'If there is nothing to your liking, Miss Potts, I am sure the cook can prepare you something else?'

She started and turned to him, another flush of colour on her cheeks. 'No, Your Grace. It is quite the opposite. There are so many delightful options that I do not know which to pick.' She smiled and he was pleased that her good humour had returned and that, unlike the late Marchioness, Miss Potts was quick to recover from upset.

She glanced at Millie. 'What do you suggest?' she asked in a whisper.

William's nerves bubbled up. He always hoped the magic question would arrive that would bring Millie back to speaking. He waited with anticipation to see if she might answer Miss Potts. Unfortunately, she didn't, but she walked closer to her new governess and pointed to the plate of scones and jar of strawberry jam beside it.

'Ah! A fine choice indeed. I believe that is what I will have,' she replied with a wink. She added two scones to her plate followed by strawberry preserve and clotted cream to each and turned to him. She eyed the table, no doubt uncertain where to sit.

'Perhaps a seat here,' he said, pointing to the chair to the right of where he usually sat at the head of the table. 'Just opposite Millie.'

She nodded and settled in, sitting quietly until he and Millie were seated at the table with her. Tea was brought out and poured for them and they settled into a companionable silence as they ate. Seeing Miss Potts in the very chair Cecily would have sat in would take some getting used to, but it was necessary. Millie needed to recover and know she was safe and supported in order to find her voice again.

'Do you have any specific items for our areas of study today, Your Grace?' Miss Potts asked as she slathered her scones with a generous portion of strawberry preserve and clotted cream. He almost smiled. It reminded him of his cousin. Lady Buchanan also had a penchant for sweets for breakfast, but retained a fine figure. It seemed Miss Potts was the same. He baulked at his own thoughts. Why was he noting her figure? Lack of sleep had to be impacting his judgement. There was no other explanation for it. She was Millie's governess after all.

Miss Potts took a bite and he regrouped before answering, 'Since you seem to enjoy the outdoors as much as Millie, perhaps some science and geography for this morning and some reading this afternoon. You could choose a new book from the library.'

'That sounds like a fine schedule for us to settle into, does it not, Lady Millie? We can explore the grounds each morning and work on our geography, science and histories, then come indoors in the afternoons when it gets warm to work on our reading and mathematics. We could even schedule a nap to rest if you'd like.' She cast his daughter a wink before glancing over at Millie's favourite bear that occupied the seat next to her. 'Even bears need their rest.'

Joy exuded from her and her sunny personality soaked into the room, leaving him and Millie with smiles all around. Millie even nodded and gave a giggle as if she, too, couldn't wait for such fun to begin. It filled William with a sense of peace and happiness he had not felt in far too long. In that moment, he knew his instincts about Miss Potts had been right. She was just the right fit for his daughter...and perhaps even him. He cast the thought aside like the ridiculousness it was and enjoyed the rest of his meal.

* * *

'Shall we walk off some of our lovely breakfast?' Miss Potts asked Millie after their plates had been cleared.

His daughter nodded and smiled, clutched her teddy by the hand and slid down from her chair. She gave him a little hug before scampering after Miss Potts, clutching her hand, and leaving the room. William's heart soared and he let out a long sigh.

Soon, he spied them through the window. They were walking through the grass heading back to the lake. What should he do with *his* day? It had been some time since he had felt settled enough to wonder, let alone plan time for himself. There had been task after task to manage over the last year. With Cecily's and his father's passings and Millie to tend to while moving and inheriting a title and estate with its many responsibilities, William had lost a bit of himself. Seeing Millie settled, even if it might be temporary, helped him feel as though he was regaining his footing, himself and his life.

He rose and decided to complete his outstanding tasks from this morning as he mused how he might have some of his own enjoyment this afternoon. He was off to draft a letter to his cousin to head off any further matchmaking. He knew Lady Buchanan. She believed silence was agreement and the last thing he wanted was for her to believe he was ready for a match with one of the ladies she and Mrs Chisholm had presented him with on their list. He shuddered. Just the thought of such a match put an extra spring in his step and he hurried off to reply to her, so he could send out a messenger with the letter before midday. Time was of the essence.

Chapter Six

Somehow a week had already passed in her new post as governess and Hattie was proud of the joyful daily routine they had settled into and the rapport she and Lady Millie had built with one another. Each morning, they met in the parlour and walked about the lake before breaking their fast with scones and jam with His Grace.

Then they returned to the lake for a daily adventure and exploration, coupled with lessons in science and local geography, which Hattie had been able to learn all about thanks to the hearty library His Grace had given her access to during her stay. Trudy would swoon at the stack of books Hattie had in her chambers. The thought of it made her smile.

After a midday meal, they napped and then rose for lessons in reading, literature and mathematics. It was hard to believe so many days had passed and that Hattie might only have one week left with her new charge.

She had grown so fond of her that Hattie dreaded the idea of leaving.

The Duke of Wimberley seemed pleased with her work and dedication to his daughter when she provided him updates each eve, so Hattie had high hopes she might be invited to stay on longer, but not too high hopes, as she couldn't bear the disappointment if he didn't extend her contract of employment. Nor did she wish to think about having to leave little Millie or this place.

In just a short time, the Manor and its occupants had grown on her, even His Grace, who often kept to himself during the day. Despite his best efforts to remain serious and distant, she had seen glimpses of his kindness and warmth in the exchanges with his daughter and servants when he forgot himself and let his mask slip out of place.

She and Millie had already enjoyed their morning meal and her young charge had been eager to return to the pond to search out the same tiny duckling they had rescued from danger their first outing together. Hattie watched as Millie played at the edge of the pond, splashing her hand in the sparkling water. Sunlight streamed through the trees out in the distance and the little girl met Hattie's gaze and smiled at her. While Hattie could still take three strides and reach Millie with ease, Hattie was trying to let more physical distance between them build as time went on so she could gain confidence and assurance.

It had taken almost three days for her to dare let go of Hattie's hand and walk more than a full stride away from her. The poor girl was still scared of the world after losing her mother and grandfather in such a short period of time and Hattie understood. Losing her mother and becoming an orphan had shaken her to her core when she was only a bit older than Millie. It would take time for the little girl to heal and realise the world still had wonderful adventures to offer and happiness could be trusted once more.

Hattie plucked colourful wildflowers as she watched Millie pick up the rocks along the bank and examine them. Each one seemed to fascinate her as did much of the outdoors. They would do a review of the flowers they had been studying today and make a beautiful thank-you bouquet for the cook, Mrs Updike, who had agreed to help teach them both about the intricacies of cooking a tart after they came in and washed up from their morning excursion outside.

While their 'reviews' each morning consisted of nods, pointing and head shakes rather than words from Millie, she *was* learning. It was evident in the girl's bright eyes and smiles. Hattie continued to pray each day that something unexpected would unlock Millie's silence, but nothing had so far.

A flutter of birds flew from a cluster of large bushes on the other side of the lake. Hattie turned and watched to see what had startled them. It wouldn't be the first time a deer or fox had trotted out this way looking for their own morning meal. A small hare hopped out of the bush and Hattie smiled. Evidently today it was a bunny looking for some fresh clover. She turned back to look for a blue spray to add to the bunch in her hand. Spying the perfect cornflower-blue cluster, she bent over to pluck it when Millie let out a shriek.

Hattie lurched up, dropping the flowers to the ground, and saw two men approaching them from the very bushes the birds had scattered from. Millie screamed again as the men continued towards her. Hattie's pulse raced. What was happening?

'Come to me, Millie!' Hattie shouted, rushing to Millie. She clutched the little girl's hand and then moved in front of her to shield her from whoever these odd men were who had emerged from what appeared to be out of nowhere. They moved towards them with purpose and looked strange…while they had the clothes of a farmer, they had fine shoes and the clean-shaven faces of gentlemen. Hattie didn't know what to make of them, so she started moving backwards slowly. When the men picked up speed and called to her, she turned to Millie. 'Run as fast as you can to the Manor. Don't look back. Just run,' she said firmly, clutching her arms.

Millie paused, her eyes wide with fright. Hattie tried to reassure her with a timid smile. 'Run inside and point out here to get help. I will distract them. Now go!'

Millie nodded and then darted off. The men exchanged words and one of them peeled off and attempted to go after Millie. Hattie's heart dropped. Where these men kidnappers? What would they want with a young girl? Perhaps they hoped to collect a ransom from a new duke? Anger replaced her fear and Hattie ran towards the man chasing Millie rather than away. She hoped to intercede and block his progress. She had to give the young girl enough time to reach safety and get help.

'Miss, I only wish to speak with her,' he began as Hattie blocked him.

'Who are you? This is private property. Go! Leave her be!' Hattie countered, matching his movements in hopes of keeping him away from Millie. He frowned at her.

'Not until I get what I want. Now move!' he commanded.

'No,' she replied, squaring her shoulders. The other man had almost reached them now.

'Bloody hell. Go get her, Jay. I'll take care of this one,' he replied. He lunged for her, but Hattie moved quickly, evading his grasp and causing him to stumble. He cursed and the other man darted off. Hattie lifted her skirts and ran after him, making good progress. She pulled on his jacket and he whipped back an arm, which connected with her shoulder, making it sting. Not sure what else she could do to slow him down, she launched her body at him and ended up on his back. They both crashed to the ground, landing in a rather large mud puddle caused by the rain from the night before.

The man cursed at her and shoved her away just as Hattie heard men running towards them. One of the footmen tackled the other man to the ground, while the other, now splattered with mud, was easily seized. Hattie sighed in relief, her heart still thundering in her chest as she leaned back on her arms and gathered her breath. The Duke of Wimberley rushed to her, his gaze roving over her. 'Miss Potts? Are you hurt?'

'No,' she panted, out of breath from her efforts. 'Millie?' she spluttered, her full question implied.

'She is fine,' he answered. 'You gave us a fright. It was quite a scene from inside.' He offered his hand to help her to stand.

She paused before accepting. Covered in mud, she must *look* a sight. *What must he think of me?* It was not exactly what a proper governess would do, but she'd acted on instinct. Embarrassment warmed her cheeks and she reluctantly reached up her muddy hand and accepted his clean one. His grip was strong, warm and sent a shiver along her entire body.

Once she was back to standing, his gaze assessed her again before he released her hand. His gaze dropped away before he spoke again. 'Please go inside while this is dealt with, Miss Potts. I will speak with you shortly.'

There was a tightness in his voice that set her on edge. *Blast.* She could only hope her behaviour hadn't ruined her chances to stay on. She batted the thought away. She was being ridiculous. None of that mattered. The most important thing was Millie was safe.

Once Miss Potts and his daughter were inside, the Duke of Wimberley faced the intruders, who had finally ceased their struggles against the footmen who held them in check and the other men from the household who had joined them. While William wasn't prone to rage or even a quick temper, at this moment he wanted to roar. Roar so loudly that the whole valley would hear it. How dare these men attempt to harm his daughter and Miss Potts? How dare they trespass upon his property and threaten those under his care?

While he didn't know who they were, he knew exactly what kind of men they were and what they were doing here. He'd seen his fair share of them back in the city. London was crawling with them: reporters, gossip scribblers, private detectives. They were all the same to him. They were paid for information and ferreted around to uncover it by whatever means they could, legally or otherwise. They dug through refuse, intercepted correspondence, paid servicemen for updates and peered in windows when they could.

This pair had evidently risked trespassing as a means of getting what they wanted. William stared off in the distance as he counted down from five and exhaled, pausing to regain his composure. Millie was safe and inside now, but his pulse still raged, hammering loudly, reverberating through his body. He hadn't felt such a rush of emotion since he'd learned of the details surrounding Cecily's death. He shook off the memories and approached the two men held by the footmen and nearby groundskeepers. When he spied the black notepad and pencil on the ground, he frowned. Despite not knowing them by name, he knew exactly who they were now from the list of possibilities: gossip hounds.

'Explain yourselves,' he commanded, his voice harsh and biting.

A brief silencc followed until Reggie, a man who had worked the grounds since William was a teen, twisted the arm of one of the men tighter behind his back. 'His Grace asked you a question,' he growled.

'I...' he began and then groaned as Reggie tugged

his arm again. *'We...'* he added, 'are from *The Times*, Your Grace.'

'For?' William asked impatiently, his temper rising now that it was confirmed they were reporters. 'What has you willing to terrify my daughter and her governess after all we have been through?'

They paused. Reggie looked as if he might turn his arm again and the older reporter spluttered out a quick answer. 'We were informed of the arrival of a woman. That your private carriage had been sent out to Stow and returned a few days ago. We wanted to be the first to report on your new bride...and to see how she feels about settling into the shoes of your late wife and her many proclivities.'

The younger reporter shot a glance at the other and chimed in with his own accusation. 'Word has it your daughter may not even be yours. Care to comment, Your Grace?'

That same rage from a minute ago that made him want to roar churned in his gut. He clenched his fists by his sides and reminded himself that his whole household was watching, even his daughter. The *ton* was thorough and constant in their desire for gossip. Now they were inventing brides and casting doubt on his daughter's lineage.

'Care to provide us details?' the younger of the two reporters asked again.

William cursed under his breath. Then he walked slowly over to the young man, who smirked at him. William stopped in front of him, the man's game finally becoming clearer. He wanted William to punch him. Needed him to. All to sell more papers.

Well, he wouldn't be helping them. Not today.

'I will not dignify your question with an answer,' he replied, his voice dark, heavy, and menacing, 'but I will grant you the ability to leave alive…this time. Next time you may not be so lucky.' The man's smirk fell.

'Deposit them far from the property. Very far,' William ordered. 'Do not come back again,' he warned the reporters. 'Otherwise I will set the dogs on you and I will not be responsible for what happens after that.'

The trespassers were dragged away to a wagon by the groundskeepers where they were unceremoniously tossed on the back and secured by the footmen. His other driver, Fitzroy, had emerged from the stables by then and jumped up to drive them off the property.

Mr Simmons approached William's side and they watched the wagon rumble down the long drive. While William knew such gossip hounds were relentless and without scruples, the doggedness of this duo concerned him. No one had dared encroach on the Manor before in such a fashion. He worried more might be coming, especially if such lies and gossip were floating on the wagging tongues of the *ton*.

His belief that the fascination for him and his family had subsided briefly before the ball to celebrate his succession had been faulty. It seemed they were even more determined to write stories about him, even if they were nonsense. So much so that they risked trespassing to gain enough to weave together a fabricated tale. He sighed. The payout from the papers must be sizable for them to take such risks. This time the cost had been his daughter's well-being as well as that of Miss Potts.

He cursed under his breath.

'When will they leave us be?' William asked aloud, unable to keep the weariness from his voice. No doubt these men were most likely the first to arrive for such a story, not the last.

'I do not know,' Simmons replied. 'And we do not have dogs, Your Grace,' he added. 'Shall I get some?'

William turned and caught the small smirk on the old man's face. He couldn't help but grin back. He appreciated Simmons's attempt to turn his mood and for his practical and calm nature.

'Perhaps it is not the worst idea,' he replied with a bit of a chuckle. 'Send out an enquiry to the farmers nearby. Perhaps they will have a litter coming soon that we could pull two pups from. And none of those fussy dogs, Simmons. I want a hound or a hunter. Dogs large enough to alert loudly and give chase to the next set of reporters that wander on our property.' He crossed his arms against his chest. 'Then I can enjoy watching them run.' He flashed a full smile to Simmons, who gave a smirk as well.

'I look forward to seeing such a display, Your Grace.'

'As do I. Please also send for the doctor to come check on Millie and Miss Potts. Although I think they will be fine after they settle from the scare, I would feel better to know for certain they were unharmed.'

'Of course, Your Grace. I will see to it now.'

'Thank you, Simmons. This Manor wouldn't work without you.'

'Well, I hope to never be without it,' he replied, his voice softening in a rare display of affection, before he turned to leave.

William stood in silence as the wagon disappeared around the last bend to the main road. He settled himself with one more deep breath before he went inside. He had to be calm, not enraged, despite how he felt. His daughter would not benefit from him being out of sorts. He climbed the steps, made the walk to the kitchen and found her with Mrs Updike, rather than in the parlour, sitting in a small chair pulled in from the other room.

Millie stared out the window at the lake, one of her

favourite places in the world. Her legs swung in the air as she nibbled on a biscuit, her upper lip showing evidence of the milk she'd consumed already. Cook stood behind, watching her as she sipped from a cup of tea.

'Everyone settled?' he asked.

Millie paused and turned to him. She smiled, which set his heart at ease.

'Yes, Your Grace. Nothing a biscuit and warm milk cannot cure,' Mrs Updike replied.

While he was pleased to see that was the case now, what of next time? Would she be hurt? Should he take a bride to show he'd moved on from the scandals of Cecily to stop this pestering and invasion of their privacy? It was the last thing he wanted to do, but for Millie… he would do anything. He sat next to her and Mrs Updike brought him his own plate of biscuits and some strong tea and set it before him without even asking.

'Thank you,' he replied, moved by the woman's ability to know exactly what *he* needed, too. He took a sip, letting the warm tang settle through him. His pulse was nearing normal despite his racing thoughts. 'Miss Potts?' he asked.

'Went to change and clean up, Your Grace. Quite a spill she took. Never seen anything like it,' Mrs Updike replied with pride. 'Quite a brave lass.'

'She is,' he agreed. He popped an entire biscuit in his mouth and savoured the soft, delicate way it dissolved on his tongue as he chewed. He needed to speak with his new governess and to thank her. The woman had risked her own well-being and safety to protect his daughter. What more could one ask of a governess? He chewed slowly on another biscuit. Or of a wife, for that matter? He set the biscuit down as an idea bloomed.

He had after all given up on the idea of marrying for love after Cecily. But what if he married for Millie instead? Married a woman who was unexpected and unjaded by Society. A woman Millie knew and adored already.

He frowned. What a ridiculous idea. For starters, it was too great a risk. He hardly knew the woman and rash decisions never worked out well for him if Cecily was any indication. He was being irrational and nonsensical…emotional. He was still startled by what happened to Millie. He batted the idea away and pulled his daughter to his side, kissing the top of her head. When she looked meaningfully at the remaining biscuit on his plate, he nodded. 'It's yours,' he murmured.

She took it from his plate and ate it, and they sat in silence, looking upon the glorious sun streaming down around the lake. He would worry about all that much later. First, he needed the doctor to check both Millie and Miss Potts to make sure they were well. Once that had been accomplished, he would be able to think far more clearly.

Chapter Seven

'May I speak with you for a moment, Your Grace?' Doctor Kemplar asked as he tucked his stethoscope back into his medicine bag and snapped the metal clasp shut. He was in the hallway outside William's study and evidently finished with his checks on his patients this morning: Millie and Miss Potts.

William's heart skipped in his chest for a beat and he stood behind his desk. He knew Dr Kemplar well and *this* tone was reserved for serious conversations. The last time he'd used this tone with William, he'd told him his father was close to death after a decade-long battle with his lungs. Fear tightened every muscle within him.

William nodded and tucked his hands in his trouser pockets. 'Of course, Doctor,' he replied with a forced calm he didn't feel. It was either that or curse so loudly the chandelier would rattle from the rafters.

The Doctor entered the study and closed the door

behind him. He settled in a chair opposite the large desk and William sat down, grateful for the barrier between him and whatever news he was about to receive.

'While Miss Potts seems fine despite a few bruises and a strained shoulder, your daughter…' He paused and shifted in his seat. 'I am gravely concerned. While she has no physical concerns, her refusal to speak despite the time that has passed leaves me feeling… uncertain.'

'Uncertain?' William asked.

The Doctor's brow creased and a frown pulled down the corners of his mouth, making his large white moustache twitch. 'Continued exposures like the one today may cause her to never speak again.'

William froze. *Never?* The idea of never hearing his daughter's voice again sent ice through his veins.

'Over the years, I have seen children shocked into silence by such traumas before, but they have always spoken again before now. It has been over a year, has it not?'

'Yes, it has.'

He nodded. 'And you have enlisted the help of those doctors and specialists I have recommended?'

'Yes,' William answered. 'All of them.'

He sighed. 'That is what I feared. In that case, I think you should prepare yourself that she may never speak again, especially if these types of occurrences continue.'

'Did what happened today impact her? Was she close to speaking again?'

He shrugged. 'While *I* do not know if she was close to speaking again, Miss Potts and I spoke at length about her experiences with Lady Millie while she had been with her over this last week. I believe they were making progress, but such…disruptions…like today will set her back. It is such sudden scares and traumas that will compound on themselves. I cannot say that I know what the long-term consequences will be or if she will become worse than she is now.'

All the Doctor's words overwhelmed William. He shook his head, trying to understand what the Doctor was *not* saying. 'What exactly do you mean by "worse than she is now"?'

'She is isolated, Your Grace. She only knows those within this household. The fact that she took to Miss Potts so quickly is quite miraculous. She is wary of strangers, which will make moving within the ranks of Society challenging when she is older, especially when she will not speak. She was shy of me even this morning when I checked upon her and I have known her since the day she was born.'

'What can I do?' William asked, leaning forward in his chair. 'You know that I will do anything for her,' he said, his voice catching and his pulse increasing. 'She is my world.'

The Doctor nodded, his gaze softening with sympathy. 'I know you would move heaven and earth for her, Your Grace. All you can truly do is stabilise her world as much as you can. Keep her days structured, have those around her be consistent and reduce events like today where she sees her safety threatened as best you can, so it does not set back her improvement. Then, maybe one day we will have a chance of unlocking what has held her silent.'

Illness threatened, but William swallowed it down. After a beat, he stood and extended his hand. 'Thank you, Doctor. That is exactly what I will do.'

Even though I have no idea how to do it.

'Of course. Send for me if you have need of me in the coming days.'

'I will.' William watched the Doctor leave his study and moments later he heard the front door of the Manor open and close. William set his palms flat on his desk and let his head hang down. He closed his eyes and cursed. Cecily, all of Society and the *ton* could hang for all he cared. He hated them all…but he loved his daughter more. He had to unearth a solution for the mess he was in and quickly. Doctor Kemplar wasn't prone to exaggeration. If he felt Millie was in danger of never speaking again, William needed to do something about it.

Now.

Restless, he left the study and walked down the hall to the library. While he'd never loved the room as a boy, as he preferred to be outside playing cricket, boxing or exploring the acres surrounding the Manor, he revelled in the peace it brought him now as it reminded him of his father, whom he missed dearly.

As a father himself now, he understood why this room was his own father's refuge and sanctuary. Surrounded by walls of books and knowledge, William felt safe and as if he could conquer anything, even the current situation. He walked into the room and settled into his father's favourite oversized, highbacked chair and let the lush, velvet cushions envelop him.

He glanced at the small round table next to him and rested his palm on the book he had been reading on those nights he couldn't sleep, but also couldn't bear to work: *Grimms' Fairy Tales*. He smiled at the fanciful choice he had made and the surprise he felt when he'd seen it here among the hallowed shelves of his father's history, geography, science and fiction works.

He had no idea his father'd had interest in such books, so William had plucked it from the shelf one evening and had been reading its stories ever since. He stared up at the familiar family portrait where his parents, young and vibrant, stared back at him. He also studied his younger self and the older brother long lost to him. He smirked. What his brother would have said to him now, he could clearly imagine.

'Stop your gloaming. Just because life has given you a bit of a knockabout does not mean you're down and out. Dust yourself off and get back in the fight.'

That had been one of the last conversations he'd had with his brother and William could still feel the warmth of his brother's hold as he'd tugged him into his side and ruffled his hair. Sebastian had always been the fun, charming older brother meant to be Duke, unlike William, who was never a fan of Society and its trappings. Easy-going and well loved, Sebastian's passing ten years ago had been what had killed their mother. She had passed but a year later. Though she would never admit it, part of her light drifted away when his life had been extinguished, as it had from all of them, but her loss was deeper. She was his mother after all.

Father had focused his energies on building after that. So much so that he'd become obsessed with perfection, almost to the point of creating financial strain, but William had righted the course of their expenses when he'd come to his father's aid during his last months of decline. Now he just needed to right the course for Millie's future. But how to do it?

He ran his fingertips restlessly over the fine gilded-script inset on the cover of the book, tracing its letters. He stared at the cover and his fingers stilled. 'Cinderella'. He shook his head. Could it work? Could the solution be so simple? He smiled at the portraits of his father and brother. How they both would smirk at him now if they could see his scheme. It was brilliant and yet mad enough that it might work.

William *would* take a wife to quiet the reporters and the *ton* in their quest for gossip about the newest Duke. Well, at least he would *pretend* to.

And he knew exactly who his fake future bride would be.

Now he just needed to talk Miss Potts into it to see if she would be willing to play the part of a fake princess like the woman in the story of Grimm's cinder girl.

Hattie settled in the chair opposite His Grace in his study, having been summoned by Mrs Chisholm and brought to him post-haste. When the housekeeper closed the door for privacy, Hattie almost jumped out of her skin. She was a cluster of nerves and pain since the incident this morning.

She winced when her shoulder touched the back of the chair. She edged forward in her seat and readjusted the sling that held her left arm still. Her heart roared in her chest. She risked a glance at the Duke of Wimberley and he was frowning. Deeply frowning. She dropped her gaze, pressed her lips together and swallowed. Now he appeared to be scowling as he studied her sling.

'You need not worry, Your Grace,' she rushed out. 'I will still be able to tend to my duties for your daughter. It shall only be a few days.' She smiled weakly and leaned back in her chair as far as she dared with her injured shoulder and waited. He appeared very angry. But at her? Why? Was he annoyed at the time it took for her to come see him? Or perhaps he was angry about her unladylike behaviour in tackling the trespasser? She wouldn't apologise for it. Millie's safety was more important than propriety.

'Does it hurt?' he asked, his voice soft with concern as he glanced at her shoulder.

Startled, it took her a moment to reply. 'It is strained and sore, but I was lucky. Only bruises other than my shoulder. The doctor said a couple of days in this sling and my arm will be fine. I am just relieved Lady Millie was unhurt.'

He exhaled and sat back in his chair. 'As am I. And I am glad to hear your injuries were not more serious.'

She nodded and swallowed, still uncertain as to where their conversation was headed.

He shifted in his chair. 'I am grateful for how you interceded on my daughter's behalf to protect her.' He shook his head and a bit of a smile emerged. 'I cannot say that I have ever before seen a woman face off against two men in such a way. It was brave, Miss Potts. You and Millie could have been seriously hurt or...' His voice trailed off and his scowl returned.

She sat frozen.

'Which makes what I am about to ask of you...difficult. But knowing how much you care for my daughter, I thought I would dare it, for her sake, especially after speaking with Dr Kemplar. Despite how dubious a request it is.'

Dubious? Her eyes widened and she leaned forward, uncertain about what he would say next, but intrigued to know. What dubious needs could a duke like him have? If only Ophelia was here, she would know. She had the keenest imagination of anyone Hattie knew.

'I would like to extend your offer of employment not only as Millie's governess, but also as my fake betrothed. I think a Lady Penelope Denning would do nicely,' he said, his words rushing out. 'But if you prefer another name, I am open to such possibilities. Do you think you could do that?'

She could have sworn he said something about pretending to be his betrothed, but surely she had misheard every word. 'I am sorry, Your Grace. I do not think I understood you properly. I would love to remain on as Lady Millie's governess, but that last part...

Did you say you wish for me, an orphan from Stow, to also pretend to be your betrothed as some other person entirely?'

A beat of silence passed and then His Grace sat back in his chair, his hands sliding down the curved wooden armrests before covering the painted gold flowers at the ends. He met her gaze. 'Yes, Miss Potts, that is *exactly* what I wish for you to do.'

Not even Ophelia would have anticipated this request. Hattie was torn between the shock of silence and the wild laughter of disbelief and confusion. He stared at her and waited.

She asked the only thing she could think of. 'Why?'

'A fair question,' he replied and stood. He walked along the outline of the room as he thought and tucked his hands in his trouser pockets. She couldn't help but notice the fine cut of them and how they, along with the slim cut of his waistcoat and jacket, accentuated his muscular build. She slid her hand over the new stain she spied on her dress to cover it as best she could.

This whole scene was ridiculous. Why would *this* man need a woman like her to be his pretend betrothed? He was a duke, he was handsome and had all the time and wealth in the world at his disposal. He could find an eager wife in the time it would take him to blink.

He paused in front of the portrait of the late Marchioness and faced Hattie. 'In the simplest terms, Miss Potts, I cannot take a new bride, but the *ton* will give me and my daughter no peace until I am adequately… unavailable to help quash the rumours they create to sell their gossip sheets. I cannot ask a woman of high Society to fill such a role as they all know one another and will talk about such a ruse and embarrass me.

'So, my hope was that you being from Stow and far removed from here and someone who cares for my daughter and whom my daughter adores would help me with this…endeavour.'

'You mean lie to everyone?'

'Yes.' For some reason, his truthful reply astonished her. He supplied no excuse for what he had asked. 'After speaking to Dr Kemplar, I feel I must do something drastic to protect my daughter. He said we cannot risk more situations such as this morning. She is too fragile and such occurrences will only set back her progress and recovery.'

Hattie nodded and looked down at her hands briefly before daring to glance up and ask the question that was plaguing her to her core. 'Again, Your Grace, why me? Who in the world would look at me and believe I am a lady of…anything?'

He smiled at her, a deep full smile that made the air flutter in her chest. 'It is no secret my daughter adores you, Miss Potts. You are willing to risk your life to keep her safe as I have seen this morning. Also, you are not of the *ton* and, from what I can see, do not have a deceitful bone in your body. In short, I trust you. And I believe with the right clothes, hair and training in the ways of Society, you would be quite...believable.' His gaze roved over her slowly, hesitating on her face. 'Quite believable, in fact.'

Warmth flushed her cheeks. She couldn't utter a word.

'I know it is an unseemly and deceitful request, Miss Potts, but I do it for my daughter. As you know, she has not spoken since my wife died over a year ago and losing her grandfather recently has hit her even harder. We cannot grieve and heal with the circus of people around us and all these reporters and fortune hunters nipping at our heels for information to sell to a gossip sheet. All I want is peace for us, for Millie, so that she can be happy again. So she can be the laughing, joyful girl she once was. Can you understand that?'

His direct and unvarnished plea unsettled Hattie. How could she deny the young girl anything? Certainly there was no harm in asking questions. Asking wasn't agreeing to anything.

'And your staff? Do they know of your plan?'

He smiled. 'Not yet, but I believe they would be willing to go along with the ruse if you were. For Millie's sake, of course. They are also quite fond of you from what I can see.'

'And how are you planning to make people believe I am this…?'

'Lady Penelope Denning?' he supplied. 'Have you ever read the story "Cinderella"?' he asked.

'No. I haven't.'

'It is where I got the idea. It is the story of a girl who is overlooked and treated poorly after her father dies. She dresses up for the royal ball in disguise with the help of a few fanciful creatures. The Prince falls in love with her, not knowing who she really is. She is transformed into a princess. Although I do not believe you will require anything as fanciful as birds and a glass slipper to transform you into my fake bride-to-be for the evening, I believe you can play the part.' He smiled and chuckled as if what he said made all the sense in the world.

She stared at him blankly.

'Here,' he said and set a book before her. 'Read the story. Think over what I have said. Even if you refuse to be my fake betrothed, I still wish for you to stay on as governess for Millie. I just wanted to try for you to be both and minimise any additional exposures to strangers for my daughter's sake.'

She was stunned by his belief in her, so much so that she tumbled into her next question without hesitation, leaning forward. 'And if I agreed, when would I be presented to your friends as this Lady Penelope Denning?'

'Next weekend at the ball celebrating my succession as Duke of Wimberley,' he replied, holding her gaze. He said it with confidence and certainty as if a mere week was all the time anyone would need to prepare her for such an event. She was quite certain His Grace, despite being as young as he was, had lost his faculties.

'Seven days?' Miss Potts asked after staring at him blankly. Her brown eyes widened further in alarm.

William shifted in his chair. 'Yes,' he answered simply. His pulse increased with each enquiry she made. He hadn't expected to even be able to keep her in the room this long, let alone have her asking questions as to *how* this whole scheme might work. He should have planned for more success and thought the next steps of his plan through.

Especially when the woman might just say yes. Hope flickered in him.

'How would that be possible?' she asked.

'As you have noted, I am a duke. You would be amazed at how quickly I can acquire anything I need. People fall over themselves to please me.' His answer sounded entitled and snobbish, but he needed to prove his point.

She scrunched her nose at him and his answer, which made her look even younger, and he chuckled in amusement.

'I did not say it was not distasteful, but it is true. Arrogance aside, whatever you need, or whatever the household needs to make you into Lady Penelope Denning, can be acquired and acquired quickly.'

'You do not worry that the people supplying what you require will expose your scheme?' Her brow furrowed.

'There is a tight circle of those who I know have great discretion and I would not stray outside of those trusted few for what is needed. Dressmakers, stylists, and those versed in etiquette will support us in our ruse.'

She looked down at her hands in her lap and fidgeted with her gown. Her hands were small, delicate and strong, much like her. The more he studied her features, the more surprising little treasures of loveliness he discovered.

Another minute passed. There was something else concerning her, but he did not know what it was.

She finally glanced up and met his gaze, looking every bit as timid and small as the brown wren she appeared to be when she'd first emerged from his carriage a week ago. 'As much as I am…honoured by your belief in me, Your Grace, I do not believe anyone would look at me and not see what I truly am.'

'And what is that?' he asked, not understanding her meaning.

'I am an orphan from Stow with no real family or breeding.' She said this with certainty and finality as if this single sentence explained all.

It didn't. He waited for her to continue. 'I do not quite understand,' he finally said, hoping for more.

'I know nothing of the finer ways of Society,' she continued. 'Travelling here was the first time I have been in anything other than a cramped stagecoach. Before my employment here, I had never seen the inside of a fancy estate outside of what my imagination had allowed me to create from the books I have read. Those in your world would root out our deception before it even started. No one would believe I was a lady of any means or import despite all the finery you wrap me in.' She released a shaky breath and her shoulders relaxed as if she had finally confessed to a horrible crime: that of her birth.

The uncertainty and vulnerability of her words shifted something deep inside him. How long had it been since anyone had been so honest with him and exposed such to him? Far too long.

It made him more determined than ever to believe in her more than she believed in herself. He wanted to be her champion and for her to know how grateful he was that she was willing to embark on this with him for the sake of his daughter.

'I do not know you well, Miss Potts, but from what I have seen of you, I think you underestimate yourself. You came to Blithe Manor alone, to a place you did not know and to work for a family you also did not know. You dared stretch yourself to a place of discomfort to change your life. You can do this, too. It is for a fortnight starting from today. One week to prepare and one week to stay on here in case there are questions the *ton* needs answers to, then it will be done and you can be simply Miss Potts, governess, once again.' The more he talked, the more he believed in his own success, and hers, which could change his daughter's life as well as his.

'I want desperately to have something more, Your Grace.' She met his gaze and continued. 'For myself and my friends. I just do not know if this…this dishonesty is the way to achieve that.' Her fingers worked nervously in her lap and she shifted in her chair. Her struggle was palpable and it moved him. Most ladies in her situation would have cast aside any moral discomfort with dishonesty and agreed readily, but not her.

And he was beyond intrigued to know why. This would change her life.

'What is it you are most worried about, Miss Potts?

Do you have want for more money? I can offer you a handsome lump sum outside your salary as governess. I know this is a risk you take. What amount would properly compensate you?' Perhaps it was the money, but she didn't seem driven by material things based on her simple wardrobe.

'No, not at all, Your Grace,' she stumbled out. 'Whatever you wish to offer is more than enough. I just do not wish to stain what little reputation I have or bring shame upon those around me when the truth comes out. My reputation is the only thing I truly possess that has worth.'

'And how do you know the truth would be exposed?' he asked. 'I would tell no one.'

She tilted her head at him. 'The truth always comes out. There is no way to prevent it,' she replied as if this was the most obvious known fact in the world.

It was his turn to shift uncomfortably in his chair. She did not know the *ton* as he did. She believed the truth was the truth and lies were lies. 'The *ton* operates on a certain level of grey and untruths, Miss Potts. I am somewhat pleased that you have no understanding of the way in which it and the people within it operate.'

'I am unsure as to what you mean.' She narrowed her brow.

'You speak of lies and truth as if they were black and white with nothing in between. What I suggest to you is that the wealthiest of society and those within it choose to often ignore the truth and embrace the grey in between what is truth and fiction for their own gain.'

She sat quietly. 'You mean to say that people might guess as to your lies, but not say them?'

'Exactly.'

She shook her head. 'Why would they be willing to do that?'

'Because it suits them…and in my case because they do not wish to lose favour with a duke like me.' He shrugged. It sounded deplorable when he said it aloud.

He hoped he was right. There were several truths he hoped never came out and this ruse was one of them.

'It is a confusing world you live in,' she replied.

'You are not wrong.'

She continued to contemplate in silence. 'And what about Lady Millie? Will it not confuse her to have me as her governess and this Lady Penelope?'

He smiled. 'I have given this some thought. Before she fell into silence…' he paused '…she loved to play dress up and make believe she was a princess.'

'I often did the same, your Grace, when I was her age and lived in the orphanage. Not a princess, perhaps, but I pretended I had another life. I venture she loved playing dress up with your wife and all her finery. I know I would have.'

The joy on her face and belief in the goodness of

Cecily was not something he dared dispute. Cecily had never had time for such trivialities as playing dress up with her daughter, but Miss Potts didn't need to know that. He swallowed back the truth. 'Yes, exactly. Millie loved it. I believe she would enjoy our scheme. We can tell her you will be playing pretend on the night of the ball.'

She nodded, but her smile faded and she shifted in her chair.

'What can I do to sway you?' he asked. His pulse quickened. He had to secure her in this. He was determined she say yes, now more than ever. For himself, for his daughter and for her, now. He wanted to help her to build belief and confidence and somehow this seemed the way to do it.

She thought quietly for a moment. 'If you can promise me some starting money and a recommendation letter for my future employment and one for my two friends, so that we can begin a new life outside Stow if this plan does not work out or you no longer wish for me to be your governess if it fails. I cannot be blamed if it does not fool everyone. I have doubts about how believable I will be in such a role and I do not wish to risk losing everything. My success is too important to me. But another chance such as this may never come along for someone...like me, Your Grace.'

'Will you promise to dedicate yourself to its success and not sabotage our plan?' he asked.

She baulked, pressing a hand to her collarbone. 'I would never sabotage anything, Your Grace. I always put forth my best,' she stated, sitting up straight and pulling back her shoulders, wincing when her sore shoulder touched the chair back. 'I just doubt that I can learn to look like or act like a lady of such breeding, especially with only a few days to prepare.'

The woman had pride and a strong will. He sat back, studied her once more, then cast caution aside by telling her the words on his heart. 'Perhaps not yet, but you could, Miss Potts. I believe in you.'

'I am honoured by your belief in me,' she said quietly, colour flushing her throat and cheeks. It was apparent she was not used to kindness or compliments. He would have to tread carefully.

'I will agree to those terms, Miss Potts. Take the night to think upon what we have discussed before you make your final decision. You have had a horrible day and I have overwhelmed you with my request. My apologies for my poor timing. I can only say that Dr Kemplar has thrust me into urgency on the matter.' He rose and brought her the Brothers Grimm book he had been reading that had inspired his offer. 'Take this book and have a think about it. Come and see me in the morning to let me know what you have decided.'

'Thank you, Your Grace. I will.' She accepted the book. He didn't let go, but took their proximity to say what was now in his heart.

'And, Miss Potts, I believe you could do anything you set your mind upon based on what I have seen today. Thank you again for what you did for Millie. It was...extraordinary.'

Her eyes widened and she flushed a beautiful, deep-rose pink before she gifted him a timid smile and nodded. 'Of course, Your Grace.' He let go of the book and she clutched it to her chest before turning to leave. He smiled. Who would have thought this little brown mouse of a woman from Stow might be his saving grace?

He returned to his study and gazed upon his father's portrait. He knew his father would find humour in what that little book had brought about. Perhaps his library was a lovely place of respite and where solutions to all of his problems resided after all.

Chapter Eight

Hattie left the room and headed to her chambers. To say she was stunned was an understatement. She couldn't have been more shocked if he'd confessed to this being an academy as Ophelia and Trudy had teased her about before she'd left to start her adventure here as governess. How she longed for their counsel now. They would know what to do. She didn't.

Her mind was racing, her thoughts colliding with one another, and her uncertainty was as big as the Manor itself. She sealed herself safely into her chambers, pressed her body against the back of the door to ensure she was indeed awake and not dreaming, and closed her eyes. She couldn't possibly pretend to be some Lady Penelope Denning.

Could she?

She opened her eyes and moved away from the door and allowed herself to soak in the calm beauty of her room. She set aside the book the Duke had given her on her nightstand and walked to the large, gilded dressing mirror. Standing before it, she tried to imagine herself with the trappings of a fine silk gown, sparkling jewels, a fancy bandeau woven through her tresses and pristine gloves matching her dress. She gathered up her hair in a twist with her good arm and couldn't help but giggle at the thought of such an idea.

Trudy would have pursed her lips at her and Ophelia would have cheered on her foolishness as she had when they were little. On rainy days, the trio of them could while away a whole afternoon pretending to be anything other than where they were or what they were: orphans alone in the world. Their favourite game they nicknamed 'the day'. It was *the day* they would be adopted all together by a fancy, wealthy family that loved them instantly. They used old ribbons to tie back their hair and a sheet from their beds as a long train as one of them pretended to be their new mother, a regal yet kind woman eager to love them just as they were.

Hattie's chest tightened. That day had never come. No one had ever adopted any of them. No wealthy family had saved them. They had aged out of the orphanage and saved themselves. Together. She tugged up the cuff sleeve of her dress and ran her fingertips over the worn string bracelet with three purple glass beads around her wrist. Hers was identical to the ones Ophelia and Trudy had and the three of them had worn them for years as wish bracelets. Once broken, their wishes were supposed to come true. While none of them had been worn away and broken just yet, they teased how Ophelia would forcibly break hers so her wish of finding her prince would come true soon, as she had grown restless of waiting.

Hadn't they all?

Hattie smiled as she ran her fingertip over the lop-sided pale-purple beads. They had saved for weeks to purchase them from the milliner's shop years ago. Hattie's wish had never changed: she wanted independence and the safety that regular work provided. Securing steady work like she had now was her dream as it would allow her a sense of safety she had never had and she could support Ophelia and Trudy, too, if all continued to go well. They were her family. She would do anything for them.

Her chest tightened. Just as His Grace would do anything for his daughter.

While his request appeared absurd to her, part of Hattie understood where it had been born from: love mixed with desperation. She had felt that way before many times. To know a duke with all his wealth and standing would share such a feeling and experience with someone like her was a revelation and a surprise. She never would have expected His Grace to suffer from the same problem. Wealth had always seemed like a solution and an escape from where she had been as a child, but perhaps she had been all wrong. Perhaps wealth could not fix all that was broken.

She completed her ablutions and dressed for bed, still mulling over the events of the day. Her body and shoulder ached and Mrs Chisholm came in with a steaming draught with a powder to help her sleep. She lingered nearby.

'Do you have need of anything else, Miss Potts?' Mrs Chisholm asked.

Hattie fidgeted with her hands. If anyone knew of what His Grace had proposed to her, it was his housekeeper. Did she dare?

'Advice?' Hattie said, hesitating a moment before continuing. 'I am confused and I have no one to counsel me here.'

Mrs Simmons smiled sympathetically. 'Is this about your conversation with His Grace?' she asked.

Hattie sighed in relief, knowing she didn't have to break any confidence by speaking with her. 'Yes. And I want to help His Grace and Lady Millie, but I…' She paused. 'I cannot imagine anyone would believe me to be a lady of breeding. Look at me.' Relief over sharing her insecurity and fear freed her, if only for a moment. She plopped down on the edge of her bed.

Mrs Chisholm watched her. 'May I?' she asked, gesturing to the bed.

Hattie patted the space next to her and wiped a tear from her cheek. The day had been simply too much.

'I believe you could, Miss Potts. You are a handsome woman. You just lack the confidence, if I may say so.' She patted Hattie's hand and Hattie's heart skipped in her chest. No one other than Ophelia and Trudy had ever thought her pretty. Her cheeks warmed.

'But it is also a great deal to ask of anyone and, if I am honest, I was surprised he asked it of you. It is a compliment to you. He must trust you. His Grace has difficulty asking for help.'

'Really?' Hattie asked. 'Why?'

'He didn't always have such difficulties, but when his older brother died ten years ago, he changed. Hardened. I think he was angry about losing him.'

'How did he die?'

'Carriage accident. Then, when his wife died in a carriage accident in a…similar fashion…just last year…it was difficult for him. Such a loss seemed to bring it all up again. He closed up, isolated himself in London and then here after his father passed.'

'So much loss,' Hattie murmured, her heart swelling with compassion.

'Too much. But he has been lighter since you arrived,' Mrs Chisholm added with a smile. 'You have made Lady Millie happy, which in turn has made him happy as well.'

Her cheeks burned hotter under her praise. 'Thank you.'

'So, whatever you decide, you have a post here as

governess, I know that much. He told me so.' She winked at Hattie and clutched her hands, and the warm, soft feel of them over her own made her think of her mother. A lump filled her throat and her eyes welled again.

'Have a sleep on it,' she said, squeezing Hattie's hands before releasing them. 'Your heart will know the right decision in the morning. It works for me every time.'

'Thank you for the advice, Mrs Chisholm,' Hattie replied, wiping a tear from her cheek. 'I will do that.'

The older woman rose. 'And be sure to take your tonic. It will ease some of the ache and help you sleep.' She glanced at Hattie's shoulder.

'I will. Thank you.'

After the door closed quietly, Hattie pulled back the covers and crawled into bed. The cool sheets and soft mattress enveloped her and she sighed aloud. She propped herself up with the numerous pillows, sipped on her tonic and opened to the first page of the story 'Cinderella'. Soon the words were blurry and she submitted to her body's need for sleep.

Hattie knocked on the door to His Grace's study the next morning, her pulse hammering in her throat. She had awoken early, ready to speak with him and she could wait no longer.

'Enter,' His Grace replied.

Hattie opened the door slowly and it squeaked on its hinges.

'Simmons, please see if that door can be oiled and I have some correspondence for you to—' He turned his head to her and his words fell off into an abyss. 'Miss Potts,' he spluttered out. He haphazardly folded the broadsheet he was reading, pulled his feet down from where they had been crossed at the ankles and propped on the corner of his desk, and stood.

Blast. She knew she should have waited. She gripped the edges of her skirts. What had she been thinking?

'I am sorry. It is an early hour. I just wished to speak with you, Your Grace. I tend to be an early riser and I did not think—' She did an awkward curtsy although she had no idea why. They were far beyond such ridiculous formalities. She righted herself quickly and as she took in the sight of him her throat dried.

Lord, he was handsome.

His untied cravat dangled about his neck and his loosened tunic gaped open, revealing a clean 'v' of skin at his throat and a sliver of his fine collarbone and chest. His brown hair was dishevelled as if he'd been running his hands through it and he had a shadow of stubble darkening his face. Once again, she was reminded he was no elderly Duke, but a man in his prime. A man only a handful of years older than her.

A man who was also her employer.

Her face heated. But she was also a woman in her prime.

Even a dead woman would notice his fine features.

Hattie almost giggled aloud as Ophelia's often-used phrase popped into her head. She pressed her lips together instead, gripped her hands in front of her, and prayed that the candlelit room was too dim for him to see the hot blush that was now heating her entire body. She stared at the fine rug for a few seconds to regain her composure. When she glanced back up, His Grace had shrugged on the jacket that had been hanging loosely on the back of his chair. His hair had also been somewhat smoothed.

But it didn't matter. Her eyes couldn't unsee what he had looked like before: disastrously handsome. How had she not noticed it before? How could she not notice it now?

'Miss Potts?'

She started and met his gaze. He furrowed his brow. She had missed his question. *Blast.* Woolgathering was going to be the end of her.

'I came to speak with you about…yesterday, Your Grace. I have a few questions before I make my decision.'

'At five in the morning?' He lifted a brow at her.

Her gaze slid to the large mantel clock to her right and cringed. Was it really that early?

She flushed again. 'My apologies. I slept soundly from the tonic Mrs Chisolm brought me and I wanted to talk to you about...the proposal you made to me yesterday as soon as I woke...' She paused, uncertain if she should say it aloud or not. 'I did not even check the time.'

His eyebrows shot up higher and he smirked. 'My proposal to you?' he asked.

All the colour drained from her face when she realised her faulty word choice. It made it seem as though she believed his offer for her to be his fake betrothed was a real offer of marriage.

'I...' she began, unsure how to unwind her words.

'I am teasing you, Miss Potts. I know what you are referring to. Come, sit.' His smile was warm and welcoming and she released a shaky breath. She smiled back at him, relieved by his good humour. She sat in the chair across from his desk.

'What questions do you have?' he asked as he settled into the large chair behind his desk and leaned forward, letting his arms rest on his desk and linking his hands together. 'Oh, and did you enjoy the book and the story of the Cinder girl?'

'Truthfully, I fell asleep before I finished all of it, but I believe I understand the gist of it. You wish to transform me into a princess, or, in this case, Lady Penelope Denning, for the evening to fool the *ton* and then I shall be returned to my governess position.'

'Yes. Exactly. For one evening, I will show you off to the *ton* as my future bride. Then, you will return to…wherever we decide you are from to await our wedding after a very long engagement.'

'And then you hope the *ton* will forget?'

'While I know they will not forget, I hope it will at least buy us some peace and quiet for a bit.'

Her stomach flipped. 'You do not worry they will want more?'

'How do you mean?'

'You have had men trespassing for just the name of a possible bride and to revive gossip about your family. Will they not want more than one opportunity of seeing us together at your upcoming ball? What if more than one event is required?' This was the question that plagued her: that it might not be a one-day affair. She couldn't imagine surviving more than one evening pretending, so she needed to know what his expectations were. She was not the actress Ophelia was.

'Does this worry you?'

She stared down at her hands. 'Yes,' she replied, daring to meet his gaze again. 'I am a horrible liar, Your Grace. I am afraid I will be discovered if people ask too many questions.'

He studied her. 'How do you know this?'

'That I am a horrible liar?'

'Yes,' he asked.

'My friends Trudy and Ophelia have told me so. And they've known me for years.'

'Would having them here make you more believable?'

She almost gasped. 'No, Your Grace. It would make it harder. I don't wish to lie to them as well.'

'Would you be embarrassed to tell them if you agree to this?'

'Yes,' she faltered, her cheeks heating again.

'Then why consider it?'

'Because I want the chance to better my life and theirs with my continued employment here…and I also want to help your daughter. I know perhaps more than most how she feels right now.'

His gaze softened and a muscle ticked in his jaw before he swallowed and nodded. 'May I ask?' he said softly before clearing his throat to continue. 'How she feels? How you felt after losing your mother?'

Goose pimples rose along her skin. Such an intimate question from him shook her, but his need to know the truth burned bright, hot and deep in his eyes as the light caught them from the candles lit sparsely around the room. She dared not deny him for he needed to know for Millie's sake. She gathered herself for a moment before she spoke the truth.

'I was eight and close to your daughter's age when I lost my mother. I suppose the best way to describe it is like that tiny duckling we found at the lake my first morning here. It was alone and crying out for help on the other side of the lake, desperate for its mother. Then it was overjoyed at being reunited with her once we brought them together and couldn't stop quacking. But, for me...for your daughter,' she continued holding his intense gaze, 'it is as though she is the duckling that never gets reunited with her mother. She just cries for her and aches for her...every day.'

His features tightened and he stared at her before he silently stood and walked over to the hearth, turning his back on her. He leaned his hands on the mantel and cursed, dipping his head before pushing back from it and running a hand over his face. When he turned to her, his eyes reflected in the firelight bright with unshed tears.

A chill came over her as they stared upon one another with such a ferocity she felt naked and exposed. She had revealed too much to him about herself and his daughter and she wished to take the words back, but she couldn't.

'Thank you for your honesty,' he said, blinking, his tone husky and full of emotion.

The fire crackled and silence settled between them.

'I am grateful for it and I feel compelled...no, that it is not right.' He hesitated. 'I *want* to tell you about Cecily, my late wife. You should know what you are stepping into in some sense and it may help you understand why I have dared ask this of you.' He tucked his hands in his trouser pockets.

'Mrs Chisholm told me she died in a carriage accident,' Hattie offered. 'I am sorry, Your Grace.' And she was. 'I can see how it pains you to speak of it.'

He released an awkward chuckle and shook his head. 'Ah, thank you, Miss Potts, but I think you mistake me,' he offered. He wiped a hand over his mouth and his brow furrowed before he continued. 'It is not grief, but her betrayal that pains me...angers me,' he replied, his words sharpening, darkening with emotion. 'She had affairs with other men and she died with one of those men, breaking the vows of our marriage, in a carriage accident that night.'

Hattie stilled and her throat dried. She could have sworn her heart stopped in her chest. That was the last thing she had expected him to say. Her cheeks heated. Why would a woman do such to her husband, especially to a man such as him? No wonder he did not wish to remarry and held himself at such a distance from Society. Hattie stared down at her lap, uncertain what to do. What did one say after such an admission?

'And because of her choices,' he continued, 'my daughter has no mother and she does not speak, and we live as we do now attempting to recover from the damage she inflicted upon us under the *ton*'s oppressive gaze. It enrages me. So, it is not *grief* that keeps me silent, but the shame and anger of her betrayal and the scandal that has engulfed us since then.'

Hattie's heartbeat thrummed in her ears as she looked upon him. 'I am so sorry,' she replied. 'I did not know. I thought—'

He met her gaze and gave a wistful smile. 'That I was a grieving widower?'

She pressed her lips together and nodded.

'Well, at least now you know I am not.' He sighed. 'I grieved for the loss of the marriage and the woman I believed I had married early on in our union. Now, I am merely a protective father hoping to shield his daughter from further harm.'

'You do not worry I may fail in this charade and bring you worse scandal?'

'No,' he replied without hesitation. 'I have every belief in you, Miss Potts.' His words were certain and steady. 'Dare I ask if you have decided if you will take part in our ruse?' he asked.

Her mind screamed not to risk such foolishness and deception and to just remain the governess, but her heart, her heart smothered out that reluctance when she thought of what he and Millie had suffered and that she might help her recover. 'Yes. I will help you.' Hattie's words came out quietly like a tremble against the air.

His shoulders relaxed, his gaze softening further. 'Thank you,' he said, walking closer to her. 'And as I said yesterday, I promise to protect you in all of this, Miss Potts. Your reputation will not be harmed.' He reached out his hand to shake hers. 'To seal our agreement.'

She nodded and, as her hand slid into his, the warmth and intimacy of it after what she had shared about herself sent a pooling heat through her entire body despite how brief the touch was.

She swallowed and prayed she could protect *herself* in all of this. The Duke of Wimberley was slowly becoming the most dashing man she had ever met and the most dangerous employer she had ever had.

'We have not a moment to waste,' he said. 'I will speak with the servants, let them know of your agreement, and return. Wait here.'

He was gone before she could even nod in agreement. Her hands trembled and her stomach flipped. Her agreement had set this whole farce in motion. She imagined how Ophelia would have clasped her hands in glee and droned on about how romantic it was to pretend to be a future duchess and how Trudy's raised brow of disapproval would have disappeared into her hairline entirely this time. Hattie fought the urge to giggle out of nervous uncertainty. She had never done anything so reckless or daring in all her life.

And she wasn't sure if she'd done the right thing at all.

But when she thought of Millie with her wide startled eyes yesterday morning and how this brief ruse might help her as well as Hattie's future, she couldn't argue against her choice. Always playing it safe had yielded her nothing, while daring a risk, such as coming here, was proving to pay dividends. She hoped it stayed that way and she hadn't gambled too much too soon.

This was the beginning of a new chapter in her life and in Ophelia's and Trudy's lives. This marked the beginning of permanent employment that could give them some measure of safety and happiness… finally…and little Millie could be left to grieve and heal properly and find her voice once more. Perhaps even the Duke himself could heal his broken heart. Despite what he had said, Hattie was no fool. He *was* a man struggling with grief. The sadness over losing his dream of a happy marriage was evident and hiding beneath his rage.

Hattie waited in the silence of the study in the same small chair, listening to the crackle of the fire and the distant voice of His Grace, who must be speaking to his household. She was tempted to rise and join them, but didn't dare. Some of them might be displeased with their arrangement. After all, he would be asking them all to lie, too. She shook her head. What a turn her life had taken in such a short time. Who knew what other turns were in her future?

Despite her trepidation and the shock of the news the Duke had shared with her about his late wife, Hattie could hardly wait to see what would happen as Lady Penelope Denning. She tapped the toes of her boots on the rug, restless for what was next. Her body ached for movement. She stood and walked about the room, letting her fingertips glide along fine furnishings and ornate crown moulding until she reached a large window looking down on the drive. She smiled when she realised it looked down on the very spot where she had first alighted from the Duke's carriage and met him and his staff a week ago.

Now she would be the pretend future duchess. It was enough to make her laugh aloud, but she didn't…for a future duchess would have far more decorum than that, would she not? She stared out in the distance. The sun was rising and the last vestiges of the darkened sky were disappearing, leaving only an endless swathe of a tangerine-rose-coloured sun pushing through the treeline as far as she could see. It was glorious and her heart was full of hope, a feeling she had not had in so very long she could hardly name it at first.

Then the familiar knot of dread that followed any

flickering of hope set in. What if she couldn't be this Penelope Denning? What if everyone laughed at her and she brought shame to the Duke or brought scandal and more rather than less intrigue to his doorstep? And—how did one greet a marquis or a lord? And would she need to learn to dance? Her stomach soured. She had little idea what one did at a fancy ball, especially one befitting a duke. Her nerves and pulse increased, threatening to drown out her initial enthusiasm.

But what if you are brilliant?

She could hear Ophelia's words in her head now encouraging her, and Hattie bit her lip.

What if she *was* the jewel of the ball? This man believed in her, so much so that he was risking his standing in Society and had everything to lose, while she had little to lose other than her reputation, which was small despite how protective she was of it.

She had to at least try to believe in herself and so she would. She closed her eyes and made the promise to herself.

I will believe that I can do this for Millie's sake and for my own.

'Miss Potts?' the Duke called from behind her.

Hattie squared her shoulders and turned. Her stomach lurched at the sight of him at the doorway with a sea of servants standing behind him in the hallway.

Her smile faltered before she set it in place. She'd had no idea they would be joining him upon his return and that so many would already be awake. She chastised herself. But, of course, they would be. Their day started even earlier than her own.

'We are ready, Miss Potts,' he said with confidence and authority, smiling at her as if this was the biggest adventure of her life. 'Let us begin.'

And in that moment, she realised it was. Her throat dried. All these people knew of their charade and wanted to help? How was that possible? How would they ever keep this secret? It was required for this plan to be successful.

His Grace cleared his throat and Hattie glanced in his direction, realising he was indeed waiting for something. Had he asked her something and she not noticed?

Blast.

What would Ophelia do?

Greet everyone.

'Good morning,' Hattie said in the loudest and most certain voice she could muster. 'Thank you for whatever it is you are all about to do to transform me…for Lady Millie's sake,' she rushed out at the end.

A silence followed. Her cheeks heated. Had she said the wrong thing?

The butler was the first to respond. 'We would do anything for her, Miss Potts. We are grateful for your help in this…endeavour.' He nodded, which was as close as the man had ever come to a smile.

'Yes, Miss Potts,' the housekeeper added. 'Whatever you need…just ask.' She truly did smile at Hattie, which put her at ease, and she smiled back.

The rest of the servants nodded or gave smiles of encouragement as they looked upon her.

'What shall we do first, Mrs Chisholm?' His Grace asked.

The woman assessed Hattie for a moment and said simply, 'Wardrobe, Your Grace. We simply must do something about all that brown.'

Hattie looked down at the brown dress she had chosen this morning, which was the same one she had arrived in a week ago. A flush entered her cheeks. Perhaps it was a bit drab, but the colour hid every stain, which is why she had selected it.

His Grace's lip quirked up. 'Yes, Mrs Chisholm. I could not agree more.'

Hattie prayed the floor beneath her would open and swallow her whole. Sadly, it didn't.

Chapter Nine

William could not have been prouder of the efficiency of his staff and how they rallied around his plan to transform Miss Potts from a little country mouse into the fictional lady of his creation: Lady Penelope Denning. What began as a mere desperate filament of thought to ease his daughter's suffering had grown into a full-fledged woman of his imagination. Now, he needed each part of his plan to fall into place seamlessly.

Thankfully, the first piece of his plan was in motion. The late Marchioness's favourite modiste, Mademoiselle Dashiell, arrived following the evening meal after being summoned by his driver Eddie earlier in the morning. Despite his fear that Miss Potts might baulk at the idea of the process, she reported to his study with a timid smile after Millie had been gathered by her nurse for bed and been whisked away by the dressmaker to her chamber. The next two hours were spent on measurements of Miss Potts and selecting fabrics from the array of samples.

The mantel clock chimed nine o'clock when the ladies arrived at the door of his study once more for his final approval, since it was his coin being spent and significant coin at that. He tried to pretend he knew what he was looking at and cared about the choice of colours before him. While he would have paid anything for the peace of mind this successful ruse would bring, he didn't wish for the Mademoiselle to know that. The dressmaker's prices were high enough. He remembered the bills for Cecily well. He prepared himself for the exorbitant fees he would pay now for the Mademoiselle's skill plus the hasty timeline for completion...and the added cost for her continued loyalty and secrecy.

A sea of colourful fabrics covered what remained of his desk in the study and Mademoiselle Dashiell, Mrs Chisholm, and Miss Potts looked up at him in expectation as he studied the fabrics. The oddity of having such trifles on his father's old desk was not lost on William. He wasn't sure if his father would laugh at the absurdity of it or clap William on the back for discovering a solution to finding his way through his present issue of being an unmarried duke in the *ton* with gossip hounds at his doors.

'I quite like this series of blues and emeralds,' Mrs

Chisholm stated to Mademoiselle Dashiell, running her fingertips over the fine silks, muslin and embroidered fabrics of which he had limited knowledge, other than what they felt like between his fingertips and the cost of each, silk being the most expensive if his memory served.

'You have fine taste, Mrs Chisholm,' Mademoiselle Dashiell agreed, her words sounding more like a rolling purr with her heavy French accent.

'Your Grace?' Mrs Chisholm enquired, looking at the fabrics and then him with expectation.

Rather than answering, his gaze landed on Miss Potts who sat wedged between the two women wide-eyed and silent. She hadn't said a word since they'd entered the room.

'Which fabrics do you prefer, Miss Potts?' he asked.

Although he didn't believe it possible, her eyes widened further as she studied the fabrics again. She appeared on the edge of full alarm. After another beat of examining them, she met his gaze. She started to reply and then clamped her mouth shut, her brow furrowing.

'You shall be wearing them,' he added. 'Certainly you have an opinion.'

She swallowed and edged forward in her seat. The other women looked terrified by which ones she might pick. Evidently, wearing brown as a signature colour of one's wardrobe did not build confidence in one's fashion sensibilities.

'May I?' she asked, nodding to the fabric swatches. Once in her hands, she studied each one with care and scrutiny. After a few minutes, she set them back on the desk. 'I have never seen or touched such fine fabrics before. Although any of them would be beautiful, I think the wine-coloured fabric would suit me best for His Grace's celebratory ball. It shall favour my colouring more.'

The other woman baulked. 'Such a colour in early spring?' Mrs Chisholm asked. She shook her head. 'I do not know, Your Grace.'

'It would make you stand out. The other ladies will no doubt favour the softer tones this time of year,' the Mademoiselle chimed in, glancing back and forth from the swathe of fabric to Miss Potts's face, considering the woman's suggestion rather than dismissing it entirely.

'If I have won the heart of a duke, would I not be prone to such decisions to flaunt myself, especially with other women about?' Miss Potts asked.

They faced her and her cheeks bloomed with colour. 'I am only thinking of the Lady Penelope Denning you have created. Did I misunderstand your description of her and your wish for her to be like a Cinderella of those fairy tales, Your Grace?' she asked.

William couldn't help but smile. 'No. You interpreted my words and the story to precision. She is right. *This*,' he said, lifting the dark-burgundy material, 'would be the choice of a bold, confident woman who has stolen my heart and wished to shock the ladies of the *ton* by not conforming to Society's expectations.'

Mademoiselle Dashiell smiled. 'Then, this is the fabric I will use and I know just what style of dress I shall make. I will commission a handful of others of softer colours for daily use in case you receive callers after the event, Miss Potts. My team of seamstresses shall set upon it directly and be back for a fitting in two days' time. That way, alterations can be made prior to the ball on Saturday.'

'Thank you, Mademoiselle. Be sure to send along the bill,' William answered, relieved that the browns had been eradicated from Miss Potts's wardrobe. Now, it was on to the next item on Mrs Chisholm's list.

'Of course, Your Grace,' she purred, batting her eyelashes at him.

His stomach churned. It would be one hell of a bill, but it would be worth it, he reminded himself as she gathered up the fabrics and left.

'And now for the rest of you,' the housekeeper said. 'Miss Potts,' she added when the woman failed to rise. 'Follow me,' Mrs Chisholm commanded.

Miss Potts sent William a mournful glance before

leaving the room and he couldn't help but chuckle. Heaven only knew what she would be subjected to now. He glanced at the bay of windows and noted the pitch-black sky and smiled. What had begun as a day of uncertainty had ended with a plan in place.

They had six days to prepare for a ball and for the big reveal of Lady Penelope Denning—for once, he could hardly wait for the day of a fussy ball to arrive.

Hattie closed her chamber door with hesitation. While she was relieved to have survived the measuring, poking, prodding and fabric selection with Mademoiselle Dashiell, what was coming next was of greater uncertainty. Slowly, she followed the low murmurs and headed towards the elegant bath nestled within her chambers. The large porcelain tub with its extravagant claw feet was filled with steaming water and rose petals of all things. Hattie commanded herself not to gasp. She could not wait to tell Ophelia about this.

She would never believe her, of course. Nor would Trudy. Hattie was staring at it and she didn't believe it. Who lived like this? Evidently the late Marchioness had.

'Good evening, Miss Potts. We have prepared a bath for you as requested by Mrs Chisholm. Are you ready?' the elder of the two young maids asked with a timid smile.

Hattie stood at the threshold and breathed in the fragrant steaming rose-scented waters and sighed. *This* would not be so bad after all. When Mrs Chisholm had declared Miss Potts was to be 'scrubbed and refreshed down to the bones', Hattie had feared for her well-being. Now, she was relieved. The woman merely wanted her to have a proper bath and have her hair washed.

Despite feeling shy about disrobing in front of two women she did not know, Hattie did so with some speed and then stepped into the hot water. She did sigh then. It was exquisite. She eased herself into the water, letting the heat spread through her as she eased back. To her surprise the water was deep enough to cover most of her and only her head, neck and shoulders were exposed. She leaned back, closed her eyes and relaxed, feeling the ache in her shoulder which, while she didn't need the sling today, was still tender. She was lucky she had minimal bruising, which wouldn't show in a gown. Then she felt fingers threading through her hair. She started at first.

'I shall just remove your hairpins and ribbons, Miss Potts. Then we will wash your hair and scrub you down.'

She stilled. While the first part sounded just fine,

she wasn't so sure about being 'scrubbed down'. She was perfectly capable of scrubbing herself. Gently the pins were pulled from her hair one after another.

The comb pulled less gently. Hattie winced. 'Sorry, Miss,' the younger maid whispered. 'I must get the tangles out before we wash it.'

'Of course,' she murmured and then cringed as the girl worked the tangles out with a bit more force than she expected.

Hattie closed her eyes. *This was all for a better life.* One week of pretending stood between her and a new life for Lady Millie, herself and hopefully for Ophelia and Trudy, too. All she needed to do was become someone else entirely. How many times had she wished such as a young girl in the orphanage? Honestly, this ruse might be more natural for her than she ever expected or wished to admit to.

The three of them had whiled away many a rainy afternoon in the orphanage pretending to be the long-lost daughters of a lady of high esteem in a household where they had all they wished for: care, safety, love and the extravagance of having a family, which was what they all had desired more than anything else in the world. Even now, if she allowed herself to imagine it for a moment, she still wanted it: a family of her own. A husband, children and a place they all could call home.

One final tug yanked Hattie back and she opened her eyes, her brief daydream vanishing. 'Ow.' She winced, unable to ignore the force.

'Apologies, Miss,' the younger of the two women said, releasing her hair and coming into view. She bit her lip and wrung her hands, her grey eyes widening. The poor girl couldn't be more than seventeen.

'I know my hair must be a fright,' Hattie chuckled, trying to put her at ease. 'Do what you must.'

'You have beautiful hair, Miss,' she said. 'I am new here. Susie left to get some hair oils to soften and condition it. I am still learning.'

'Oh?' Hattie replied, dropping her voice. 'Then we shall get along well. I have only been here a bit over a week myself. Perhaps we shall muddle through together? I'm Hattie,' she said.

The girl smiled and nodded. 'I would like that. Thank you, Miss. I'm Emma.'

The girl lifted the comb and Hattie sat back, relaxed to know she was not the only one who was nervous and uncertain about…everything.

'I think it is brave of you to help His Grace and his daughter as you are,' Emma stated, running the comb gently through Hattie's hair.

'Oh?'

'Yes. Some of those women of the *ton* are absolutely

horrid.' Then she gasped. 'I should not have said that. My apologies, Miss.'

Hattie covered her mouth and then chuckled aloud. 'Perhaps not, but I do not disagree with you, even though I cannot say I have met anyone with any great means,' she replied with a wink.

The older servant girl entered the chamber and the two of them reset their features and fell silent before the woman entered the bathroom. Hattie smothered her smile and closed her eyes, so she wouldn't give herself or the young maid away.

Perhaps everything would be fine after all.

The older girl lifted one of Hattie's arms and started scrubbing with some force. She cringed.

Well, *maybe*, anyway.

Chapter Ten

'Good to see you, Cousin. Thank you for joining us for dinner this evening on such short notice.' William pressed a kiss to Lady Daphne Buchanan's cheek as he greeted her in the parlour. Simmons nodded to him and closed the door, so they could speak in private. Daphne was essential to the success of William's plan. He prayed she would not baulk at his request for help in making Miss Potts into Lady Penelope Denning.

'I see widowhood continues to suit you,' he added, smiling at her. And it did, much as being a widower did him. It was something they had both shared and borne together: the loss of a spouse who had made them miserable for all intents and purposes despite how much they had initially loved them. Daphne had fallen for an older bachelor who held little regard for monogamy, much like William's wife. In a way it had made him and Daphne depend on one another over the last year. She was the only one who truly understood and he was grateful for her friendship. He hoped what he was about to ask of her didn't strain their relationship.

She smirked at him. 'As it does you,' she quipped. 'So, what is all this secrecy about, Liam? My mind is a whirlwind of theories. I can hardly wait to see which one of my speculations is correct.' Her eyes sparkled from the light of the glowing sconces in the room as she clasped her hands together in excitement.

'Sherry?' he offered.

She tilted her head and nodded, her sandy-blonde waves catching the light. 'Of course. This must be good for you to ply me with my favourite drink *before* we dine.'

He poured, handed her the glass and gestured for her to sit on the sofa before he sat down next to her. 'I need your help,' he said.

She took a sip of her drink and studied him. 'You look painfully serious. With what?'

He released his breath. 'Creating a fake betrothed and making her believable to the *ton*…by this weekend's ball.' There, he'd said it in one big rush. He felt better already.

She watched him for a beat and then threw back her head and had a hearty laugh. 'You are good. I almost believed you,' she said, wiping one of her eyes.

'I am serious, Cousin.'

She set down her glass on the end table next to her and her eyes widened. 'What?'

'We have had an eventful week and I am desperate.'

She stilled and placed a gloved hand gently on his forearm. 'Start from the beginning and tell me what has happened. Leave nothing out. We will figure it out together, Cousin. We are family.'

Telling Daphne everything hadn't been as hard as he first believed. She had listened and nodded throughout, interrupting only once to add in a curse of frustration when he relayed to her the events with the trespassing reporters at the lake and how they had scared the wits out of Millie and Miss Potts.

'Scoundrels, all of them,' she added, even after William had moved on and outlined his plan in full to her.

He sat in silence and allowed his body to reclaim the calm and relief he felt now. Whether she agreed to assist him or not was out of his hands, but to have finally shared all his worries, hopes and fears with someone who knew all he and Millie had been through relieved him in a way he hadn't anticipated. His cousin was an ally, no matter what her answer, and he would respect her choices, no matter what they were.

'And this Miss Potts,' she asked. 'She has agreed wholeheartedly?'

He paused. 'Perhaps that is too strong a word, but she has agreed to do her best for Millie's sake.'

'And?'

He shook his head. 'And what?'

'What incentives have you given her? For her to agree to take such a risk, it had to have been something impressive?'

While Daphne was not a snob, William wasn't sure how she would react when he told her the truth of Miss Potts's upbringing. He also felt a surge of protectiveness in him for the woman, which was odd to acknowledge, despite its truth.

'Liam?' she asked, extending the length of his name to show her concern.

'I promised her a good reference for herself as well as her two friends in case it did not go to plan and she was no longer able to stay on as governess here. I also offered her an additional lump sum that she can use as she sees fit.' He rubbed the back of his neck, which had begun to ache. It didn't seem like much now when he thought of the risks she was taking. He felt a bit like a cad.

'That is *all* she requires?' she asked. Her brow furrowed, and she took a sip of sherry before resting the tumbler in her lap. 'Why did she not ask for more? This is quite a risk.'

'I do not believe she thought to. She is…kind and

has had little. She grew up as an orphan. It was initially why I selected her as governess. I thought…' He paused and shrugged.

Understanding bloomed on Daphne's face and she gifted him a soft smile. 'That she would understand Millie as she lost her mother.'

'Precisely.'

They sat in companionable silence for a few minutes before the mantel clock chimed eight times loudly, reminding them it was time for their evening meal. William viewed his cousin's silence as her answer and decided to take the rejection in stride. It had been a long shot and she had her own reputation to risk. He didn't blame her for not wishing to be a part of such subterfuge. Success could not be guaranteed and if they failed the *ton* would scrutinise them relentlessly.

'Shall we?' he said, standing and offering his arm to escort her to the dining room for their meal. 'I know Millie will love seeing you, as will Miss Potts enjoy meeting you.'

Daphne set down her drink, rose and accepted his arm. 'So, you have your governess dining with you? That is unusual, is it not?'

He shrugged. 'Yes, but you know we are not a household that stands on such formalities.'

She chuckled. 'I do.'

'But I do it for Millie,' he rushed out. 'She is quite taken with her.'

'Oh? Is she the only one? Or perhaps you are quite taken with her yourself?' she whispered and lifted a brow at him as they walked out of the parlour.

'Cousin, you know I am not interested in an attachment of any kind.'

She smirked at him as they walked into the dining room, and she leaned close to his ear. 'Perhaps, but you also did not answer my question, *Cousin*.'

William would have rebuked her quip if they were not already deep into the dining room and headed towards their chairs. Millie smiled and rushed to Daphne, colliding with her legs and hugging her. His cousin stooped and kissed his daughter's cheeks one at a time and lavished her with praise and well wishes before she disengaged and stood.

She glanced to William.

'Lady Buchanan, let me introduce you to Miss Potts, our new governess. Miss Potts, this is my cousin, Lady Daphne Buchanan.'

Millie rushed back to her seat as Daphne and Miss Potts exchanged pleasantries. Seeing the women side by side was strange. Despite having similar builds, their features and colouring were in sharp contrast. Daphne was blonde, green eyed and wore a soft periwinkle-blue gown while Miss Potts was brunette with equally dark eyes in her signature plain-dress style. Today it was dark grey. While an improvement over her brown dress, it left little to enhance her looks. He wondered what they would make of each other.

William shouldn't have worried. The women chatted along easily at dinner and, despite not joining in, Millie's gaze was bright and interested as she listened and watched them talk. At times, his daughter smiled and even turned to him, as if she, too, approved of their dinner companions. It set William at ease in a way he hadn't expected and their dinner together ended far too soon. Even though he'd missed his usual time at dusk with Millie due to their extended meal, she kissed his cheek and left with her nurse willingly for bed. The dinner had been a success even if his cousin hadn't agreed to help him.

Miss Potts excused herself not long after and the evening ended the way it had begun, with him saying goodbye to his cousin in the parlour. He helped her with her coat and she faced him as she fastened the clasp at the throat. 'I have thought over your plan, Liam. I will help you.'

At first, he didn't move. But then he hugged her fiercely, pressing a kiss to her cheek. 'Thank you,' he said.

She laughed. 'I do not know if it will work, mind

you,' she added. 'But I will help you in whatever way I can. I will compile a list tonight of what she needs to know and I will arrive tomorrow to begin preparations.'

'Thank you, Daphne. I owe you.'

She smiled widely as he opened the door for her. 'Yes, Cousin, you will. And I cannot wait for the day to collect such a favour.' She winked at him and he laughed as he watched her walk down the front steps towards her waiting carriage.

William closed the door and turned to find Mrs Chisholm and Mr Simmons standing behind him. Although a bit startled, he wasn't entirely surprised to see them waiting in the wings for news of how his dinner went with his cousin. He smiled. 'She has agreed to help us. Lady Buchanan will return tomorrow with a list of what Miss Potts needs to know.'

Mrs Chisholm clapped her hands together. 'That is splendid news, Your Grace.' Even Mr Simmons appeared to sigh in relief. The outcome of the evening could not have been better.

'Mademoiselle Dashiell is also supposed to return tomorrow for the fittings of gowns for Miss Potts. Having Lady Buchanan here to oversee such matters will be helpful,' Mrs Chisholm added.

'Ah, yes. I agree,' William added. 'Things are coming together. And how are the actual preparations for the ball itself proceeding? I know I am asking a great deal of you both right now.'

'All is on schedule, Your Grace,' Simmons replied.

'Excellent.'

'Miss Potts wished to speak with you before you retired this eve, Your Grace,' Mrs Chisholm said. 'She is in the study awaiting you.'

William's heart thudded in his chest. What if she had changed her mind? The momentary thought of it sickened him, but he wouldn't know unless he went to speak with her. There was no need to put it off.

'Thank you. I will see her now.'

Mrs Chisholm dropped her voice low. 'I believe she is nervous after meeting your cousin. Perhaps if you told her how she will be assisting, it will put her mind at ease.'

He sighed. 'Yes. Thank you both.'

They nodded and replied kindly, and everyone travelled off in different directions. In hindsight, perhaps William should have told Miss Potts why he had invited his cousin to join them for dinner this evening beforehand, but he didn't wish to raise hopes in case Daphne had not agreed to assist them in their scheme. The fact that she had was a delightful surprise. William had thought his chances of success were negligible. He was utterly pleased to be wrong.

He entered the room with a spring in his step. Miss Potts stood before the window, looking out at the crescent moon that hung high over the hillside.

'Good evening, Miss Potts. I hope you enjoyed dining with Lady Buchanan.'

She turned and the emotion in her face knocked the wind out of him and he came to a stop. The next words died on his lips.

She attempted a smile, but it fell flat. 'I did. She is lovely, Your Grace. I feel horrible about the idea of deceiving her…and everyone else for that matter.' She rubbed her injured shoulder.

'Does it still plague you?' he asked, gesturing to her arm.

She looked down at her arm as if she hadn't even known what she had been doing and stopped. 'I am fine. It is much better. I am just anxious, I suppose.'

'That makes two of us,' he replied with a chuckle. 'Would it make you feel better to know that Lady Buchanan knows of our ruse and plans to come tomorrow to assist you in preparing for the role?'

She froze and her lips parted. 'She will?'

'Yes. She told me before she left this evening.' He walked towards her. 'I should have told you, Miss Potts, before dinner, but I did not know if she would agree. I did not wish to get your hopes up only to disappoint you.'

'I suppose that is a relief. Does she believe I can do it? Play this part?' she asked, hugging her arms around her waist.

While William wasn't sure of the answer, he could see the answer Miss Potts needed to hear. 'Yes,' he replied, despite the fact it might well be a lie. 'She does.'

Miss Potts nodded and sat down on the cushion of the window seat. 'That is good to hear, for when we met her for dinner, I wondered how in the world I could be as polished as she.'

He approached and settled on the window cushion seat with her, being mindful to leave adequate distance between them. 'I think you will be surprised at just how easily you can transform into our fictional character once you have on fine dresses and learn the etiquette required of a lady.'

She stared at him, her brown eyes clouded with doubt. 'How can you be so sure?' she asked.

'It is a fair question, I suppose. But when I think of how quickly you won all of us over here at Blithe Manor, it makes me certain of your success. All you must do is believe in it yourself.'

As he said the words, he wondered if it was indeed that simple. For he had believed in marriage, his wife and in a joyful future, but look where he had ended up. Why did he believe in her so? It defied reasoning.

She nodded. 'I will try, Your Grace.' She rose.

'Thank you for speaking with me. I will be ready for Lady Buchanan's arrival tomorrow.'

'And, Miss Potts…' he rushed out, reaching for her fingertips to halt her advance. The feathering touch sent an unexpected tremble through him and she stilled, as if she, too, were affected.

She turned to him. 'Yes, Your Grace?'

He cleared his throat and gestured for her to join him, so she settled back on the window seat. 'Lady Buchanan also helped me fashion a fake history for you. I wanted to get your approval of it before I share it with the household.' He did not know how she would feel about the story they had crafted and he hesitated to continue.

She smiled at him and smoothed her skirts.

'You were sent off to finishing school out of the country and have just returned.'

Her brow crinkled. 'But what of the many years before that? How will such an absence be explained? And why would my parents not be in attendance at the ball celebrating with us?'

Why had they not thought of such? 'Perhaps you lived abroad prior to that as well?' he offered.

Her throat flushed and she shifted on the cushion seat. 'Perhaps if you stick closer to my true history it will be easier for me,' she began, unable to meet his gaze. 'What if I was an orphan. A daughter of a nobleman and his mistress…maybe he did not know of me at all. And…on his deathbed, he goes in search of me, his only heir. He finds me, sends me off to finishing school, but dies before I meet you so you would never know any of my family?'

When she lifted her gaze to meet his, there was a desperation and truth in her glistening brown eyes that sent a jolt of compassion and longing through him. His chest tightened as he realised the cause of it.

'Is that part of your own story, Miss Potts?' he asked quietly.

She nodded and wiped away a tear. 'Yes. I was a product of an affair. I never knew my father. He never claimed me and my mother died of a broken heart, I think.'

'And you wished he would come back and find you? Claim you as his daughter?'

'Yes,' she began. 'More than you can ever know,' she finished, a sob cutting off her words.

His throat constricted. How could a father abandon his daughter? He couldn't imagine such cruelty. He reached out and grasped her hand and squeezed it. 'I am sorry beyond words. I wish—' he began. Her crying intensified and he set aside his boundaries of employer and employee and pulled her into his arms, consoling her. The feel of her soft, petite frame within his own stole his breath and he savoured it far more than he should have. But it had been so long since he had been held and needed in such a way by a woman, he savoured it, relishing the tenderness of her vulnerability.

After a few more moments, she pulled back and wiped her face. 'I am sorry, Your Grace. I forget myself and I…'

'You do not need to apologise for anything, Miss Potts.' He handed her a handkerchief, shuddering from the loss of her in his arms. 'I dare say we do not have the usual employer–employee relationship.' He attempted to steady his own emotions and his pulse. 'But I believe we have settled on a fake history for you that is quite believable, have we not?'

She nodded. 'Yes,' she chuckled. 'We do.'

'Then I shall share it with the household?'

'Yes,' she said dabbing her cheeks, rising once more from the window seat. 'Goodnight, Your Grace. Thank you for your kindness.'

'Thank you for yours, Miss Potts. You take a great risk for my family by taking on this charade.'

She nodded and began to walk away.

'Do not forget about the dress fittings tomorrow,' he called to her.

Her shoulders slumped. 'Oh, yes.'

He smirked. 'Do you not enjoy the idea of new gowns?' he asked, intrigued by her lack of enthusiasm.

'No, Your Grace,' she said, facing him. 'Just the idea of being pricked with more needles.'

He chuckled and she left the room, leaving William optimistic for the morning and the success of his ruse. Perhaps their success was as simple as just believing.

Chapter Eleven

'And which letter is "M" as in milk, your favourite drink?' Hattie asked, smiling at her young charge as she sat on the small reading-room floor rug upstairs. They stared down at the written alphabet 'map' they had constructed full of pretty images and the large capital letters of the alphabet.

Each day they added pictures to it and reviewed it like a trivia game in the afternoon before Millie's nap. Hattie was impressed by how quickly Millie had taken to it. Seeing her progress each day was breathtaking and its own reward.

Millie looked at the map, walking around it thoughtfully and searching. Once she saw the letter she sought, she smiled, bent down, and pressed her index finger on the 'M' before gazing up at Hattie for approval.

Hattie clapped in excitement. 'Yes! And what else in this room starts with the "M" sound?'

Millie laughed and pointed to herself.

'Wonderful!' a female voice from behind them called out.

Hattie turned in surprise to see Lady Buchanan standing in the doorway watching them. *Blast.* Hattie flushed and scrambled to stand to properly greet her.

'No, no, my dear, let me join you both. It looks like glorious fun!' She smiled and set aside the reticule and gift she had in her hand on a nearby table.

Millie rushed to the woman's side and flounced into her lap as soon as Lady Buchanan was sitting on the rug with them. Millie hugged her and giggled in happiness.

'What an intriguing way to review one's letters,' Lady Buchanan said, studying the large sprawling parchment before them. 'I am impressed by how taken my niece is with you, Miss Potts.'

Hattie smiled. 'Thank you so much for your kind words, Lady Buchanan. I have loved my time with Lady Millie. I find I am learning as much as she.' It was true. Each day, Hattie learned so much about how to teach and how Millie learned and adjusted her plans accordingly. 'Some days what I plan does not work, but she loves her letters. I think she may be a lover of books like her grandfather, the late Duke of Wimberley.'

Millie hugged Lady Buchanan's neck and the woman returned the little girl's hug. 'And the late Duke would be thrilled. He loved to read and learn. And he was incredibly kind, just like His Grace, my cousin.'

Hattie nodded and dropped her gaze. 'Yes. His Grace is kind. Much more so than I expected, if I am honest.' She lifted her head and smiled as she fidgeted with her hands in her lap.

'Then why did you look so pained when I said it?' Lady Buchanan asked with a smirk. She ran a hand down Millie's hair.

'I fear I will disappoint him with our ruse,' she replied, her stomach clenching as she admitted her fears aloud. 'I know nothing of being a proper lady.'

'But that is why I am here!' Lady Buchanan said, smiling.

Just then, Millie's nurse came to gather her for her afternoon nap.

'Perfect timing, Miss Bellows,' Lady Buchanan offered, righting herself to standing. 'Miss Potts and I were just about to begin.'

She pressed a kiss to Millie's cheek and Millie waved goodbye to Hattie before she clutched Miss Bellows's hand to go down for her afternoon rest.

'Now, come with me, Miss Potts, and let us begin. We do not have a moment to waste.'

Hattie accepted her outstretched hand. 'Thank you, Lady Buchanan. Where shall we begin?'

'You can begin by calling me Daphne,' she said with a grin and wink.

'Only if you call me Hattie, my lady.'

'Done. Now, let us begin with greetings,' she said, tucking Hattie's arm within hers as they travelled down the hallway. 'Then we have fittings to attend to. The Mademoiselle should be arriving soon. I cannot wait to see what she has created for you.'

William peeked into Millie's room. She was fast asleep, cuddling her favourite teddy bear. The afternoon sun beamed in her windows and the glow of the rays gave her a little halo above her head and on her pillow. He smiled and eased her chamber door shut quietly. The chatter of muffled female voices carried down the hallway from Miss Potts's chamber. His pulse picked up speed as he stared at the closed door. He knew he shouldn't, but he wanted to see how the preparations for Lady Penelope's wardrobe were coming along. They had been hard at work since the Mademoiselle and her assistants, as she called them, had arrived and shuffled Miss Potts and his cousin into her chambers.

He glanced down the hallway. No one was about. It wouldn't hurt to listen to how things were going. He was paying for everything after all. Despite having no interest at all in what his late wife had commissioned for her gowns, he felt an odd, vested interest in Miss Potts's new wardrobe. How she looked might well impact how well their plan was received and whether it took root as truth at all. He rubbed his neck, gave in to his urges and walked towards the chamber door, pausing to listen.

'I do not think it low enough,' Daphne said. 'A woman of such confidence would show her decolletage, not hide it.' She huffed and Mademoiselle muttered a curse in French which made William smile.

'Perhaps a compromise?' Miss Potts offered. 'The neckline could rest between where you both would like it to be and it could dip a bit further in the back?'

'That could work,' the dressmaker purred in her French accent. 'You have a fine swanlike neck, Miss Potts. With the right jewelllery, it will be quite stunning.'

'And if we wrap your hair just so,' Daphne said. 'Yes, yes, that would be perfect.'

William smiled at the way Miss Potts was managing the strong personalities.

'Is there anything you have need of, Your Grace?'

He froze and cringed before lifting his head to face Mrs Chisholm, who stood furrowing her brow at him from down the hallway. Then he cleared his throat before heading away from the door. He reached her and tucked his hands in his trouser pockets. 'Ah, no, Mrs Chisholm.'

She smirked at him. 'Are you sure, Your Grace?'

He sighed and looked heavenwards. 'I was merely… listening to the progress.'

'Would it help if I sneaked in and reported back to you?' she asked innocently.

'Yes,' he replied.

'Then, consider it done.'

He sighed in relief. 'Thank you.'

She headed down the hallway, knocking on the door before entering. She gifted him a nod before she disappeared within the chamber.

After a longer conversation than William anticipated, Mrs Chisholm emerged. William glanced greedily through the open crack of the door, hungry for a glance at the progress being made in creating Lady Penelope. All he could see was a splash of the wine-coloured fabric and a bit of Miss Potts's fine-looking bare shoulder before Mrs Chisholm sealed the chamber door again. He clenched his fist by his side in frustration before attempting to neutralise his face.

Mrs Chisholm clapped her hands together and smiled. 'It is coming along beautifully, Your Grace. You will be pleased. Mademoiselle Dashiell is working her magic with the fabric and cut, and Miss Potts is doing well in managing the situation.'

'And do you think...?' He paused. The question was on his tongue, but he hesitated to ask. His fear overpowered his hesitation, and he hurried out what he wanted to know. 'Do you think people will believe our ruse? That she is a lady?' he asked in a low tone. 'It is not too late to abandon our endeavour.'

Truth be told, he was nervous, far more so than he wished anyone to know. A great deal was at stake. He could ruin the reputation of his cousin, that of Miss Potts and his own. What had appeared a grand idea earlier in the week now threatened to be his very downfall as the ball celebrating his succession drew closer.

Her eyes softened. 'When you look at her on Saturday, you will believe just as everyone else will.'

'May I see her?'

'While the ladies do not agree on all this afternoon, they are adamant that you do *not* see Miss Potts in her gown before the ball. They wish for you to be surprised, when she is announced to everyone...to add to the believability. You *will* be pleasantly surprised. I assure you, Your Grace.'

Perhaps it made sense. It would capture his true reaction and feelings. He hoped they would be good ones. Everything was riding on how believable Miss Potts would be as his fictional creation, Lady Penelope Denning.

Chapter Twelve

Hattie's pulse throbbed in her neck and she clasped her gloved hands as she stood in front of the closed ballroom door, willing herself the courage to knock. Nerves jumped under her skin. For the thousandth time she wondered *why* she had agreed to this ruse of becoming Lady Penelope.

Over the last few days, she had been poked with sewing needles as dresses had been altered, squeezed into the most uncomfortable underclothes one could fathom, learned far too much about the gossip of the *ton* and attempted to remember confusing rules about cutlery etiquette for dining. And now the worst of all she had to learn remained…she swallowed hard and rolled her shoulders that ached with tension. She had to learn to dance.

And with a duke…*the* Duke.

She groaned inwardly. She needed a pep talk from

Ophelia and Trudy, but they weren't here. She bit her lip. What would they say?

Go in with your head held high. You can do this.

She imagined Ophelia's sweet voice and how she would hold her hands and encourage her.

If you do not go in, I will open the door and shove you in.

She smirked at what she imagined Trudy would say.

Hattie lifted her head, squared her shoulders and knocked lightly on the door. She could and would do this. She had made an agreement for Millie's sake, which she would honour. If this plan of theirs wasn't successful, Hattie would still leave with a recommendation of employment from the Duke for herself, Trudy and Ophelia, her pay, and a lump sum to begin anew elsewhere. Either way, she would be protected, she reminded herself. And this…this was simply another adventure.

Even if she fell flat on her face, she was doing something new and different. Right? The click-clacks of heeled steps on the hardwood floors echoed louder towards the door and her eyes flew open.

Her heart began to race. Her body heated. Was it too late to flee?

Stand your ground, Hat. It is only dancing.

Trudy was right. Hattie needed to stand her ground.

The door opened and Lady Buchanan stood before

her with a smile. 'Just in time, my dear. I was cueing up the pianoforte.' She winked, clutched Hattie's gloved hand and pulled her joyfully into the enormous and equally gorgeous ballroom. Hattie's limbs felt tingly and light at the sight of it. The grandeur of the space stopped her in her tracks and she stood staring at the room before her that was being transformed for a ball.

'It is absolutely gorgeous,' she murmured as she took in the large wooden floors gleaming with the afternoon light splashing along them and the high ceilings and moulding. The most glorious crystal chandelier she had ever seen glistened above her and tables with pristine white cloths and silver had been nested in between the windows. An area for musicians had been assembled near the pianoforte and the grand dual staircase that led to the top floor curled gracefully to the dance floor like the open arms of a mother's welcoming embrace.

'That, my dear, is where you will make your grand entrance,' Lady Buchanan said, pointing to the landing at the top of the stairs.

Hattie gulped. 'There?' she asked.

'Yes. We all will. You will be announced at the top of the stairs and then come gracefully down.'

'And I will be with you, Miss Potts,' His Grace added, emerging from the other end of the room. Hattie had not even seen him. He cut a fine figure in his suit and gloves. Her throat went dry. His handsomeness was becoming quite a distraction.

'It shall not be so bad,' Daphne offered.

'And if I fall down the stairs?' she murmured.

'You will do no such thing,' Daphne added, rubbing Hattie's shoulder.

'Are you ready to learn a few dances, Miss Potts?' His Grace asked. 'My cousin tells me it is important for us to appear comfortable with one another as dance partners for the ball, so that we are believable as a couple. The only way to do that is practise, but I must confess I do not enjoy dancing as much as I should.'

'Do ignore him, my dear. His Grace is a fine dancer, but lacks confidence, which is shocking, I know. While in all other areas he is a touch arrogant, he is *not* on the dance floor,' she teased, and he shot her daggers.

Hattie laughed, immediately put at ease by their banter. It reminded her of Ophelia and Trudy when they were at odds about something ridiculous. Hattie relaxed her hands by her sides. 'What shall we learn first? I am hopeless at all dancing and have never been to a ball.'

They stilled and studied her. 'Never?' The Duke of Wimberley asked.

'No, Your Grace. There are not many reasons to go if one is not invited and there were few invitations for such frivolities growing up in an orphanage.'

He shook his head and a bit of colour heated his cheeks. 'Apologies. It was a foolish question.'

His discomfort somehow put her at ease. Instead of feeling embarrassed, it felt good to tell the truth and to not hide it from them. 'You would not have known, Your Grace. Our worlds are quite…opposite.'

'You are gracious, my dear,' Lady Buchanan replied as she settled in at the pianoforte. 'Why don't we begin with learning the steps of an English country dance? If that goes well, we will build in the Scottish reel.'

Drat.

Hattie wrung her hands. 'How many dances are there to learn?'

'Really only two, Miss Potts. The quadrille and waltz are too scandalous…for now.' He winked at her.

'Scandalous? Why?' Hattie asked, laughing.

'Too intimate, my dear,' Lady Buchanan said. 'To have a man unknown to you clutch you at the waist and dance so closely isn't deemed civilised…until those at Almack's say otherwise, which will probably be soon. The world is changing after all. Must keep up with the times.'

'I have seen you waltz, Cousin,' His Grace teased.

'Yes, you have, and let us leave it at that,' she replied, sending him a sharp look.

He held up his hands in supplication. 'I shall say no more.'

Soon a joyful tune resonated through the large empty room. 'Now, imagine the room is filled with other couples.' She ceased playing. 'This will not be helpful to her if there are not others to be dancing around,' she said, frowning. 'I had not thought of it until now.'

Hattie's throat dried. 'Perhaps I could learn them before we add others. To limit some of my humiliation,' she added.

Lady Buchanan began the music again. 'Right you are. One thing at a time. But there is no humiliation, Miss Potts. His Grace will guide you. It is his job as the lead. Is it not, Cousin?' She lifted her brow and he nodded.

'Yes, of course. If you struggle, I am to blame, if that puts you at ease.' He flashed her a smile and stretched out his hand. 'Let us begin before my cousin finds yet another reason to chastise me.'

Hattie returned his smile and stepped forward. She slid her gloved hand into his and the moment his warm, strong fingers wrapped around hers she felt safe in a way she hadn't expected. He squeezed her hand in encouragement and his eyes were warm and full of belief. 'Mirror what I do,' he said, moving in step with the music.

She hesitated.

'You shall be wonderful, Miss Potts, as you have

been with everything else you have encountered here,' he encouraged. 'This shall be no different.'

She nodded and a shiver ran down her spine. How long had it been since anyone other than Trudy and Ophelia had believed in her so? Emotion tightened her throat as she followed his movements and mirrored them as best she could. If she wasn't careful, she was going to start believing this ruse of theirs.

'Well done,' Lady Buchanan called. 'Keep going.'

His Grace picked up speed with his movements as she progressed and soon their steps and turns were in time with the pace of the music. She tripped at a turn and he clasped her at the waist to prevent a fall.

'I'm sorry,' she stammered, staring up into his blue eyes, so close due to his hold along her waist.

'No apologies needed, Miss Potts,' he replied in a low tone. It sent a trill of vibration through her.

His Grace righted Hattie and released her. She patted her eyes, trying to regain her focus and composure as she smoothed her dress. She turned to face Lady Buchanan as the music had ceased and the woman stared upon her expectantly.

Blast. She had missed the woman's question. Hattie smiled in hopes the enquiry might be repeated.

'That is why the waltz is so scandalous,' Lady Buchanan called out to her with a wink. 'It dashes your reason. Shall we try again?'

Hattie's ears warmed and she nodded. The woman was right. Hattie hardly knew where she was. She breathed deeply, squared her shoulders and accepted His Grace's hand. But this was just a taste of what Saturday would be. All eyes would be on her. She needed to stop being Hattie Potts and start living like Lady Penelope Denning, who wouldn't be nervous around anyone.

Not even her fake betrothed, the dashingly handsome Duke of Wimberley.

Stop it, you cad.

William adjusted his grip on Miss Potts's gloved hand and turned them. What was wrong with him? He had no right feeling anything towards Miss Potts. It didn't matter how lovely she felt in his hold, or the way her soft blush warmed her cheeks, or the sweet floral smell of her as she twirled by him. She was his employee, his daughter's governess, and doing him the favour of a lifetime by attempting to be his fake betrothed. If he wasn't careful, he would ruin everything before the charade had even begun by feeling something for this woman.

Fool, he cursed himself.

He could no longer trust his judgement when it came to women and he would do well to remember Cecily and his initial burst of feelings towards her. The thought of his late wife and her betrayal cooled his veins. His initial passion and attraction towards her had set him in motion to where he was now and he needed to temper whatever emotion and impulses he felt for his new governess and focus on the task at hand.

Miss Potts turned and faced him again and offered a timid smile, which he returned briefly before chastising himself.

Stop it.

While he needed to *pretend* to care for her for the sake of the *ton*, he couldn't *really* care for this woman. He'd trusted with all his heart before and it had destroyed him and hurt his daughter. But she, Hattie Potts, and the delicate open way about her, as soft as a flower in spring opening to the sun, threatened to pull him in and he couldn't risk such distraction…or the disappointment when the moment passed. And he was sure it would. It was better to remain detached and to prepare oneself for whatever might complicate his life next as the last few years had been one complication followed by the next without relief in sight.

'Cousin, if you keep frowning at your betrothed, no one will dare believe this speedy attachment of yours,' Daphne called out as she continued playing. He glanced up to find her studying him, a deep V forming in her brow.

Had he been frowning? He glanced down at Miss Potts and smiled before casting a glance over her shoulder to his cousin. Evidently his need to cool his feelings had set him to scowling.

'Much better. Now you merely need to have fun,' she added with a wink before looking back to the sheet music before her.

'Yes, Cousin,' he replied in a droll tone. Miss Potts cracked a smile.

'What?' he asked.

'I enjoy your banter with your cousin, Your Grace. It reminds me of home.'

'Oh? How so?' he asked as he carefully guided her in a twirl. 'You are improving,' he said as she easily navigated the turn and the steps coming out of it.

'Thank you. My dear friends Trudy and Ophelia are always teasing one another and sometimes I would just sit and listen to them or join in the fun. It is wonderful that you have each other to lean on.'

He cast a look at Daphne and nodded before meeting Miss Potts's gaze. 'It is. We have been through a great deal together as we lost our spouses within a month of one another.'

'I am so sorry to hear of your combined losses, but it is wonderful you had each other to weather it.' Her soft brown eyes held so much compassion and sympathy, so much care. He wondered how she managed.

The music came to an end and he released her. He bowed deeply to her and she matched it with a curtsy of her own.

Clapping sounded from the doorway and William turned to see his daughter and her nurse watching. At first, he faltered, worried about what his daughter would think or feel. She smiled and clapped before running over to him for a hug. He scooped her up in his arms and swung her about as if they were dancing. She giggled and the sound warmed him down to his toes. This was the happiness he wished for her… always.

'Are you excited about this weekend's ball, my sweet?' he asked as he held her in his arms.

She pressed her nose to his own, their own special greeting with one another, and nodded with another giggle.

'I am pleased to hear it,' he said. 'Your aunt and Miss Potts will be joining us as well. What do you think of that?'

She smiled and played with his cravat.

'And I shall be dressing up that evening,' Miss Potts began, looking at him with meaning.

'Ah, yes, yes! I almost forgot. I will be escorting Miss Potts and we will be playing dress up like you do sometimes.'

Millie's eyes widened and she clapped her hands together.

'I will be Lady Penelope Denning,' Miss Potts added, lifting her head and body up tall, 'and I will be dressed like a princess, or in this case, Cinderella.'

'Hmm,' His Grace added. 'I do not think she knows the story of Cinderella. Shall I read it to you tonight before bed?' he asked Millie.

She nodded and wriggled out of his hold. She rushed over to Miss Potts and tugged her hand.

Hattie beamed at the little girl, stooping down. 'Speaking of reading, Your Grace. I believe it is time for our afternoon stories. May we end our session a bit early?'

'Perhaps Millie could stay with us as we review the curtsy and practise fan etiquette,' Daphne offered, walking over to them. 'As the daughter of a duke, Lady Millie must learn such things as well.'

'Fair point, Daphne. What say you to practising your curtsies?' William asked Millie.

She nodded and smiled.

'Curtsies it is,' he said.

Miss Potts groaned. He chuckled. 'It is not so bad, Miss Potts. I promise.'

She lifted her brow. 'Fan etiquette?' she asked.

'Yes,' Daphne answered, dropping her voice. 'You would be surprised what trouble you can get yourself into by sending the wrong message.'

'Like what?' Miss Potts asked.

Daphne spread out her fan with a flourish, opening it fully, and fluttered it to cover her face except for her eyes.

'That means "follow me",' William offered.

Daphne tilted the open fan to cover only one of her eyes and fluttered it again.

'I am engaged,' he supplied.

Miss Potts's gaze widened. 'That's what those mean? I had no idea.'

'Do you use a fan often?' Daphne asked.

'Never,' she replied, a furrow creasing her forehead. 'Perhaps a good thing. Who knows what I would have been telling people?'

Daphne chuckled and handed her and Millie a fan of their own. Millie struggled to open it at first, but then squealed in delight as it slid open in her small hand, which gripped it fiercely.

Miss Potts opened hers in a small 'v' and peered over it at him.

'Do you love me?' he blurted out.

Her face flushed and she froze. 'Your Grace?' she asked in confusion.

It was then he realised his error. It was his turn to feel his face flush with heat. He cleared his throat and stammered out. 'My apologies. I did not mean…' He paused and began again. 'What you are doing now with your fan,' he gestured, 'it means "do you love me", Miss Potts.'

Daphne giggled behind him and Millie joined in. He shot them a glance of annoyance.

Miss Potts had the good humour to join in the laugh as well. She snapped her fan closed. 'Oh, my. Indeed, this is a weapon, is it not?' She held the closed fan down by her side.

'More than you know, Hattie. And here I was beginning to think this ruse was affecting you, Cousin.' She gave him a wink.

'Not yet,' he answered, forcing a smile.

Millie tugged on Hattie's hand again. She smiled down at his daughter. 'I believe I can no longer postpone our afternoon stories. Can the curtsy practising wait until tomorrow?' she asked.

'Of course,' he replied, eager to wrap up the awkward exchange. 'Keep practising though, Miss Potts.'

She chuckled. 'Of course. I will be perfection with my steps and be wary of my fan on Saturday…' she paused '…just as Lady Penelope would be.'

And as he watched her walk out, swinging arms with his daughter, the pit in William's stomach grew. If this Saturday's ball didn't go well, they all had a great deal to lose. He just wasn't sure who would lose the most.

Chapter Thirteen

Violins and music cascaded up to Hattie's chamber and her stomach flipped…twice. The night of the ball had arrived, and so had everyone in London, or so it seemed. She eased over to the east window of her bedroom chamber and peered out. Carriages lined the long drive, which was illuminated by lighted stakes at regular intervals to guide drivers as they approached Blithe Manor. She pressed a hand over her stomach.

Why had she agreed to this?

A steady flow of guests arrived in gowns, suits and jewels that glistened in the flickering glow of the lanterns as they climbed the steps with grace.

The chamber door of her room squeaked open.

'Is all of London here?' she asked Mrs Chisholm, who had gone to retrieve some additional necessity that Hattie couldn't remember. Her mind was blanking from lack of focus and nerves.

'Almost,' Daphne replied with a chuckle and Hattie turned. Her heart soared with gratitude and relief to see her new friend arrive for support.

Lady Buchanan stilled at the sight of Hattie and stared briefly before bringing a hand to her mouth and looking to Mademoiselle Dashiell who was making yet another 'final adjustment' to Hattie's hem.

A blush warmed Hattie's cheeks and her pulse increased. 'Is it too much?' Hattie rushed out. 'I may have misjudged when I insisted on this shade,' she continued. 'I know nothing of the *ton* or Society and I fear I may ruin His Grace's plan,' she continued. 'It is not too late,' she added. 'I can change and pretend we have not done any of this. No one will know,' she finished. She struggled to take a breath. She didn't know if it was from nerves or the exquisite binding of the new undergarments the Mademoiselle and Lady Buchanan said were 'essential' to showcase her figure.

Daphne dropped her hand from her mouth and smiled. 'Mademoiselle,' she said softly, 'you have created a masterpiece. Truly. No one will be able to take their eyes from you, Miss Potts.' Her eyes glistened as if she might cry and Hattie's throat tightened. Could it be true? Could she be beautiful enough to fool everyone?

'Don't you mean Lady Penelope?' Mademoiselle quipped and smirked before fluffing out the back of Hattie's gown and standing. 'Turn and look in the mirror for yourself, Miss Potts. You are stunning, *ma chérie*.'

Hattie closed her eyes. 'I cannot,' she murmured. Uncertainty swirled and festered in her stomach like a crowd of butterflies desperate to free themselves from their cocoons.

What if she wasn't enough? What if she was still… lacking…after all they had done for her and they just didn't want to tell her the truth?

'Yes, you can,' Daphne said, grasping her shoulders and gently turning her. 'Open your eyes,' she said.

You can do this. She counted down. Five. Four. Three. Two. One.

Then she opened her eyes.

Hattie blinked once and then again. Her lips parted in surprise. Was *this* woman looking back in the gilded standing mirror truly her? Hattie lifted a hand to her stomach—so did the woman in the mirror. She felt the gentle pressure of her trembling fingers on her hip as she slid her hand to the edge of the embroidered fabric of her gown. It was her. She had never seen a more glorious dress in all her life and she had never looked as beautiful. While she knew the modiste was a gifted seamstress, Hattie had never seen or dreamed of anything so exquisite. She had also never understood how a gown could transform oneself until this moment.

How a fine frock could thrust you into a power you had never known before.

Simply put, it was magic.

She *was* Cinderella.

'I cannot believe it. You have made me her. I am no longer Hattie Potts, orphan from Stow, but Lady Penelope Denning, a woman of means, substance and standing.'

'And great wealth,' Daphne quipped with a wink. 'Do not forget you are from a prominent family overseas and have returned after studies at a fine boarding school. You are a hidden treasure revealed.'

'And that.' Hattie smiled and the uncertainty of before transformed into excitement.

For a night she could be someone else just like she and Ophelia and Trudy had always dreamed about. For a few hours, she would escape the disappointment of her past and revel in the finery and acceptance of being someone else with influence and means...and beauty.

She turned her head and couldn't help but smile. Her dark hair was wrapped in a jewelled bandeau of small crystals and rubies woven with skill through her tresses. It twinkled when she turned her head and caught the light. And the jewels! Rubies dangled from her ears and trailed gently along her collarbone from the necklace around her neck. She ran her fingertips over them, stunned by the petite oval stones and their rich, wine colour that warmed her fair skin. The three women stared at Hattie's reflection.

Daphne was the first to speak. 'I think His Grace will be quite pleased with how compelling and how very believable you look. I dare say you might be more successful than he is prepared for.'

'Is that good or bad?' Hattie asked.

'It is good, *ma chérie*,' Mademoiselle offered. 'It is always good to keep a man of power and influence on his toes, is it not, my lady?'

'My, yes, it is,' Daphne murmured. 'I can hardly wait to see his face.'

The mantel clock chimed as if it, too, agreed with Lady Buchanan's statement. 'Is it time?' Hattie asked.

Daphne cast a glance back at the clock and then walked to the window where she peaked out at the drive. She quirked her lips. 'We shall give ten more minutes and then present you. I shall go ahead and go down, my dear, and make sure that my cousin has not attempted a hasty escape.'

Hattie froze.

'Only teasing,' Daphne began and then paused. 'Mostly teasing. He would not abandon his own ball… at least I don't *think* he would. I'd best go and check on him.'

Before Hattie could utter a word of protest, Daphne, her tether of safety, vanished from her chambers.

'You will take their breath away, Miss Potts,' Mademoiselle said, smiling at her.

'Are you sure?'

'I believe you may be my finest creation,' she said, lifting her chin as she smoothed out a turned-up edge on one of Hattie's small cap sleeves.

Hattie's shoulders fell and she swallowed hard. If this did not work, she would be failing everyone.

'What happened to that confident powerful woman I saw emerge when you first glanced upon yourself in that mirror?' Mademoiselle asked. 'Bring her back. *She* was Lady Penelope. She is who you must become. The dress can do much for you, but you must bring the woman to life.'

Hattie looked at herself. Mademoiselle Dashiell's words were true. Hattie had to not only *look* like a lady, but act like one. She lifted her chin and harnessed the power and magic she'd felt the first moment she'd gazed upon herself in the mirror once more.

She would become Lady Penelope Denning.

For Millie. For Ophelia. For Trudy. For His Grace.

And if she were honest…for herself.

For once, she wanted to become the woman she had always wished to be. A woman who was adored, beautiful, wealthy and with a family, even if it was only a pretend one. Her father could become the man of her imagination's creation, since she had never known him, and her mother could be the strong, resilient, nurturing spirit she had always longed for rather than the woman who had given up on her life and died from heartbreak when Hattie was a child.

Hattie would be worthy of what she wore and how she was treated this evening.

'Shoes?' Mademoiselle asked, smiling at her. She held two options for Hattie and each was beautiful.

'Which one will I be less likely to fall in?' she asked.

'That does not sound like something Lady Penelope would worry over,' Lady Buchanan stated with a smirk as she closed the chamber door behind her. Hattie had not even heard her return.

'You are right,' Hattie replied. She studied each shoe and opted for the one with the higher heel and embellished flowers cascading across the toe.

'They will swoon for you,' Daphne stated. 'William is waiting. I do not believe I have seen him this nervous since his wedding day.'

Hattie's stomach flipped as she slipped her stocking feet into the satin shoes. They felt so marvellous she almost sighed aloud.

'Ready?' Daphne asked.

While her heart screamed she was not at all prepared, Hattie nodded as if she was. The sooner the charade began, the sooner it would end, and if she could muster up the adequate amount of courage, she might even enjoy herself. This was her chance to be someone rather than an orphan and governess. This evening anything was possible, even a great deal of happiness.

But she had to let herself receive it. For it was there for the taking.

Hattie slid her hands into the silky-smooth long gloves the modiste had made of the same wine-coloured material as her dress and stepped forward as the chamber door was opened for her by the maid.

Daphne turned to her and smiled. 'Follow me, my lady. The *ton* awaits.'

William felt like an awkward schoolboy as he waited at the threshold behind the curtains at the top of the stairs. The ballroom below was awash with colourful gowns, glistening jewels and the golden glow of candlelight. Soft music played in the background as the *ton* mingled with one another, no doubt whispering about when he, as the Duke and host of the ball to celebrate his succession, would appear. So much depended on how believable Miss Potts was this evening. If she was convincing as Lady Penelope Denning, then his family might finally have some sense of normalcy and peace. If she was not, then the scrutiny around him, his wife's scandalous past and his family would only intensify.

A wave of loneliness washed over him. How he wished his parents and brother could be here to share this moment, but the irony was if they were here, he wouldn't be inheriting such a title. How he would trade it all to have them back. He longed for their love, support and guidance. At least he had Daphne. After Cecily's death, many of his so-called friends had created some distance from him. For even if the *ton* did not speak of the indelicacies of his late wife in public, they were whispered about in private. Everyone had known of Cecily's proclivities.

He stifled a curse. Tonight had to be successful. It was time for positive gossip to spread like wildfire among the peerage about his family name and legacy. For his sake. For Millie's sake.

This had to be a new chapter and a fresh step forward.

He closed his eyes and began to will just that.

'Your Grace?'

Miss Potts.

Her voice was soft yet confident. He smiled, eager to see what Mademoiselle Dashiell had created and why Daphne had been so insistent on him not seeing his pretend betrothed for the evening until this very moment.

He turned.

Everything around him stopped. He could not hear or see anything but her. He stared. Was this gorgeous creature Miss Potts, his governess? He gazed at her, taking in every detail of her. Her gown, the darkest of merlots, flowed along her form, accentuating her fine figure by cinching in and out of all the right places. A whisper of rubies glittered from an exquisite trail along her neck and teased the light as they twinkled from her delicate earlobes and hair, and her skin radiated like soft cream with her chestnut hair bound in some glorious twist of waves upon her head.

His throat dried. He had never seen so much of her before. Her shoulders and collarbone and whisper of decolletage thrust his mind and body into places he had not expected. Lust surged in him and he did his best to tamp it down before his body reacted too strongly. While he did need to appear attracted to her, as his pretend betrothed, he did need to maintain decorum.

She is Millie's governess. She is Millie's governess.

He chanted it over and over in his mind. But she surely did not look like one tonight. He opened and closed one of his gloved hands by his side as he regained his composure. 'You look breathtaking, *Lady Penelope*,' he finally said, his voice low and husky. He cleared his throat.

'Thank you, Your Grace. I am astonished by what Lady Buchanan and Mademoiselle Dashiell have accomplished. I feel like a princess.' Miss Potts smiled, wide and full, and her beauty expanded further, threatening to reach out and touch him. Another surge of lust rushed through his limbs, making his entire body flush with a need he had not allowed himself to feel in…evidently far too long a time: desire.

His mind cast about for something to say to distract himself. 'I agree. You will be the talk of the ball this evening. Shall we?' he said, gesturing to the ballroom below.

Her eyes widened. 'Now?'

He chuckled. There was the Miss Potts he knew. 'Shall there be a better time?'

She paused, considering his words. 'I suppose not, Your Grace.'

'Remember, while you should address me as Your Grace as governess, you should address me as William as my betrothed when we are alone and others listen in.' He winked. 'And I will address you as Penelope.'

'Of course, I forgot…' She paused and tried out his given name. 'William,' she said slowly as if she'd never said the syllables in such a way before. His name from her now-rouged lips sounded sacred and he liked it more than he wished to admit.

He stepped forward and caught the gaze of the head musician to signal a pause, so he could be announced, and he turned back to Miss Potts to explain what was to come. 'He will announce me. Then I will step out and say a few words of greeting and introduce you to everyone. You will then emerge from behind here, smile, greet the applause with a slight curtsy and accept my arm. I will guide you down the stairs and the swarm of the *ton* will begin.'

Her eyes widened. 'And what will I say to everyone?'

'Tell them who you are the way we practised. They will be so entranced by your beauty they most likely will not remember a word of what you have said. Oh, and be mindful with that fan of yours,' he teased, glancing down at the matching wine-and-cream-coloured fan dangling from her gloved wrist. He winked at her and she laughed, which put them both at ease as the music came to a stop and a quiet fell over the crowd.

Chapter Fourteen

Hattie couldn't breathe. Her heart thundered against the crushing silence below.

'Ladies and gentlemen, may I introduce William Sutherland, Duke of Wimberley.'

Applause filled the air as His Grace stepped out on to the landing and, after almost a minute, the clapping finally abated. He was talking, but Hattie couldn't process the words. *Focus. Focus.* The crowd laughed and she realised he must have said something to lighten the mood, which reminded her to breathe.

'Do not forget you are Lady Penelope Denning,' Daphne whispered in her ear. 'Chin up, chest out, shoulders back and remember you are the most beautiful woman in the room and betrothed to a duke. *No one* can rival your beauty, charm, or power at this moment. Let them fawn over you and allow yourself to soak it all in. It is not every day one becomes a pretend future duchess, is it? And do not accept a word of harshness or judgement from anyone. Look down at them and move on, if needed.' She clutched one of Hattie's hands and squeezed it.

Hattie smiled and nodded. Then she heard the Duke say her name—well, Lady Penelope's name. All the blood rushed from her head to her feet, but she remembered Lady Buchanan's words. *No one can rival your beauty, charm, or power at this moment.* Hattie lifted her chin, pulled back her shoulders, put out her chest and stepped forward one beautiful shoe at a time as though she was Cinderella herself until she was next to the Duke.

A collective intake of breath fell over the crowd below and then a silence followed.

Hattie held her smile and let her gaze drift over the sea of beautiful ladies and gentlemen who gaped up in surprise at her. Her pulse raced along, but she focused on the amazing transformation of the room to distract herself. It was far more pleasing than anything she had read in any book and it was real. She was no longer the girl in the orphanage praying for a different life, she had one…for a moment at least.

Savour it, she imagined Ophelia whispering in her ear. *You are glorious, Hat. Allow yourself to enjoy it.*

And so she would. She smiled once more and turned to His Grace, bowing slightly. Applause broke through the silence and she released a breath. When His Grace smiled at her and gestured for her to step forward, she smiled back and did so to more applause and a few unexpected cheers.

Her toes and fingertips tingled. She had never been in such a crowd or been the centre of such attentions. Was this what he was used to? It was hard to imagine such a world, but here she was thrust into the centre of it. To her surprise, she had been initially accepted, so the first part of their ruse was complete. His Grace offered his arm to her once more and she slid her gloved hand around his forearm. The sheer warmth and strength emanating from him steeled through her and steadied her as they took the first stair step together.

'Well done. They adore you already, Lady Penelope,' he whispered as they continued down step after step.

'My heart may explode from my chest,' she said with a bit of a giggle. She took her time, letting her slippered toes and heels anchor safely on each carpeted stair to avoid a trip or fall.

'I could not ask for anyone more beautiful or kind to be my betrothed this evening,' he murmured close to her ear. 'Thank you.'

A delicious shiver went through her as the warmth of his breath edged along her cheek and the soft lobe of her ear. She glanced at him. His gaze of sincerity and the intensity of his words shifted something deep within her. The long dormant desire for more awakened in her, like a new bud wishing to open under the warmth of its first sun.

They descended from the last step and settled on the hardwood of the ballroom floor. Her reply died on her lips as His Grace lifted her arm and led her out to the opposite side of the floor. She pressed her lips together as they moved to the very spot they had practised from earlier in the week as the opening strings began to play. This was their dance and their moment to prove to everyone that their farce was real. There was no escaping the hundreds of pairs of eyes upon them.

'Penelope,' he breathed, pressing a kiss to her gloved hand.

'William,' she replied, the 'm' hanging precariously in the air as she gazed into his blue eyes.

Then they stepped back from each other, bowed and began the dance as the first couple. Soon after, other couples, those of highest rank first, fell in place around them. Hattie moved with ease between her partners—all of the men were poised and graceful in their measured movements—and soon she was smiling and laughing, as she was handed from one nobleman to another until they had woven through the entire set and ended up with each other once more.

'I am pleased to see you enjoying yourself, my lady,' William stated.

'Far more than I expected,' she replied in a low tone. 'Pretending is fun.'

'Then, let us continue for one more and then take refreshment.'

'Sounds glorious, William,' she replied, offering a small bow and wink before they began their next set.

The evening became a blur of dances, introductions and pauses with His Grace and Lady Buchanan. They were keen to check in with her at regular intervals and Hattie was grateful for their attentions to ensure she was settled and comfortable. The hours passed quickly and as a crack of thunder and lightning sounded, there was a small hiccup to the music and dancing.

'Stay as long as you desire, everyone. No need to rush out only to be caught in a downpour,' His Grace called out good-naturedly.

Laughter followed and the musicians began an enthusiastic reel, which men and women settled into with ease. Hattie stood by His Grace's side and sipped wine from her glass. 'We may be dancing all night,' she quipped. 'The rain is sideways,' she added, nodding towards the rain now pounding along the large windows.

'It is, but we cannot send them off now, can we? Especially when you are such a smashing success. They are all believers in Lady Penelope Denning and our… attachment. You have charmed all of them…including me.' He gazed upon her, taking a step closer. His forearm pressed against her own and the liquid heat from such a meagre touch coursed through her.

Her stomach flipped. Perhaps the wine was rushing to her head, but the way he said the words and the gaze accompanying them made her believe for a moment that he desired her and that she *was* Cinderella destined to live among them all here for ever with Ophelia and Trudy by her side.

His fingers trailed along her collarbone and her pulse jumped. Surely she was mistaken. He would never think of her in such a way. She was an orphan, a no one, and he was her employer. She took a small step back despite how she savoured his touch and the idea of his affections.

'My apologies. That was inappropriate…' he added, running a hand through his hair. 'I am grateful to you, that is all. I will see to our guests.' He disappeared into the crowd before she could reply.

The evening continued in a swirl of music, dancing and revelry, and after a time even the most steadfast guests began to exit the dance floor and prepare to leave as the clock struck two a.m. The worst of the storm had dissipated despite the errant rumblings of thunder and lightning that seemed determined to linger.

'Shall we bid our guests farewell?'

Hattie turned to His Grace and smiled. His playful good humour had returned and Hattie was grateful for it. She disliked awkwardness and wished to celebrate all they had accomplished that evening with Lady Buchanan and the staff of the Manor. Without all of them, they wouldn't have been able to succeed in such a scheme.

'Of course,' she replied, accepting his offered arm.

Guests filtered out in intervals as the carriages manoeuvred through the muddy mess that had become the drive leading to the Manor. Even from the doorway, Hattie could see several of the horses were still a bit skittish and jumpy from the storm as they wove through the line of carriages and guests hurrying to reach them and return home for rest.

Several of the horses pawed at the ground and shook their heads against their reins and blinders, eager to escape the storm and the crush of carriages crawling around the drive as they were loaded with guests. A crack of thunder and lightning flashed, sending one pair of horses from a fine carriage in the middle of the drive that had just been loaded with its guests into a jump as the driver closed the door for the ladies within. The horses kicked up as the man rushed to them, attempting to grab the reins and leap up to the driver's seat to regain control. One of the horse's hooves hit him squarely in the chest, sending him sprawling back into the muddy drive with a thud.

Hattie sucked in a breath and grabbed His Grace's forearm. 'William,' she said, urgently interrupting him. The desperation in her voice must have shocked him. He stopped speaking mid-sentence and turned to where she pointed.

He cursed before shouting, 'The carriage!' to all those before him and closer at hand. He rushed past several men, who then followed him in pursuit of the runaway carriage that was picking up speed as it approached an upcoming curve in the drive. The women within the carriage screamed as they clung to the doors for safety and men ran behind, trying to catch up with the carriage as the wheels splashed mud back at them, impeding their progress.

His Grace was fleet of foot, closing the distance between him and the carriage with impressive speed. Soon, he was alongside the back wheel and Hattie cringed. It was a dangerous spot to be in as the carriage began its turn, but he stuck to his position and did not falter, but increased his efforts. He reached the first horse and grabbed for the reins. The horse picked up speed and the back wheel of the opposite side of the carriage tilted off the ground. Hattie's heart thundered in her chest. The carriage was tipping.

'William!' she cried out over the din of the noise

and commotion around her. Before his name had even echoed across the drive, the carriage tipped and William disappeared beneath it.

Chapter Fifteen

William awakened to humming, a woman's humming. It was a sweet tranquil sound and followed a soft rise and fall like the movements of a dance. It might have soothed him if every single fibre of his body didn't ache like the devil. His eyes felt heavy and weighted, but he blinked them open slowly, which hurt more than expected.

It wasn't even that bright. It was dusk or perhaps dawn, it was hard to tell, but he was in a bed and streams of yawning light fell across the room. It was a stately room and looked familiar, but not entirely. Where was he? And what had happened to him? He groaned and shifted.

The humming ceased and the floorboards creaked. A woman appeared above him and smiled. 'Your Grace!' the woman said, her beautiful face beaming down at him. 'He is awake, Daphne. Can you ring for Mrs Chisholm?'

Your Grace? Was she speaking to him?

He stared up at her. She looked familiar, but he could not place her. Her features were handsome, but subdued. Her chestnut hair fell softly about the shoulders of her blue dress and her wide brown eyes were warm and searching as she smiled. There was a kind, gentle way about her he liked. 'Hello,' he said and coughed. His throat was dry and it pained him to speak. Had he been shouting? He clutched his throat and coughed again.

The young woman pressed a gentle reassuring hand to his forearm. 'I will pour you some water. Do not trouble yourself to speak. We are just pleased to see you awake.'

'Yes…' another woman appeared at his bedside '…you gave us a scare.' She smiled brightly at him. She was blonde, quite pretty, and seemed familiar, but in a different way. He stared at her. What was her name? He should know her. He was certain of it.

But his mind was blank and void of any answers. It also ached horribly. He touched the side of his head and cursed.

'You took quite a spill, but the women in the carriage are fine, merely shaken from the accident. They have you to thank. But, please, no more gallantry like that for a while, Cousin, you gave us all quite a scare.' She clutched his hand in hers.

Cousin?

He studied her some more, eager to remember her name. If she was his cousin, he knew her. The other woman returned with a glass of water. He struggled to sit up, even with their aid, as every muscle screamed out in agony against the movement and his head began to spin, but he sipped from the glass and swallowed before collapsing back on the propped-up pillows behind him.

Another woman rushed into the room. 'Your Grace!' She was older, plump and carried a tray of food and tea. The smell of it turned his stomach and he baulked, putting up his hand. He shook his head and she set the tray aside and approached, smoothing her hands down her apron. The woman had soft grey eyes that put him at ease.

Once he swallowed down the nausea, he cleared his throat. 'I am sorry to be rude, but who are all of you? And where am I?'

The silence that followed lasted longer than he would have liked and his pulse increased, creating a throbbing in his body, especially his head. He closed his eyes and hoped they would answer before he passed out. He heard low whispers, but nothing he could decipher with his head pounding as it was. A hand gently clutched his and he opened his eyes again.

'William?' the blonde woman asked. 'Do you not remember me? I am your cousin, Daphne. Lady Daphne Buchanan. We have known each other since we were children.'

He studied her.

William? Was that his name? He didn't feel like a William, but that was no matter now. What mattered was the black blankness of his mind.

'I know I should know you as you appear familiar to me, but, no… I do not remember you…any of you.' His pulse increased. 'What has happened? Why can I not remember…anything?'

'You were in a serious accident two days ago,' she explained. 'It must have affected your memory. I am sure it is only temporary.' Her hand tightened around his and he was grateful for her certainty. 'You are William Sutherland, Duke of Wimberley, and these are your chambers. You reside here at Blithe Manor with your daughter, Millie.'

His chest tightened. Awe came over him. 'I have a daughter?' he whispered. Surely he would remember her above all else, yet nothing came to mind despite how he searched his mind for her. Panic bubbled in him.

'We must send for Doctor Kemplar,' his cousin said.

'Yes,' William replied, swallowing back the fear rising in his throat. 'I believe that would be best. I'd like to know why I cannot remember a whit about who I am or the life I have here.'

Hattie paced the hallway. She took laps up and back along the corridor outside William's chamber, taking turns in passing Daphne, who also struggled to remain seated. Mrs Chisholm had given up waiting outside the door long ago and had busied herself in preparing for anything and everything His Grace might need now that he was awake. Maids and footmen were scurrying about the house in precision, following one order after another. Since the night of the ball and the carriage accident that had followed, the Manor had been vibrant with a frenetic energy, which had now reached a fever pitch.

William's belief that the interest in his life and future at Blithe Manor would become more subdued after the night of the ball and his announcement of her as his betrothed, even if it was entirely pretend, had only fanned the flames of interest. His accident that evening had sent the gossip mongers and *ton* into a full-blown frenzy. Social calls and gifts for 'improving his well-being at this difficult time' were aplenty. The latest of which was an oversized Persian rug poor Mr Simmons was still trying to create space for in the crowded receiving room and parlour where the bountiful gifts, flowers and well wishes had been set out for display.

Stacks of invitations and enquiries had arrived, most of which were addressed to her, Lady Penelope Denning. Another silver salver for her correspondence had been placed in the parlour and it was now as overflowing as His Grace's. Only the gloves she wore kept her from nibbling on her nails and chewing the cuticles down to the quick. What had begun as a ruse had taken on an unseemly life of its own and Hattie had simply no idea what to do or how to stop it.

She wrung her hands and turned on her heel when she reached the small library upstairs and began another pass by His Grace's chamber where the doctor was still assessing his injuries. What would she do if he never regained his memory? If only she could talk to Trudy and Ophelia. Surely they would offer their supportive counsel and help her devise a solution. For the hundredth time, the pang of missing them curdled her stomach. She clutched her hand by her side in a fist and wished she could wrinkle her nose and have them here.

The doctor's voice grew louder and the sound of his footsteps on the hardwood floors of William's chamber stilled her. She glanced at Daphne, who had also ceased her movements. Collectively, they held their breath as the door to William's room opened and the doctor stepped out. He closed the door gently behind him and sighed. Once he realised he was not alone, he cleared his throat, lifted his chin and nodded. 'May I have a word, Lady Buchanan?' he asked, looking at Daphne through his monocle.

'Of course,' she replied. 'I would appreciate an update on His Grace's condition.'

Hattie held her ground as he walked to Daphne and spoke with her in low tones. Her gaze clicked up to Hattie.

'Perhaps some tea, Doctor? I shall ring Mrs Chisholm and we can take refreshments in the parlour and talk further. Miss Potts should also join us.'

'Is that appropriate?' he asked in lowered tones. 'While I know she is Lady Millie's governess, I do not see—' He paused, sending a half-hearted smile toward Hattie.

'All will be explained, Doctor,' Daphne promised.

Hattie followed Daphne and Doctor Kemplar down the stairs and tried to prepare herself for whatever they needed to discuss about the ruse she was still caught up in. The one-night-only portrayal of Lady Penelope Denning, betrothed to the newly minted Duke of Wimberley, was now extended into an encore performance lasting far more days than any of them had anticipated. His Grace's injuries threatened to draw it out even further.

They settled into the parlour and Mrs Chisholm brought in the tea tray and refreshments herself. Hattie smothered a smile as the housekeeper lingered, no doubt hopeful to hear a word or two about William's condition before departing. Unfortunately, the doctor was nothing if not fastidious in maintaining patient confidentiality. He did not utter a solitary syllable until the tea had been poured, biscuits selected and settled on their small plates and the door to the parlour sealed closed.

Hattie half-heartedly bit into a shortbread biscuit, usually her favourite, although it was lacking in taste this morning. The doctor took a sip of tea, settled back in the oversized chair he had selected opposite of her and Daphne, where they sat on the sofa. 'Before I begin, Lady Buchanan,' he said, 'I must know why Miss Potts needed to be here.'

Daphne smiled at him. 'Have you heard about the announcement of William's betrothal to a Lady Penelope Denning?'

'Ah! Yes, I did as a matter of fact. I was hoping to meet her. Her presence may help His Grace's recovery.'

'It just so happens she is with us, Doctor. Right now.' Daphne gestured to Hattie.

'I do not quite understand,' he said, his smile faltering.

'In short,' Hattie offered. 'His Grace asked me to pretend to be this Lady Penelope in an effort to quell the *ton*'s interest in his personal life after the attack at the lake, and the *ton* now believes I am such.'

'What?' he asked, his gaze moving between the two of them.

'And the household? They know of this?' he asked.

'They are all in on the charade,' Daphne added. 'Now, we need *you* to be a part of it as well.'

'So, you are this Lady Penelope?' he asked Hattie. 'People know you as such?'

'Yes,' she replied quietly. 'It is shocking what a new wardrobe, hair styling, and a fake history can do. I have continued to be her at the manor when members of the *ton* visit, and they continue to believe me to be her.'

'Good lord,' he murmured. 'That complicates the situation.'

'Could you help us in maintaining this ruse? For His Grace's sake? And Millie's?' Daphne pleaded.

He shrugged and sighed. 'I suppose we must as much as it goes against my reliance on the truth in most matters.'

Hattie's heart skipped in her chest. 'Thank you, Doctor.'

'I fear your ruse may be the least of your worries at present. I am sorry to relay that His Grace's injuries have left him completely without his memory. While

I have seen such cases before, they are usually caused by battle or war trauma. His case is a unique one.'

'And your plan for his care, Doctor? What can we do to help him regain his memory?' Daphne asked the questions before Hattie could even open her mouth.

'Well, that is the tricky part. I cannot say for certain when…or if…his memory will return.' He sipped from his tea again and his cup clanged loudly when he settled it back on its holder.

Hattie's stomach dropped to her feet and her throat dried.

'But you must keep his schedule and routine here as it has always been. He must know you are here for him and support him as he recovers. In the past, my patients have responded best to routine, subtle reminders of their past selves and small pushes to engage with their world, even if they are frightened or ill at ease.'

'Even if he does not remember us?' Hattie asked.

'It is even more imperative to do so because he does not remember.' He paused. 'And while I know it is unorthodox to do so, Miss Potts, you should remain here as long as possible. Your presence as governess to Millie will help her and your role as this Lady Penelope will help protect His Grace's reputation and privacy.' He smiled at them. 'It will do him well to have you both along with his daughter by his side every day.'

'It will not upset him?' Daphne shifted to the edge

of the sofa. 'If he does not remember and has to see us each day.'

'On the contrary, my lady. It will help him know he is not alone. Right now, he is confused and angry about what has happened. He wants to will himself healed, but we all know the body does not work in such a way. His daughter has shown us that.' He dropped his gaze to his lap.

They fell into silence. Only the mantel clock ticked behind them as a reminder that time was passing. Otherwise, Hattie felt frozen in the moment. What was she to do? She glanced at Daphne, but she stared down at her hands which she rubbed together in her lap. Her shoulders were rolled, which was in stark contrast to her usual regal posture. She cared deeply for her cousin and after the loss of her husband the worry she felt now about William had to be profound. As if hearing Hattie's thoughts, Daphne sniffed, sat up straight, lifted her chin and pulled back her shoulders, assuming the full height and prowess of the Lady Buchanan they all knew.

'Then we shall rally around him until he regains his memory, Doctor,' she said in a firm confident voice. 'Miss Potts and I shall set a schedule for his day along with some activities that will boost his spirits and hopefully bring him back to us as he once was.'

Hattie nodded and reached over to clasp Daphne's

hand. She glanced up to Hattie, her eyes glistening with tears. She squeezed Hattie's hand and then wiped her eyes.

'Yes,' Hattie agreed aloud. 'That is exactly what we shall do, starting right now.'

'I shall return daily to check in on his progress. I have told him about his daughter's condition. It was a shock to him, but he had to know. Telling him the truth…well, aside from you as Lady Penelope, should be part of his recovery. You may have to wait until he reclaims his memory, so you can work out a way to untangle your fake courtship with him, so it does not damage his reputation.'

Hattie stilled. 'And if he does not remember?'

'You and Lady Buchanan will have to make a decision then. But until that time, he must know what society does so he does not stumble upon it on his own. One of you must tell him about his recent losses of his late wife and father. It is imperative for his recovery and should help him regain his memory.'

Hattie nodded.

'The staff will also need to be told,' he said, rising to leave. 'Everyone will be needed for his recovery.'

'Of course, Doctor. We will gather them together and speak with them now,' Daphne said, also rising to see him out. Once he crossed the threshold of the parlour, Hattie dropped to the sofa, sinking into its cushions.

What was she to do? This ruse was now not only impossible to undo, but His Grace's recovery might well hinge on her performance. Why had she ever agreed to this scheme to begin with? Lies never did her any good. Today was the ultimate example.

'Curses,' she mumbled, closing her eyes as she let her head rest against the back of the cushion.

'I could not agree more,' Daphne muttered as she closed the door to the parlour behind her.

Hattie cringed and opened her eyes. 'Apologies. I did not realise I spoke aloud.'

'No need to apologise. It is exactly how I feel. I can hardly believe what has happened, but at least we know how we must move forward.'

Hattie sat up. 'We do?'

Daphne stopped pacing. 'Of course! Continue as if *this* is his life.'

'And when he regains his memory and realises I am not his true betrothed and that we have all duped him? The doctor said the truth was also important in his recovery. Would it not be best to tell William the truth about who I really am now rather than continuing on with this charade?'

Daphne nibbled her lip and looked at a portrait of what Hattie assumed was Blithe Manor upon its original completion, as trees did not tower over the drive then as they did now. 'He will know that we did it to preserve his future, his daughter's future and the future of the Manor and be all the more grateful for it.'

'He will?' Hattie asked, sliding to the edge of the cushion. She could not imagine anyone would be grateful for being deceived, especially a man like William. It seemed he had suffered enough deceit.

She shrugged. 'Perhaps *grateful* is a bit strong, but he will understand. There is no malice in our undertaking. We are simply following the Doctor's orders.'

A knock sounded on the parlour door and then it opened. Mrs Chisholm and Mr Simmons came in and bobbed their heads to Daphne.

'Thank you for coming.' Daphne nodded. 'If you don't mind closing the door, we have a rather urgent matter to discuss with you…as well as your co-operation to request. It is all in the name of His Grace's recovery,' she continued. 'And we will need you to speak to the staff. We must all agree. His Grace's recovery is at stake and our united front is imperative.'

As the door eased closed, Hattie's heart jumped.

Our united front is imperative. Her decision had been made for her.

Her throat dried. There was no escaping being Lady Penelope now.

Chapter Sixteen

William punched his pillow not once but twice, but it didn't make him feel any better. How could he *not* remember who he was or his family? Or his child? What kind of father looked upon his daughter and felt…nothing? He couldn't even remember the woman he had proposed to. The very woman he had chosen to marry. Nor could he remember his parents, his family, or his first wife. What if he never remembered anything?

His heart rate quickened, heat flushed his body and he threw off the bedcovers, trying to catch his breath. He sat up, closed his eyes and splayed his palms by his sides, clutching the bed beneath to gain his bearings, commanding himself to breathe. He refused to give in to panic.

Not yet anyway.

His breathing deepened and finally after another minute his pulse slowed, his heart beating at a far more regular rhythm than before. He opened his eyes and stared around his ornate and sprawling chamber. Had he picked such lavish furnishings? He supposed it didn't matter. In all accounts, he was a stranger in his home. A guest in his life. If it hadn't been so damned tragic, he would have laughed aloud at the irony of it all. But he wouldn't wallow. Something told him he wasn't the sort.

So he lifted his chin, rose from bed, stretched until he could almost reach the large canopy top of his bed and completed his ablutions. It was ungodly early based on the darkness of the room, moonlight gleaming in from the expanse of windows, and a single torch flickered along the wall in his chamber. He appreciated the kindness of the servant who'd left it lit for him each night to make him comfortable in the very home he did not recognise.

Especially since he had no idea where he was. Even after a handful of days, he couldn't fathom this huge manor was his. That *he* was a duke. Although he might not be for much longer. He scrubbed a hand through his hair. How could one be a duke and care for an entire manor, estate, and the people within it if he couldn't remember one whit of his past or how to navigate his life? The entire situation was ridiculous. He dressed, grabbed his waistcoat rather than shrugging it on, left his cravat undone hanging about his neck and closed his chamber doors. It was time to do something other than berate himself.

He travelled down to the study, which he found after only two attempts, which was an improvement from yesterday when it had taken him three. He applauded himself for the small victory. Once inside, he lit two more wall sconces, settled in at the large desk and acclimated himself with the books, ledgers and items he'd kept close at hand when he remembered his life. Surely they meant something to him. He lifted the worn leather-bound estate ledger and opened it. His gaze settled on the last page with entries. His finger landed upon the bottom of the first column of numbers and his mouth gaped open. He stilled and leaned forward in his chair.

Good lord. Did he truly have that much in income and expenses? His throat dried and he sat back. Evidently, he was quite a wealthy man and a duke after all. How else did he have such fictional numbers in his accounting ledger? He shook his head and chuckled. Too bad such wealth couldn't bring his memory back.

He also had quite lavish taste or at least his betrothed did. The cost of the ball where he had lost his memory had been high. The total amount startled him and it looked as if a few outstanding bills remained. He clamped the ledger shut. Enough for expenses. He opened the top right-hand drawer. It was stuffed with post, perhaps old letters from people he once knew. He shifted through them. He gathered up the first and opened it. Most were recent notes of condolence for the loss of his father or celebratory letters on his ascension to the Duke of Wimberley. Some letters even held tribute to both. He set them aside and frowned.

There were no expected love letters between him and his betrothed, which seemed odd for one recently engaged, but perhaps he kept those letters elsewhere. So much for gleaning information about his past from his correspondence to awaken his memory of his betrothed or his life. Evidently, he wasn't a romantic or one prone to record the events of his life with any regularity. He frowned. Except for his expenses. Perhaps he had faced financial ruin before?

Although the Manor looked to be in pristine condition, as did his finances, perhaps that was not always the case. He stared upon the portrait of his late wife. Nothing stirred within him. Not one wink of recognition at the sight of the mother of his child. Not that it mattered really, since she had passed. But Lady Penelope, his cousin Lady Buchanan and his daughter did. Today he would try to spend time with them. Something had to trigger his memories. And if not, he needed to start anew. He couldn't continue as a stranger in his own life. It was lonely…and exhausting.

* * *

Hattie brushed back her hair and tucked a small decorative floral comb in the tidy chignon at the nape of her neck, a style she'd learned from her young maid, Emma. It was easy and becoming as it showed the soft slope of her neck and collarbone in the stylish new gowns William had made for her. She blinked back at herself in the large vanity mirror in her bedchamber. Continuing as 'Lady Penelope' was shockingly simple, so much so that Hattie feared she might very well forget who she truly was.

She replied to invitations with ease with a standard, kind refusal, explaining His Grace's recovery was her focus at this difficult time, but a thank you for the thought of being included. She also sent thank-you letters to those who had sent gifts, flowers and tempting treats to His Grace and the household or small tokens of kindness to Millie, her favourite of which was a teddy bear as soft as rabbit's fur with a small pink ribbon around its neck.

She clung to it fiercely as the days clicked by and her father still did not regain his memory. It was hard to determine how much it affected Millie, but Hattie knew it was most likely far more than they could see.

Worry plagued them all as the days of William's amnesia turned into over a week. What had begun as a temporary ruse until he remembered was turning into something far worse: their lives. The familiar guilt over her deception slithered along Hattie's consciousness. She was not built for such lies, but what could she do? She didn't dare tell him the truth now. Did she? No, she told herself. They had to continue as a united front.

She squared her shoulders, gathered up her courage and exited her chamber as the early dawn was breaking over the canopy of trees that shaded the long drive leading up to the Manor. Wall scones flickered in the shadows, since they had yet to be extinguished. This was still her favourite time of day and she continued to rise early even though there was no need to. Millie usually slept until eight and her nurse cared for her until they ventured on their morning walks around the lake after breaking their fast. The late spring weather continued to co-operate in the mornings, allowing them daily adventures with the ducks, rabbits and whatever other creatures ventured out at that time.

And although Millie still had not spoken, the other morning as Hattie sang a little song her mother had taught her, she could have sworn she heard a soft low hum as if Millie was wishing to join her. Hattie longed to hear the voice of her young charge as much as she wished her father would remember who he was. She sent up her daily morning prayer for just that as she descended the steps to the main level of the Manor and followed the sounds of Mrs Chisholm and the other servants bustling about with their early morning duties.

'Good morning, my lady,' Mr Simmons said, nodding to Hattie as she turned down a hallway towards the library to pick out a new book.

'And to you, too, Mr Simmons,' Hattie replied with a smile. His Grace's butler had softened even more towards her since the accident and he had been kind and encouraging in her expanded role as pretend betrothed. He had been the one to nestle a silver salver just for her correspondence in the parlour next to William's. While the gesture was small, it had great meaning, and Hattie appreciated his acceptance of her.

'His Grace is up this morning, if you would like to take tea with him in his study,' he offered.

Hattie's steps faltered and she stopped. 'Is he unwell?' Her pulse increased. He had not risen so early since before his accident and she was not certain if it suggested improvement or ailment.

Mr Simmons smiled. 'He seems quite eager to join you and Lady Millie on your walk this morning.'

Hattie's heart soared in her chest. 'That is a glorious sign indeed. Some tea would be wonderful and I will join him in his study. Thank you.' She walked with purpose down the remaining hallway until she reached the study.

William stood staring out the window upon the lake,

his back to her and in slight profile. Even now with his simple trousers, tunic and waistcoat, he was regal. He didn't need a cravat or fancy jacket to exude his rank. He simply looked the part of a duke and she had almost grown used to his handsomeness. *Almost.* She took a steadying breath, knocked on the open door and waited for William to turn from the window.

When he faced her, she met his gaze and smiled, her toes tingling. She still was never quite prepared for the attraction she felt and the winsome looks he gifted her. Ones that she reminded herself she had never earned as she was *not* his betrothed. She smothered down the guilt that bucked up in her again and assumed her role: that of the loving and devoted Lady Penelope Denning.

'Good morning, dear,' he said and came to her, pressing a kiss to her cheek and pulling her into his side to greet her as he had been wont to do over the last few days. The same longing bloomed in her chest each time, wishing it all were real and that this was her life and he her actual betrothed. She closed her eyes, savouring the feeling of being cherished and wishing what he felt for her was real and true despite knowing it wasn't. She would allow herself these moments for she knew they were fleeting. One day he would remember who he was and most likely hate her for what she had done: pretend to love him.

But part of her knew it was not pretend at all.

'How are you feeling today?' she cooed, leaning into his warm, strong hold, something she would miss when it was gone. She shoved the worry aside.

'Better now that you are here with me.' He ran a hand over her hair and his thumb skimmed the top of her ear before resting along the back of her neck. She sighed aloud and he met her gaze, his eyes curious and sparkling.

'I wish I could remember how I was able to win you, Lady Penelope.' His voice lowered. 'You are the most gorgeous creature, and I find...it is hard to subdue the—'

A knock sounded at the door and they froze before William released his hold on her. Whatever he was about to say was lost. The moment severed.

'Your Grace,' Simmons offered with a nod before he brought in their tea service. He set it on the table between the sofa and oversized chair and left them.

William cleared his throat. 'Tea?'

'Of course,' Hattie replied, creating some distance between them as they settled across from each other around the table. The distance helped clear her muddled thoughts and she focused on preparing their cups. William had a hidden penchant for a cube of sugar and splash of milk, which was exactly how he'd taken his tea before. Evidently, his body remembered much of what his mind could not.

She handed him his saucer and cup carefully, their hands brushing briefly, just enough to awaken that longing within her once more.

He is not truly yours. It is best you remember that.

She knew one morning he would remember and she would be just the governess once more at best or dismissed at worst. Who knew how he might react once he regained his memory and realised the truth behind who she was and the lies he had been told? But could she not enjoy the ruse while it lasted, especially if it aided his recovery? She sipped her tea and pretended she wasn't completely deluding herself.

Which she knew she was.

'Will you tell me of her? Of what happened?' he asked, glancing back at the portrait of his late wife over the hearth.

Hattie choked on her tea, caught off guard by his question. Perhaps the universe was reminding her of the dangerous game she played. The poor man had been deceived before. How would he feel once he realised he had been deceived again by a woman he believed loved him?

'Although Daphne has told me some of it, I sense she is reluctant to tell me all. Was it truly so bad what happened between us?' His gaze searched hers, a notch woven deep between his blue eyes as he leaned forward in his seat.

Her stomach flipped and lurched.

Why did he have to be so…handsome…and what did she dare tell him?

'I do not know if such talk will aid your recovery,' she began, cutting a fine line between the truths she knew. Her cup clattered against the saucer.

He watched her face, then his gaze drifted to her hand, noting her obvious unease. She set the saucer on her lap. His face softened. 'You can tell me. It does not matter now. You need not shelter me from it. I have lost everything already.' His voice trailed off into a whisper and he sat back, ready to accept whatever she told him.

Blast.

Where were Mr Simmons's and Mrs Chisholm's timely interruptions when she needed them?

Clarity is kindness, Hat.

Trudy's words echoed in her mind. Her friend said such all the time. Most of the time Hattie agreed with her, but at this moment she wasn't so certain.

His gaze was unflinching and she squirmed under his assessment of her. Heat flushed her cheeks and she shifted again on the sofa and placed her tea and saucer back on the table. He waited patiently for her to begin.

'I can only tell you what you told me.'

'That shall be enough,' he replied with a soft nod.

'Your first wife, Cecily, the Marchioness, was beautiful and quite popular with the *ton*…and enjoyed the attentions of other gentleman…' She paused, looking to the ceiling and trying to find some delicate way of indicating what the late Marchioness had done.

'She was unfaithful?' he asked, his voice deep with emotion.

Relieved, she nodded and met his gaze. 'That is what you told me.'

'And her death?' he continued.

'A carriage accident.'

'Hmm. And that is all?'

She hesitated again and her pulse thrummed through her body.

'Please. Just tell me.'

She held his gaze. 'She was with another man in that carriage when she died. They were…together, if you take my meaning.'

His brow lifted and he cursed before he sank back into the cushion, his face blanched briefly before he regained his colour and composure.

'And my daughter? How long has she not spoken?'

'Since the day your wife died,' she replied.

He nodded and stood. He walked to the window and looked out. The quiet hung between them and Hattie sat frozen. *Curses.* She shouldn't have told him. What man would want to know such about his late wife?

But lying would have been worse. He deserved the truth, yet she couldn't bring herself to tell him all of it…the truth about her. But she could right now while the wound was already fresh. She opened her mouth to begin.

'Perhaps I should not have asked,' he said aloud, followed by a small chuckle.

She closed her eyes and clamped her mouth shut. *Saints be.* Perhaps not. She felt horrible. This was the last thing she wished to do. 'It was I who should not have told you. Too much has happened for you to be ready for such news.'

Or any additional truths for that matter.

He scrubbed a hand through his hair and turned to her. He stilled and studied her like a curiosity one sees in a shop window, his gaze uncertain. 'And yet you chose me despite such a scandal and upheaval with my late wife? And the difficulties with my daughter?'

'Yes,' she said breathlessly. She shouldn't have said it, because it wasn't true, but the word tumbled out before she even knew it was a thought in her mind. For she *would* have chosen him repeatedly if this was her real life and she could have made such a choice.

If this were something other than a ruse carrying on too long.

'Why?' He walked to her and sat next to her, the cushion sinking under his weight, taking her hands in his own. 'Why would you choose me after all this?' His words were desperate, his eyes wide and urgent.

He needed to know and understand as if this were the most important thing in his world. She could feel his pulse through the tight pressure of his hold on her fingers.

She hesitated and swallowed hard. She could tell him everything right now. This could be the moment where she told the whole truth, not just the bits she wished to. They could start new and fresh with no deceit between them and she could return to being the governess to Millie she was hired to be. Her heartbeat faltered and increased.

'I…' she began and then glanced down at their interlaced hands. How long had she wanted this? To be cared for, to have someone look at her as if she was their world, to have…a man who adored her and a family. And, yet it wasn't real, not really, but could it be? Could this be real?

'Because you are the best of men, William,' she said quietly. Her eyes welled and she met his gaze. The words were true and yet still a lie, and confusion overwhelmed her. 'I know the situation is impossible and I wish—' she began, but he reached up and cupped her cheek in a soft caress, turning her face to his. The softness in his eyes and acceptance there made her breath catch.

And then before she could say or do anything else, he kissed the life out of her. His mouth came down hard on her own, his lips commanding and yet soft, and she felt herself tumbling through the air into some other world far beyond anything she had read in any book.

He pulled her into his arms and his warmth cocooned her. Her arms slid around his torso, his muscles rippling beneath the fabric of his thin tunic. His body shuddered under her touch and she thought it was the most magical feeling in the world. To be wanted, desired, and cherished all at once. She felt like the little cinder girl with the power of a woman for the first time and it was intoxicating.

Too soon, he pulled away, resting his forehead against her own, his breaths shallow and uneven. 'I am afraid, I must cease, my lady,' he said his voice husky and low. 'Or I may cease to be a gentleman. You have me undone.'

Hattie's stomach flipped and she bit her lip. She didn't trust herself, so she nodded in agreement, running a palm down his cheek. She was quite undone, too.

'Shall we break our fast?' he asked. 'Then I will join you and Millie for a walk about the lake.'

'Sounds wonderful,' she said, finally gathering the courage to speak.

He rose and pulled her up alongside him. She fit perfectly in the crook of his arm. He pressed a kiss to her temple before he stepped out of the embrace. His hand slid down her arm and clutched her hand, squeezing it gently before letting go. Hattie released a shuddering breath and smiled at him as she headed for the dining room. Her step was wobbly as if she were a newborn colt, the rush of feeling alive upsetting her balance.

She had set them on a course she couldn't control as it was only a matter of time before he regained his memory. She only hoped there wouldn't be too much damage, but her heart knew far better. They were headed to disaster.

But for now, it would be blissful and she would capture it for as long as she could. As Ophelia would say, what was one's life without adventure? This held the promise of being an adventure in spades and she would claim it until it shattered, for if life had taught her anything it was that it could change in an instant.

Chapter Seventeen

William followed behind Penelope and his daughter, entranced by the sweet ease between them. Penelope showed Millie flowers, animals and other curiosities as they walked and he found himself relaxing, the tension loosening from his shoulders.

Although his daughter didn't answer any of Penelope's questions with words, her eyes sparkled as she nodded, pointed, or laughed, and soon they had travelled half the distance of the lake without him saying a single word to them. Millie ran over to the lake's edge and looked for a smooth stone as Penelope instructed and Penelope stood by watching. He settled in beside her.

'Have you always had such ease with her?' he asked.

'It took some time for her to get used to me, but she is eager to learn and love. She is a treasure.' Her smile was bright and brilliant and the sunlight captured the soft caramel and rich browns of her irises.

Tiny gold flecks danced in them and he couldn't steal his gaze away.

'What?' she asked, a faint blush rising to her cheeks.

'You are absolutely enchanting, my lady,' he said. 'And I find it hard to look anywhere else.'

And he meant it. His words weren't flattery or full of empty promises. Despite himself, he found himself bewitched by her kindness and acceptance of him, his situation, and for the care she gave his daughter, especially when he was so lacking now. He reached out his hand, his thumb skimming along the edge of her palm as he wrapped his fingers around her own, a skittering fire resounding in his blood. Was this what love felt like? Or was this a heady attraction born of baser desire? Ironically, he didn't know and he surely couldn't ask, could he?

Millie rushed to them and held out a perfectly smooth stone to him and smiled. His stomach turned as this was the first time she'd come to him this way since his accident and he released his hold on Penelope's hand. His daughter smiled and thrust it towards him again and then pointed to the lake. He stood, uncertain, but smiled and thanked her, accepting the stone from her small, soft fingers, still slick from the water of the lake.

He closed his palm around it and a rush of emotion captured him. What was his life before? Did they run along the shore together or cuddle for afternoon naps? What he wouldn't give to remember. He cursed himself and his body's weakness.

Penelope leaned close and whispered into his ear, 'She wishes for you to skip stones along the water. It was one of your favourite things to do together, aside from nightly bedtime stories.'

'Ah,' he replied. 'Was I any good at it?'

'Quite, actually,' she cooed before stepping back.

'I was afraid you might say that,' he replied.

He studied the lake, his pulse picking up speed, as if this were a competition and great hopes were pinned to his success, which in a way it was. Would he be able to do it? He wanted to live up to his daughter's expectations of him, even if it was only how far he could skip rocks along the surface of a lake. He opened his palm, looking at the flat tan rock, wishing the stone within it could remind him exactly how to do such.

Sadly, it said nothing.

'Let your mind go and see if your body remembers. You might surprise yourself, Your Grace,' she said with a wink. Evidently she could read his discomfort like a gossip sheet.

He smiled and chuckled. 'Fine idea.' He tossed the stone into the air, caught it and followed Millie to the water's edge.

Millie clapped her hands in glee and he put on the

most serious face he could, studying the water, and pretending to stretch out his shoulder. She giggled and his heart swelled in his chest. Her laughter was effervescent and he wished to bottle it.

He reached back and released the stone. It skipped along the water seven times before it sank and Millie jumped up and down with joy. A flash of memory overtook him. He was a boy at the lake with another boy in the evening, a sunset budding before them, skipping stones one after another until finally an older woman came out, beckoning them to come inside for supper.

'I wager your pudding you can't beat me, Brother,' he challenged, tossing a rock into the air and catching it.

'I will take the wager and double it. Two days of desserts I can beat you,' his brother quipped, smiling. 'I can all but taste my victory now.' He rolled up his shirt sleeves, preparing for the throw.

'Agreed. And what you taste is the sourness of disappointment when I best you,' he countered, rolling up his sleeves as well.

The sun burnt a bright gold red before them, setting along the ridgeline of the valley. A breeze ruffled their hair and made the early wildflowers sway, sending a sweet smell to tickle his nose.

'My boys,' their mother called from behind them at the Manor, 'come in and get washed.'

'One more throw, Mother. Whoever wins gets two days of desserts.'

'If you don't hurry, I will eat all of your desserts,' she quipped, a smile evident in her voice.

'You would not do such to your sons,' his brother challenged.

'I just might,' she countered, gave a wry smile and turned for the house.

He and his brother dropped the stones from their hands and jogged back to the Manor until they caught up with their mother. Each of them pressed a kiss to her cheeks and bounded into the house like the hounds barking behind them, eager to come in.

William felt the warmth of the memory deep in his bones and he almost laughed aloud with his younger self before the memory faded away and thrust him back into the present moment.

'William?'

Startled, he turned to see Penelope watching him with concern knitting a fine furrow between her shapely eyebrows. He shook his head and smiled. 'I just remembered something.'

Her mouth opened and her eyes widened. 'What?' she asked, as her gaze slid away to Millie who clutched his pant leg.

'When I was a boy skipping rocks in this exact spot. With my brother and mother.'

'That's wonderful,' she replied in a rush, releasing a breath.

He reached down and ran his palm along his daughter's dark curls. Had her hair always been so soft? The weight of her tiny body pressed against his leg such a balm? While he couldn't remember the answer, he knew it had to have been a resounding yes. She was his daughter and what would ever have been more important to him than her? He looked down at her and smiled, and she wrapped her arms around his knee. While he wished he could remember her, remembering *something* was a start.

'Perhaps this means you shall remember all in time?' Penelope said.

There was a pull of hesitation in her voice that he couldn't work out, but he was too pleased over remembering something to explore it. 'I hope so. I would like to remember more joyful times like that one.'

While he knew both his parents and brother were dead, as he had probed in the early days of his amnesia for such answers, he felt the loss more keenly now that he had remembered them and felt the love at that first memory. No doubt he would remember more of his losses and grieve them a second time. He shoved the thought aside. There were more pressing issues, like his daughter, the upkeep of the Manor and his upcoming nuptials…

'Have we set a date?' he asked, reaching for her hand and enjoying how it slipped into his so easily, as if he'd done it a thousand times. He smiled. Most likely he had, even if he couldn't remember.

Blast.

Hattie's stomach curdled.

Just tell him.

He tightened his hold on her hand, and she sucked in a breath as the sensation buzzed through her again. Would it be like this every time he reached for her? Kissed her? The blissful agony and the easing ache after she breathed through the initial contact were becoming addictive. She didn't wish to tell him the truth. Ever.

And if he fell in love with her now as her then it counted, did it not? She wouldn't have to tell him who she was.

She frowned. Even she couldn't pass such lies on as truths to herself.

'Penelope?'

She wasn't being herself, was she? She was *pretending* to be a lady. One with an esteemed standing in society and fine clothes. She was not Hattie Potts who'd arrived mud-splattered with three gowns to her name in a rather worn portmanteau.

She released a nervous laugh. 'We had not set one as we were so newly engaged.'

That wasn't entirely untrue now, was it?

'Perhaps that is something we can do together that I will remember,' he teased. He swung little Millie's arm which resounded through his body and into hers.

She slowed to a stop. The guilt of pretending all was well in front of Millie also cut her to the quick.

'Are you sure you still wish to?' she asked, unable to hold his gaze. 'You do not remember proposing to me. You do not really *know* me. You should know the woman you marry.'

He released her hand and stooped to be eye level with Millie. 'Run inside and get washed before we eat. Penelope and I will be in shortly.' He kissed Millie's cheek and she skipped along the meadow to go inside. He watched her enter the Manor and rose to face Hattie. The intensity of his gaze made her take a step back.

He clutched both of her hands and closed the gap between them, his leg pressing in against the fold of her skirts. 'I know…' He paused. 'Actually, I cannot know how hard it has been for you. The position you have been put in. And I cannot pretend it is not a risk to move forward. I do not remember the first blush of love I felt for you or the first kiss we shared, or even the moment I met you…'

Hattie held her breath.

'But, since I have awoken, I have felt the awakenings of something that feels like love. A tenderness and longing…and when I kissed you this morning, it felt as though we had something magical. As though we *do* have something akin to a true romance. Can you try to trust that even time cannot thrust what we have asunder?'

She swallowed hard. The passion in his gaze, and the vulnerability in his features, made her unable to move. Would all he said fade away if she blinked? Did she imagine his words? Tears bloomed in her eyes and she was unable to stop them. He gripped her face, wiping away a tear with his thumb.

'I've upset you, which was the last thing I wanted. I am sorry, I…'

And rather than splutter out an answer, she leaned into him and kissed him. She threaded her hand through his hair and along his neck, unable to contain the feelings she had for him any longer. He answered her kiss, pressing into her gently and then with more urgency until their bodies were crushed together, although it didn't feel close enough. She shoved aside her worries and savoured being held, wanted and kissed by a man. By him. By the man she was beginning to love.

He pulled back and chuckled. 'Perhaps you are ready to move forward with setting a date after all,' he mused, his voice husky and his gaze hooded.

'Yes,' she replied. 'I am…but let us wait until you are more recovered. I do not wish to add to your responsibilities at present.'

He nodded and smiled. 'Wise indeed, my lady.'

As he gripped her hand in his and they walked back to the Manor, she rejected all worries. She would savour every moment of their time together for as long as it lasted. And if she was lucky, he might just love her for who she was, Hattie Potts, who'd become a lady while he was sleeping.

Chapter Eighteen

As the days and weeks clipped by, William's disappointment over not regaining his memory diminished. His life with his daughter, Penelope, his cousin and the comfort of his home at Blithe Manor was enough. The unknown past mattered less and less to him as he forged his way through to the future. The date for the nuptials had been selected and they had drafted a list of guests. He frowned when he saw Penelope had not added to the list yet.

He rose from his study, walked upstairs to the library where Penelope was prone to be while Millie napped, and sneaked in behind her. She had curled her legs under her as she read and the sunlight streamed in, catching the auburn strands of her loose tresses and turning them into a soft garnet. She paused and looked up, no doubt feeling the weight of his stare and smiled.

'What a nice surprise,' she said, setting her book

aside. 'I'd thought you buried in correspondence. It is rather teetering in that salver of yours.'

'Perhaps, but I noticed you had not written down the names of your guests for the wedding. Would you like to add some now?' He lifted the guest list.

She paled and his stomach dropped out. Had she changed her mind and not told him? He steeled himself. Best to know now. 'Have you changed your mind?' he asked. His heart pounded in his chest as the silence stretched out between them. He came to her and settled into the cushion next to her.

'Penelope,' he said, 'you can tell me. I would understand. Not every woman wants to marry a man who can't remember ninety-nine per cent of their life.' He laughed despite the knot of emotion tightening under the cravat neatly tied about his throat. He fought the urge to rip it off.

'I want to marry you more than anything,' she said, taking his hand in hers and holding it in the curve of her lap. 'But you do not remember my past and you should decide whether it makes a difference to you.'

'I don't understand,' he replied. 'What do I not know?'

'That I have few people to place on that guest list. I have no close family left…other than two friends who grew up like me…an orphan.'

Relief made him almost laugh. 'You believed I would not want to marry you because of that?'

'That and the situation of my birth.' She paused and frowned; a struggle waged inside her.

'You can tell me,' he encouraged. 'How did you become Lady Penelope? With no title or family and being raised as an orphan?'

'I did not know who my father was until after he died. My mother was his mistress.'

The pain in her voice shattered him and he waited to let her continue when she was ready.

A blush pinked her cheeks and she looked down. She sucked in a breath and released it before lifting her gaze to his. She squeezed his hands. 'It seems that my father was dying and no longer had any legitimate heirs, so he found me and claimed me as his own just before he succumbed to his illness. I suppose he thought an illegitimate heir was better than none. After that, I was sent to finishing school to make up for what I lacked. He died before I met you.'

Despitc the small chuckle and smirk, the pain in her words was evident.

'And if that is not something you can live with, now that you are hearing it again, Your Grace, I understand. You can sever our attachment. I know it does not add a flourish to the branches of your untarnished family tree.' She cast her glance away.

'I would never do such. While I am surprised, it does not alter my affections for you.'

'But maybe it should,' she said quietly staring down at their joined hands. 'You are a duke. Your lineage matters. Your standing will take a blow in society once everyone knows the truth of my past and that you have married beneath your station.'

'And how would they know?' he enquired.

'Once the wedding date is announced, people will ask and at a wedding with so few in attendance on behalf of my family, everyone will know. Not having a father or family is not a secret one can hide. I do not even have anyone to give me away.'

He thought of Millie marrying and not having him to deliver her to her future husband and the ache that would create in a little girl's heart…and in a grown woman's heart. He had no idea how to fill such a wound.

Perhaps it was best to admit he couldn't.

'I did not know. I am sorry.'

'I know. I just don't want to bring shame to you or for you to regret marrying a woman with such a past.' She wiped her eyes.

'It is your father who should be ashamed and embarrassed for what he has done and for losing out on knowing you,' he said, lifting her chin so he could look at her.

A small hiccup escaped her despite her best efforts. 'It is ridiculous to miss someone I never really knew,' she replied.

'No, it isn't. I miss people I can't remember all the time,' he teased.

She laughed and kissed his cheek.

'Then, it is settled. You will add these friends of yours to our guest list for me and we will marry?'

'Yes,' she replied. 'I will.'

'Then let's find some ink up here and add them now before you change your mind.' He pulled her to standing and she stumbled behind him as he tugged her along. There was no stopping him once he'd put his mind to something and his mind was set on marrying her.

It was far from Christmas Day, but every fibre of William's being was taut with enthusiasm and excitement. He pulled out his pocket watch. If his calculation was correct and Eddie encountered little rain along his journey, then the carriage from the tiny town of Stow should be arriving any time now. He peeked into the library as he walked past and was pleased to see Penelope reading as usual.

She had no idea what surprise he had in store for her, but he couldn't wait. Ever since she'd told him of her dear childhood friends, he was determined to meet them and to surprise his betrothed with their presence. He wanted to thank her for all she had done for him since his accident.

After distracting himself for another half-hour, he finally heard the turn of wheels along the long gravel drive and he jumped up from his desk. This was it. He could hardly wait to see the excitement on Penelope's face. He shrugged on his jacket, smoothed his waistcoat and coat sleeves, made a last-minute adjustment to his cravat and checked the looking glass to make sure his hair wasn't too out of place. He wanted her dear friends to like him. It was important he begin their acquaintance on the right foot. He exhaled a deep breath and travelled down the hall to the library where he swung into the room.

'We have guests, my dear. Care to join me in greeting them in the parlour?'

She paused and set a bookmark in her current read before snapping the book shut. 'Is it Daphne?' she asked before rising and stretching like a cat rising from a long slumber.

'No,' he replied without lying before disappearing. He feared his eagerness might give himself away. He started down the hallway and she fell in step behind him.

The door opened and Mr Simmons greeted them

before they reached the parlour. 'Welcome to Blithe Manor, ladies,' his butler said and William imagined him leaning into his deepest bows. 'His Grace and Lady Penelope will be waiting for you in the parlour.'

William's heart raced as he clutched Penelope's hand and pulled her into the parlour before they could hear their reply. 'I have a wonderful surprise for you, my dear, that I hope you will like.'

Her eyes lit up and she smiled. 'A surprise? For me?'

'Yes,' he replied as they stood in front of the prepared tea service. 'I could think of nothing better to repay you for all you have done to care for me and Millie since my accident.'

'You did not need to do any such thing…' she began, but was interrupted by Mr Simmons's knock before he entered the room. Penelope smoothed her gown and smiled, no doubt eager for the surprise.

When the door opened, she gasped at the sight of the two women, lost all sense of decorum and rushed to them, embracing them fiercely. There were murmurs, hugs, tears, laughter and a cacophony of squeals of delight that he couldn't decipher. But one thing was certain: his surprise for Penelope was a brilliant success. He stood back, smiled and crossed his arms over his chest, pleased by his efforts and the joyful reunion. Even if he couldn't be reunited with his family, she could be reunited with what by all intents and purposes was hers.

After another minute of wiping tears, greeting each other and fussing over Penelope's dress and hair, the women took notice that William was still in the room and quieted.

'William, I am so sorry. I was overcome with emotion and happiness. Please let me introduce you,' Penelope said, wiping another tear from her cheek and facing him.

'Let me guess,' he added. He studied them as he approached. 'I think you must be Miss Hastings,' he said pointing to the tall, rather serious brunette, 'and you are Miss Granger,' he added nodding to the rather pretty blonde with impish features and curls fighting to be free from her bonnet.

Penelope stood between them. Her height, brown eyes and hair and soft features were a blend between them. Together they were a rather stunning trio made for each other. He smiled when the two other women nodded.

'You are correct, Your Grace,' Miss Granger replied and squeezed Penelope's waist. 'And we are so grateful for your invitation, although we were surprised it did not come from Hattie herself.'

He frowned. 'Hattie? Who is that?'

Penelope blushed and faltered. 'It is their nickname for me. Has been since we were children.'

''Tis a rather odd nickname, is it not?' he asked.

'I used to adore wearing hats when I was younger,' she stumbled out, her blush deepening.

'Oh?' he asked. 'I had no idea. We must contact the modiste and have a few more made. You have few hats from what I have seen.'

'They do not travel well, so I did not bring many,' she rushed out.

'Yes,' Miss Hastings added, studying Penelope. 'They can get rather crumpled and unlike the original creation after a long trip.'

Penelope cleared her throat. 'Perhaps you might like to freshen up before joining us for tea. Would that be all right, Your Grace?' she offered, looking to William. 'It has been quite a journey for them, I am sure, and Miss Hastings can get a bit peckish,' she added in a lowered tone with a wink.

Why had he not thought of that?

No doubt because he was not a woman.

'My apologies, ladies. Of course. Let us reconvene in an hour and have tea then and get to know one another. I am sure you have many stories to tell about my betrothed.'

Miss Hastings coughed and Miss Granger hit her between the shoulder blades. 'Come, come, Gertrude,' she said. 'Let us change, so we can hear all about what Hat—I mean, Penelope's been up to since we arrived. Thank you, Your Grace, for your kindness and generosity for inviting us. We are so delighted to be here.'

They clutched each other by the waist and followed Penelope. 'I'll be back,' she called to William.

'Take your time,' he replied, watching them exit the room. They were an odd little pair, but for some reason he liked Penelope's friends immediately. But perhaps he was prone to like people with ease, but who knew. He couldn't remember much of anything three weeks prior to now, which might be a blessing in disguise.

Chapter Nineteen

'Care to explain, *Lady Penelope*?' Trudy asked in low staccato tones as she tugged Hattie to her side. Her brow narrowed in judgement.

Hattie smothered a smile and held her tongue.

'Yes, do tell,' Ophelia purred. 'This *betrothed* of yours is a delicious creature. I thought all dukes were rather old and vapid, but not yours.' She sucked in a breath. 'Have you fallen in love just like I thought you would?' She sighed dramatically and pressed her hand to her chest. 'What greater love story could there be?'

Hattie pulled them along the hallway, avoiding all their questions, but revelling in the sight, sound and feel of them being reunited. She was far too excited to see them, but she also didn't want to tell them what was really going on until they were far from William. Even though everyone else in the Manor knew she was no Lady Penelope, she couldn't risk William overhearing what she knew would be a rather detailed and thorough interrogation.

'Mrs Chisholm,' Hattie called across the hall as they reached the base of the stairs. 'Could you bring some refreshments upstairs to my chamber for our guests and show them their rooms?'

'Of course. Follow me, ladies.'

'Thank you,' Hattie replied. 'I will be along straight away, but first there is something I must do.'

'But—' Trudy began. Ophelia silenced her with a finely placed elbow to the ribs.

Trudy shot her a warning look and Hattie smothered a smile. 'I must speak with William first. Then, we will catch up…on everything.' She gifted them a smile and turned, the swish of her skirts whispering along the hardwood floors as she rushed back to the parlour.

William was still there, standing with his back to her, staring out the window with his hands tucked in his trouser pockets. What she felt for him was so pure and honest, she did not even pause to think about her actions. She scurried up to him, slid her arms around his waist and hugged him, resting her cheek against his back. She felt pure unbridled bliss. There were simply no other words for it. 'Thank you, thank you, thank you,' she murmured to him.

His chuckle was warm and low, resounding deep

in his belly. He turned in her arms. 'So you approve of my surprise?' he asked, light dancing in his eyes.

'I more than approve. It may be the most thoughtful thing anyone has ever done for me.' She pressed a hand to his cheek and he leaned in to her touch. She stood on her tiptoes and kissed him. The meeting of their lips was soft and gentle at first. Then, he pulled her in to him and the gratitude and sweetness she felt morphed into something deeper and more urgent.

Before she knew it, he was kissing the very life out of her and her limbs tingled and buzzed under the heat of his touch as his hands roamed up and down the column of her back and along her waist. She wasn't entirely sure her feet were even touching the floor any more.

Why did he have to feel and smell so good?

A subtle cough sounded from the doorway. 'William,' she whispered as he kissed along the column of her throat. He must not have heard it. 'Mrs Chisholm,' she said with a chuckle.

He stilled and pulled away with a low curse that made her giggle like a schoolgirl.

'Yes, Mrs Chisholm?' William asked.

'Your Grace,' she replied with a small bow. 'The ladies are settled and tea has been brought up to the small library upstairs in case you would like to join them, my lady.'

'Thank you, Mrs Chisholm. I shall join them shortly. We have much to catch up on.' She turned to William and mouthed 'thank you'.

He lifted her hands and pressed a kiss between the delicate ridge of her knuckles and released her with a wink.

Her stomach fluttered to the floor like a fallen petal catching the breeze and she held her breath. The man was making her fall in love with him. She couldn't stop the perilous journey she was on.

Nor did she want to.

Hattie entered the upstairs library and reading room and closed the door behind her with a click.

'If this wasn't one of the most gorgeous rooms I have ever been in, I would throttle you, *Lady Penelope Denning*,' Trudy announced, exaggerating the syllables of Hattie's assumed identity. Trudy looked up from the volume she had been skimming and snapped the book shut.

Ophelia bit her lip and rushed to Hattie. 'What has happened, Hat?' she asked, grasping one of Hattie's hands. 'We had a fright when we received your letter about you staying on, but with so few details, and then the carriage arrived for us from His Grace with an invitation to visit our friend, *Lady Penelope Denning*.' She lowered her voice. 'For a moment we thought you *had* been seduced into some sort of accommodation house and become a lady for hire.' Ophelia giggled.

When Hattie didn't immediately contradict her, both of her friends stilled and stared at her. The colour drained from Ophelia's face. 'You haven't, have you?'

'No,' Hattie stammered out. 'Not exactly.'

Trudy cocked her head and stared at her quizzically. 'Then, what exactly *is* going on?'

'It is a long story. Sit. I'll pour us some tea. And enjoy the biscuits. The food here is exquisite.'

They both cut a glance at each other before they sat at the small table Mrs Chisholm had filled with a silver-tiered tray of biscuits, little sandwiches and other tasty treats and a steaming pot of tea with three cups and saucers. Ophelia was the first to select a soft biscuit and pop it in her mouth. Her eyes widened and she sighed. The bliss from the shortbread melting in her mouth was evident.

'Delicious, are they not?' Hattie asked, pouring their tea and adding sugars and milk. Trudy's gaze followed Hattie until she settled into the chair between them.

'Spill,' Trudy said before sipping her tea.

'Well, my position began as a governess just as I had expected. His daughter, Millie, my young charge, is adorable. And she reminds me…of me…of us.' The other two stilled.

'How so?' Trudy asked. 'Not to be obtuse, but she

lives here. She has a father. How is she anything at all like us?'

'Her mother died quite suddenly, tragically, and she hasn't spoken a word since.'

'That is dreadful,' Ophelia said, setting her biscuit back on her plate. 'Poor girl.'

'How long has it been since she has spoken?' Trudy asked.

'Over a year,' Hattie replied. 'But I feel she is making progress…or at least I hope she is.'

'A year?' Ophelia whispered.

'So how in the world have you ended up as this Lady Penelope Denning when you began here as Miss Hattie Potts, governess?' Trudy examined the sandwiches and finally selected a cucumber mint.

'Reporters were hounding His Grace at the Manor and gave his daughter and me quite a fright one morning out by the lake. The men are desperate for gossip about him and his late first wife to sell to the papers.'

'That does not explain how this…' Trudy paused and pointed at her dress and styling '…came to be.'

'William had the idea of me becoming Lady Penelope Denning for the ball to celebrate his succession. He hoped it would keep the reporters at bay if I was to be his betrothed. It would give them the story they wanted, he said, so his daughter could be left alone as the reporters gave her a fright. For her benefit and for his, I agreed.'

'But he acts as if you *are* this Penelope Denning when he knows you are not,' Ophelia stated. 'It makes little sense to me.' She snagged another shortbread biscuit and popped it in her mouth. She made a small moan as she savoured it.

Heat crawled up Hattie's neck and into her cheeks. If she had possessed one, she would have used that blasted fan from the ball to cool herself, but she didn't, so her flush deepened. 'It is because he has lost his memory and believes I *am* Lady Penelope Denning,' Hattie replied and made a grimace.

Trudy choked on her cucumber sandwich and Ophelia landed a clean blow between her friend's shoulder blades. Ophelia patted her on the back and then turned a narrowed gaze on Hattie as if she were taking on Trudy's line of questioning. 'How? You have an entire household that knows you are no such person.'

'That is true, but they are pretending I am. Then there was the ball where I was introduced to the *ton* *as* her, so all of those people believe I am as well.' She looked down at her hands. Now that she was explaining all of it, it sounded rather horrid and deceitful.

'You mean many people believe you are this made-up person?' Ophelia asked, her eyes widening.

'Yes. Somehow, I was able to be her. I put on fancy

gowns and jewels and imagined myself to be the girl with a lovely home and parents who cared for me, just like we did when we were young. It was easier than I thought it would be to become someone else and pretend to have had a different past, like the one we always dreamed up. And a different life,' she mused and shrugged. Finally, she dared lift her gaze to them. To her surprise Ophelia was smiling. She clapped her hands together.

'That is truly wonderful and so romantic. You have become the princess and lady you were always meant to be. And you have found a man who cares for you and treats you as such.' She sighed, her gaze wistful. 'It is your happily ever after.'

Trudy snorted. 'It is a lie is what it is.'

'Trudy!' Ophelia said, trying to shush her.

Hattie frowned, but nodded. 'She is right. I know it is. And I know it will not last, but for now…for now it is…simply wonderful.'

'But why are the servants and his family lying to him as well?'

'To protect him. He and his daughter have lost much over the years and the Doctor, who knows I am not this Lady Penelope, hopes my presence as his betrothed will aid in his recovery. His household cares for him so much they have continued the ruse. They are all quite lovely,' she added. 'Even the fussiest of them, like Mr Simmons.'

'He must be a good man to have a staff who adore him so and for him to have caught your affections,' Ophelia added, reaching over and clutching Hattie's hand. The gentleness of it undid her and her throat tightened.

'Yes,' Hattie agreed, swallowing back down the emotion. 'He is the best of men. I only wish he cared for me as *me*, Hattie Potts. Not as Lady Penelope.'

'So, before, when you were merely the governess, he showed no interest in you?' Ophelia added, her brow crinkling. 'I find that hard to believe with the way he looks at you now. Perhaps he had some inkling of feeling for you then, but could not show it as your employer.'

'Perhaps there was something there,' she added, 'but he believes me to be his equal now. What will he do when he remembers who I am, realises I am no Lady Penelope, and that I continued with a ruse that was meant to be temporary?' Her shoulders relaxed. Saying her fears aloud to them soothed her. She hadn't had anyone to truly confide in about her fears until now.

Trudy reached over and placed her hand on top of Ophelia's and Hattie smiled when she saw their hands stacked atop one another like when they were younger. 'If he does not choose you again as Hattie Potts, then it is his loss, is it not? And no matter what, you will always have us.'

'Always,' Ophelia added. 'You survived without the love of a duke before and, if need be, you can again.'

The thought of losing him and the life she had built here, no matter how fragile and imaginary it was, awakened the frightened child in her. She knew what it felt like to have the foundation of everything she knew ripped out beneath her feet and she wanted desperately to never ever feel that way again.

'I know. I just don't want to,' she added quietly, squeezing their hands before letting go.

Chapter Twenty

William watched Penelope hug her friends one last time before closing the carriage door and waving to them as the coach pulled away along the gravel, kicking up a few rocks as it continued down the drive. She hugged her body, the features of her face tightening as the carriage turned on to the main road and disappeared behind a cluster of lush green foliage from the large oaks. Her shoulders sagged and she rubbed her upper arms as if chilled, but didn't turn to come back inside.

He stepped away from the window and went to her. He reached her side and slid a comforting arm around her back. She leaned into him without hesitation and rested her head along his shoulder.

'Thank you for sending for them and preparing such a lovely visit for a few days. It was extraordinarily kind of you.' She wrapped her arms around his waist.

He breathed in the sweet scent of her, pulling her to

him. The familiar need and desire to hold her tighter and yet never be able to have her close enough budded in his gut, setting his body on fire. 'For you,' he said, pressing a chaste kiss to her head, 'anything.'

She chuckled. 'Then, perhaps a walk, Your Grace? I feel restless now that they have gone.'

He glanced up to the sky. 'It looks like rain.'

'All the more reason for it. I love the crackle of thunder and electricity in the air.'

'You do? Yet another thing I do not remember about you.' He sighed.

'It is entertaining for you to learn me all over again, is it not?' she teased with a winsome smile.

'And what of me? Is it as enjoyable for you?' He worried over her answer.

She turned her face towards him. 'More than you will ever know.' Her gaze flickered with love and longing and something else he couldn't name. His body flared, matching her desire.

He cleared his throat, bent and nuzzled her neck. 'If you do not cease looking at me so, I will be forced to show you how much I desire you and wish to relearn every part of you.'

She nipped his ear with her teeth. 'I do hope you will.'

He nearly lost his footing. His body shuddered. 'Let us walk before I forget what it means to be a gentleman and that we are in public out of doors,' he replied, offering his arm to her. She threaded hers within his and chuckled.

'I do hope to see that as well,' she whispered so softly he almost believed he imagined it. But when he met her gaze, he saw her enlarged pupils and the want within them.

Lord above. If he wasn't careful, he would honour her request right then and there on the front lawn. He prayed for rain to cool the base need that banked and burned within him.

They made their way around the front lawn to the side of the Manor and a rumble of thunder far in the distance reminded him of the dangerous internal storm he was on the brink of as well. He did not wish to rush the delicate balance between them, and navigating his feelings for her was becoming more and more precarious.

They climbed up a series of stones marking the beginning of the garden that connected the front lawn to the lake in the back of the estate. She jostled into him as his gait was longer than her own, her bosom sliding along his forearm, and he clenched his jaw. He needed to distract himself with something—anything—other than the current images of her naked form pressed against him he was conjuring up in his mind.

'Why do you love thunderstorms?' he asked. The weather seemed a benign neutral topic.

'Because of my mother,' she replied.

His interest was piqued. She had told him little of her family. He knew more about her dear friends than her parents, even though he knew she did not know her father. 'Tell me more,' he encouraged, pleased to be distracted as they made their way across the grass. The wind whipped up, ruffling her chestnut hair and tugging strands free from the pins holding it in a knot at the base of her neck. The weather suited her as did everything else. He suppressed a smile.

'When she knew a storm was coming, she would light all the candles we had, build a fort of blankets, snuggle within it and read to me.' Her features softened and her voice was whimsical and light.

'What kinds of stories did she read to you?'

She smiled at him. 'Nothing you would like, I'm afraid. They were stories of love, romance and adventure.'

He cocked his head. 'And why would I not enjoy such tales?'

'Because you are a duke. You are serious and intellectual, not fanciful.'

'I guess I'll have to take your word for that as I do not know what I used to read.' A fat raindrop fell on his sleeve and another on his head. He ignored them and they continued.

'What was your favourite story?'

'All of them.' She smirked. 'Falling asleep to the sound of her voice, the rainstorm and stories of fancy was the best of memories. It is what I miss most about her.'

'The stories?'

'The sound of her voice, her smell and the warmth of her holding me.'

He pulled her close and swallowed back the emotion tightening his throat. 'When did you lose her?'

'I was only a few years older than when Millie lost her mother. Since I never knew my father and had no other family that I knew of, I ended up at the orphanage. But I was lucky as I met Ophelia and Trudy. Without them, I shudder to think what would have become of me. They became my family.'

'Until now,' he murmured, pulling her to a stop, 'my beloved. Now, we are also your family, Millie and I.'

He bent down on one knee. 'Since I do not remember proposing to you, I wanted…' he paused and pulled a small necklace with a simple ruby heart shaped pendant from his trouser pocket '…to ask for your hand again. You are all I could ever wish for in a wife and mother. Will you marry me, Penelope?'

She gazed down at him, her eyes glistening with

tears, as the rain started to fall in earnest. 'Yes, William. I will marry you. I would choose you over and over again.'

'As I would you, Lady Penelope.' The lightning flashed across the sky and illuminated her features. He stood, cupped her face and kissed her fiercely, his body flooded with relief and some other feeling—was this love that made him feel invincible and fragile all at once? She gripped his shoulders and matched the urgency of his affections. Rain soaked their clothes and the wind whipped around them as the sky darkened from the storm.

He pulled away briefly, grasped her hand and shouted to be heard above the rumble of thunder. 'Come with me. We must get out of the storm.'

She glanced around him. They were far from the Manor, but there was a drying shed they could run to. He tugged her hand. 'Follow me,' he shouted and pointed off to the shed.

She nodded and followed him. They crashed into each other as they skidded along the wet grass, trying to make their way to the shed in the now blinding sheets of rain. Finally, he thrust the door open and they stumbled inside, and he pushed the door closed. The scent of drying herbs filled his senses and, at first, he saw only darkness until his eyes finally adjusted

A flash of lightning streamed through the wooden

gaps of the walls of the shed, illuminating Penelope's features for a moment, and his body reacted to the sight of her. Water glistened from her skin, her hair was soaked and strands traced along her cheeks and neck, and her smile was vibrant and alive. She chuckled and clutched his jacket. 'You look soaked through, Your Grace.'

'No more than you,' he replied, grasping the hand that gripped his jacket and tugging her closer. 'There must be a blanket or something about in this shed to dry off with. Let's start along this wall and search.'

'A fine idea,' she replied through chattering teeth.

They stumbled along one wall finding only a work bench and more herbs waiting to be bound and hung. Turning along the second wall, his fingers skimmed a heavy scratchy material hanging from a hook. 'Aha! A blanket, or coat, or something that can warm us. Anything?' he asked.

'Nothing except a great deal of drying herbs. Although they smell lovely,' she announced. 'What do they use all of these for?'

He sighed. 'One of the many things I do not remember,' he replied. He was tired of the not knowing.

'That was thoughtless of me.' She rubbed his arm.

'It is not you, but my frustration. Not knowing what has and has not been…' He hesitated and then continued. 'I do not even know if I…if we ever…' He paused flustered and impatient with his situation. How long would his memories be locked away? What had he done to deserve such a punishment? He stepped away from her and raked a hand through his hair, muttering a curse as he turned away.

Silence followed and then a flash of lightning before a loud rumble of thunder. Penelope slid her arms around his waist and hugged his back. 'No, we have not made love, Your Grace,' she purred in his ear, eliciting a surge of want in him. His body shuddered against her. 'But it is not for a lack of desire to.'

He closed his eyes, blood thrummed through his veins and the battle between his body and mind raged. A better man would not be tempted or give in to such base desires until they were husband and wife. Was he that man? Evidently he was to have waited this long. But they were engaged, he had almost died, she had been there for him and he wanted her more than he had wanted anything in his life…that he could remember anyway.

He stilled. Life was short. What was tomorrow? There was no promise, no certainty and no guarantees. But there was her, them, now, and he would seize it. He turned in her arms, cradled the side of her face, and kissed her with the urgency, need and want he had been holding back. He let all his gratitude, lust and affection flow unbidden, unfiltered and unchecked in his kisses and caresses. The more he kissed her, the more he wanted to kiss her, and all he could feel was the warmth, softness and safety of her body.

He never wanted to let her go.

His palm slid over her wet hair and traced the fine, petite lobe of her ear, and she shuddered against him, which sent a whirl of response through his body. He cleared his throat to distract himself from the roar of want coursing through him. Her demanding kisses matched his and he tugged her against him, her core resting against his arousal.

She moaned in pleasure and his body flared like dry tinder set upon a flame. He ended their kiss and let his mouth roam unbidden upon the soft supple skin of her neck, nipping slowly. With every gasp from her mouth, his body surged in need. There was no going back for either of them.

Or was there? He pulled back slowly, allowing himself a few moments to collect the words he needed to ask. 'Are you sure you wish to…here? With me?' he asked, feeling tentative and uncertain.

'I know I do not want to stop kissing you,' she replied, slightly out of breath.

He chuckled. 'That is not quite the same as what I have in mind.'

Her silence betrayed her hesitation. 'I do not know

all there is to know about coupling, but I do know that I trust you…and that I want you, William.'

He was speechless. Had sweeter, more trusting words ever been spoken to him? Her honesty stilled him.

'William?' she asked timidly. 'Have I said something wrong?' She squeezed his hand, brought it to her lips and kissed the inside of his palm.

'No,' he stammered. 'I am in awe of your honesty and trust in me.'

'Then make love to me. We are betrothed, are we not?'

The hesitation and uncertainty in her voice signalled some far distant bell in his head, but he ignored it and gave in to the surge of need, desire and longing he felt for her.

'We are, my lady, and I plan to make love to you for the rest of my days.' His fingers trembled as he placed the ruby pendant necklace around her neck and secured the clasp. He smiled and pulled her into an embrace, his hands caressing every part of her, and kissed her over and over again. She responded in kind, eager to match his desire for her. No more words were spoken as their bodies became the only tool they needed to communicate with one another. And in the storm, another story was told. One they both would never forget.

Chapter Twenty-One

Hattie woke, feeling warm and sated until she remembered where she was and what had happened between her and William. Heat flushed her body and her pulse increased. Rain dripped down from the eves of the shed, the storm having passed. Streams of sun shone through the slats of the wood, and she could sense it was late afternoon. A handful of hours had passed and they had some time before they needed to return for the evening meal. She turned in William's arms, unwilling to leave him just yet. Would he be angry with her? Disappointed in her?

While their time together had been blissful, she had been unable to make love to him, calling a halt to his advances at consummating their attachment at the last possible moment. The guilt over him not knowing who she really was, not actually being his betrothed and the deep-seated fear of him one day finding out the truth and feeling she had entrapped him in some way overcame her desire to join with him. To her surprise, he was not angry, but said he could wait for as long as she needed him to and brought pleasure to her in other ways she had never known possible.

Goose pimples covered her skin as her body remembered. She never knew a man's lips could create such feelings in her or that they could travel other places than over her lips and breasts with such care and tenderness. Her body flushed and hummed to awareness of him as she remembered his touch and his kiss. She only hoped he woke with the same feelings. Either way, she knew she had done the right thing. She could not have lived with herself if she'd made love to him as anyone other than herself, especially if she ended up with child.

She would have become everything she feared: her mother.

She shivered. Hattie traced a fingertip along the fine strong curve of William's upper back and shoulder blade. Part of her now understood her mother in a way Hattie never had before and a shift of empathy grew in her. Being with William and almost making love to him was intoxicating and pleasurable, far more than she had expected. She had been but moments away from casting aside everything to lie with him. Had her mother just succumbed to her desires while Hattie had halted it but a moment prior?

Heaven knew if she hadn't had such guilt and such an alarming conscience, the ending of their liaison could have been vastly different. And if he regained his memory, discovered her with child and proved unsympathetic to her plight, she might very well have repeated the life of her mother.

William murmured and turned to her. She held her breath, uncertain of what she would find. But the affection in his gaze put her at ease. He was not angry, but gorgeous in the shadowy shades of grey of the darkness between them. He reached for her, tugging her closer to him, and she gave no resistance.

She settled into the crook of his arm and wrapped a leg around his own. She wanted to savour this moment between them as her gut told her it might be her last. For she was strong enough to resist him this time, but what about the next? Even she might lose her fortitude. She dared not place herself in such a compromising and precarious position again.

'Well, that was a storm I don't regret going out in,' he teased, kissing the top of her head as his fingers trailed up and down her arm, eliciting a warm hum beneath her skin.

She couldn't help but laugh. 'Me either, Your Grace.'

'Your Grace, is it?' He tickled her and she laughed.

'Yes,' she continued, holding his gaze. He kissed her and she leaned into him savouring the heat and pleasure it brought her once more. As they melted into each other, he finally ended their kiss.

'You remind me that I am not being a gentleman for almost making love to you in a shed on a blanket in the middle of a storm. I blame my weakness and your beauty.'

She dropped her gaze. 'I hope you are not angry. That you understand,' she said quietly, tugging the blanket over her breasts, feeling suddenly awkward despite her words.

He lifted her chin to face him. 'Not at all, my dear. I respect you and your decision. We are not wed, not yet. As I said, I will wait until you are ready. You are my treasure and I will always honour and respect your wishes.'

Her eyes welled. His kindness was almost too much. And for a moment, her lips parted, and she thought to tell him everything. About pretending, about truly caring for him, and about wanting to have a real relationship with him as Hattie, not Lady Penelope, but her throat tightened, and she swallowed back all her words.

She was too frightened to tell him. She didn't want to lose him. Not yet.

'What is wrong? Did you fear I would be angry?' He kissed her cheek and then leaned back to smile at her. 'Never, my lady.'

She chuckled and hiccupped.

'But we do have one immediate challenge,' he said, looking at her. 'Now we must sneak back to the Manor and I must pretend that I did not ravish you and do not wish to do so every time I lock eyes upon you.' He smiled and bent to nip at the lobe of her ear, sending a tremble through her entire body.

She laughed and he tickled her, sending a burst of joy that overshadowed her budding fear and uncertainty. While she might very well lose him when he remembered their relationship was a ruse, that would not be today.

Chapter Twenty-Two

William smiled as he slipped on his boots and headed down the stairs, taking them two at a time. He could hardly wait to surprise Penelope and Millie on their morning walk about the lake this morning. The golden glow of the sunrise hit his face as he reached the final step of the landing and he paused. *Glory be.*

He walked forward and stared out the large windows of the front parlour of the Manor on to the lush green lawn. A soft mist hovered above the glistening dew-covered grass and a striking golden orange with hints of pink and violet streaked across the tops of the large, towering oaks and other hardwoods for as far as his eyes could see.

It could not have been a more glorious morning. The only thing missing was spending it with his two favourite people in the world: the woman he loved and his daughter. *Loved.* He stilled at the revelation of it, but it was true. He was certain.

It didn't matter that he couldn't remember the moment they met or the first blush he had seen upon her cheeks. He loved her now and that was enough. And Millie adored her, too. They were a perfect little trio, it seemed. He could not have wished for anything more. Perhaps he was never meant to remember. Based on what he had been told of his past, it might have been a blessing.

No matter. The sunrise was wasting. He gathered his coat from the hook in the hallway, waved a greeting to Mrs Chisholm and Mr Simmons and headed out the back door. The crisp, cool, clean air refreshed him even more than he expected and he sucked in a full heady breath before setting out through the meadow.

Soon, the wet grass ringed the hem of his dark trousers and he chuckled. Penelope's dress and Millie's would be soaked through, but no matter. Mrs Chisholm would just cluck her disapproval and command them to change and sweet Millie would refuse until Penelope talked her into it.

He saw their figures far off in the distance at the opposite side of the lake. It was too far for him to discern what they were doing, stooped and looking into the thick grass along the side of the water. He called out to them, but they didn't move. Evidently, his voice did not carry across the water as he had hoped. He stopped and plucked two wildflowers, one for each of them, and continued.

Soon they were clearly in view and he called to them.

'Good morning, my sweet ladies,' he said. 'A flower to match your beauty.' He bowed and then extended a flower to each of them.

Millie giggled and rushed to him. She hugged his knees and took the flower, holding it against her nose. She smiled. His heart soared at the joy in her face. He was right to have risen early to join them this morning. He congratulated himself on his choice.

He glanced up at Penelope, who he hardly recognised in her simple, worn brown gown. Something about it was familiar. She pointed to a tiny pack of furry ducklings. 'Look! Another hen and her brood. They are beautiful, are they not? Millie found them.'

His head ached and he stilled, closing his eyes as a rush of memory flooded him.

'Perhaps you and your father could also help me this morning. When I came out, I heard a little duckling quacking. She is all alone on the other side of the pond, which is why I was in search of its mother on this side. I need to reunite them, but I do not wish to scare the tiny creature. Perhaps she knows you both well enough to allow you to move her without injury and bring her back over here once we find her mother?'

Millie's eyes widened with excitement and she tugged his hand, urging him to follow. 'Of course, Miss Potts,' he replied. 'And we know just where the mother and the duckling's siblings are. We passed the little brood on our way to you.'

Miss Potts nodded. 'Follow me, then.' She rose and began the trek back to the other side of the pond.

They reached the site where the small duckling continued to quack and shiver, cold and scared from being alone for so long in the cool wet grass. 'I do not know how to move her,' Miss Potts said.

'When I was a boy, we used to scoop them up in our coats and hold them close to our chest, which of course made our mother livid. They are not the cleanest of creatures.'

'Oh? I will try that, then.' She removed her wrap and gently scooped up the tiny duckling, humming to it as she slowly nestled it to her chest. Its tiny orange-webbed feet pushed against her chest like a tiny flutter until it decided to trust her and settled, releasing one final plaintive squeak. The poor thing didn't know what she was about. Millie let go of his leg and approached her. Gently, she ran her hand over the tiny duckling who chirped at the girl's touch. Millie laughed with glee and Miss Potts did, too.

'William, are you unwell?'

He looked up into the beautiful brown eyes of the

woman he knew to be Penelope, his betrothed, and the woman he loved, but it was also the same face as this Miss Potts from his memory. He didn't understand. He shook his head and rubbed his eyes. She gripped his arm.

'William?' her voice was overlapping with another memory that came rushing in from the past. This time he was in his study with her.

'I would like to extend your offer of employment not only as Millie's governess, but also as my fake betrothed. I think a Lady Penelope Denning would do nicely,' he said, his words rushing out. 'Do you think you could do that?'

'I am sorry, Your Grace. I don't think I understood you. I would love to remain on as Millie's governess, but that last part... Did you say you wish for me, an orphan from Stow, to also pretend to be your betrothed as some other person entirely?' She worried her hands in her lap and her eyes were wide and searching.

A beat of silence passed, then he sat back in his chair, his hands sliding down the curved wooden armrests before covering the painted gold flowers at the ends. He met her gaze. 'Yes, Miss Potts, that is exactly what I wish for you to do.'

'Why?' she asked.

'A fair question,' he replied and stood. He walked

along the outline of the room as he thought and tucked his hands in his trousers.

He paused in front of the portrait of the late marchioness and turned. 'In the simplest terms, Miss Potts, I cannot take a new bride, but the ton *will give me and my daughter no peace until I am adequately...unavailable. I cannot ask a woman of high society to fill such a role as they all know one another and will gossip about such a ruse and embarrass me, and so, my hope was that you being from Stow and far removed from here and someone who cares for my daughter and whom my daughter adores would help me with this...endeavour.'*

'You mean lie to everyone?'

'Yes.' He supplied no excuse in what he had asked. 'After speaking to Dr Kemplar, I feel I must do something drastic to protect my daughter. He said we cannot risk more situations such as this morning. She is too fragile.'

'Again, Your Grace, why me? Who in the world would look at me and believe I am a lady of...anything?'

He studied the fine features of her face. 'It is no secret my daughter adores you, Miss Potts. You are willing to risk your life to keep her safe as I have seen this morning. Also, you are not of the ton *and from what I can see do not have a deceitful bone in your body. In short, I trust you. And I believe with the right clothes, hair and training in the ways of society, you would be quite...believable.' His gaze roved over her slowly, hesitating on her face. He was certain in his next statement. 'Quite believable, in fact.'*

'You are not my betrothed, are you?' he accused, shaking off her hold with ferocity. His heart raced in his chest and he felt short of breath. All he had long forgotten rushed back. His cheating wife. The scandal of the past. The deception and lies from Cecily that had nearly destroyed him. And the lies of this woman, who he knew…yet didn't know at all.

The woman stilled. 'Millie,' she said quietly, never taking her eyes from him as if he were a threat, like a rabid dog, and a danger to them all. Perhaps he was. 'Go inside and tell cook to prepare your scones with jam. I will come in to join you later…with your father.'

The girl nodded, setting fearful eyes upon them.

'It will be fine, sweet girl,' the woman said sending her a smile before encouraging her to go, giving her a reassuring pat to her back. His daughter cast her one last glance of confusion and jogged out towards the Manor. Once she was far enough away, he set his gaze upon the woman again.

'Who are you?' he asked. He clenched his hands by his sides. 'Are you Miss Potts? Penelope?'

'Are you remembering?' she asked, her tone hopeful but timid.

'Yes,' he accused. 'And I am remembering that you are *not* this Penelope Denning, but a governess. And not my betrothed as you pretend to be.'

She took a step back. 'Yes,' she replied simply as if that single word explained everything. She clasped her hands before her and squared her shoulders. 'My name is Hattie Potts. I am from Stow. I came here in early April to be Millie's governess. Then you asked me to pretend to be your betrothed, a Lady Penelope Denning. Against my good judgement, I agreed for Millie's sake and because I wished to help you. When you had your accident and lost your memory, we agreed it best for me to continue pretending. I have wanted to tell you the truth a thousand times, but I didn't dare.'

Her truth took the foundation out from beneath him. Lightheadedness threatened and he leaned over, pressing his palms hard to his knees, and breathed. This couldn't be happening again. He couldn't be betrayed by a woman he thought he knew and loved again. Images of Cecily and this woman merged into one, a colliding of hopes, dreams and trust crushed into bits. It didn't matter that it seemed he had created part of this disaster. She had lied to him and made him believe she loved him and he her. That she was something other than what she was. He let out a guttural roar of agony. 'Go!' he shouted. 'Leave here. Now!'

She hesitated and didn't move. To his utter shock, she held her ground.

'I will not,' she stated. 'I love you…and you love me, too. We have spoken the words, no matter who you believed you said them to. That does not change…us.'

'What?' he said with a disbelieving laugh as he righted himself.

She stood before him with a lifted chin and flushed cheeks, her eyes glimmering with unshed tears as her bosom rose and fell as she breathed. 'You heard me, Your Grace. You loved me. You almost made love to me when I was a lady *yesterday*, but I stopped you as I could not bear you not knowing the truth. You said you loved me when I was a *lady*. Why does it matter now when you discover I am from a lowly birth and a mere governess? That does not change love. At least it does not to me.'

He scoffed and ran a hand through his hair. The sight of her all glorious with raw emotion glistening off her like the morning dew almost undid his resolve to cast her out. He did care for her. He had created this illusion to begin with. But the memories and fear of the past conquered all.

The knowing of what lies and deceit did to him and his family and how he had been duped before by a lying, calculating woman, who had promised to love and honour him until death they did part as his wife, undid all he felt for Hattie. He shoved his care, his love for her aside and chose safety. It was what his daughter and his position as a duke deserved and demanded.

'It changes everything,' he finally said. 'I cannot trust a liar, especially one bent on deceiving me for my rank and my wealth. I have survived that once before.'

She took a step forward. 'I am no liar. I did as you asked of me. I did as Daphne and your household asked of me by continuing on with this ruse as you recovered. I did all of this for us because I love you. But *you*...you are just like my father I never knew. Just like those drakes along your pond. Once you have claimed what you want or you feel you deserve better, women like me have no purpose for you, just as they have no purpose for those ducks. And *I* believed you were different. That you were more than a selfish, arrogant duke. But I was wrong, so wrong. Trudy was right. I should never have trusted you. I am better off without you if you believe so ill of me and who I am.'

He stood speechless as he watched her walk away. Anger, confusion and hurt duelled within him, but in the end, anger won out. He was better off without her, too. He'd known enough liars to last a lifetime. He had one last look at the sun that now burned full and bright above him. So much for a glorious morning. He stormed inside and shouted for Mr Simmons and Mrs Chisholm. He would get to the bottom of exactly how it had come to this point if it was the last thing he did.

Chapter Twenty-Three

'What has happened?' Mrs Chisholm asked.

Hattie rushed past her without a word, racing through the house with speed and purpose, then lifting her skirts and moving into a full sprint, taking the stairs two at a time to reach her chambers as fast as her clothing would allow. Hattie would not cry until she was alone.

Once she sealed the door of her chambers behind her and clicked the lock, she collapsed against the back of it, sliding down the wood to the floor in tears. Sobs, deep and loud, rose from her belly and she gave in to them as she pulled her knees to her chest, wrapped her arms around her legs, buried her face in thc familiar scratchy material and cried. She would not pretend all was not lost when it was. Even she did not possess that much strength or will for deception. Ophelia and Trudy would tell her he was not worth her tears, but she set them free anyhow. Her heart was broken and her dreams for a fine future dashed.

Everything was in ruin.

And she was alone again, exactly as she had begun.

Why had she allowed herself to believe William was different and not a selfish and dishonourable man? She paused and sniffed, staring down at her hands. She believed it because he wasn't. William *was* good, decent, and possessed a full and kind heart.

Losing him was as much her fault as his own. She had lied to him and deceived him by choice even though she knew how important the truth was to him because of his first wife. Hattie knew she was playing a very precarious and dangerous game and that it would end poorly the longer the farce went on. She was no fool, but she had acted like one. Now she wished she had told him the truth, but she had never been able to muster the courage. She feared he would have reacted as he had today.

No doubt she would have just lost him sooner. Wouldn't she have?

Her tears were as much frustration over what she had done as they were hurt over his words and actions. There was no denying it.

She had skirted along the path of fancy, revelling in the pretence of it all as if she *were* indeed *Lady* Penelope Denning. Now that the paper-doll house she had fabricated had crumbled down and disintegrated, she had no one to blame but herself. She had ignored so many moments when she could have told him the truth of who she was, but she had been desperate to keep the façade intact. Perhaps this was what she deserved, for she'd never believed he could love her as she was.

But that also wasn't true. She deserved love. And their affection for one another was real no matter her real name or her station. If only she had believed in herself and in him. None of it mattered now, though, did it? There was a soft knock on the door. She held her breath.

Could it be William?

'Hattie?'

Mrs Chisholm.

Hattie covered her mouth to prevent another sob. How she wanted to open the door and confide in her, but Hattie's embarrassment and failure and loss kept her hidden. She hid like she had in the orphanage when she didn't wish to be found.

'He does not mean what he says,' she began softly. So softly that it sent more tears down Hattie's cheeks. 'He is angry. Confused. And well…a man.' Mrs Chisholm chuckled and paused. 'I beg you. Do not leave.' She sighed.

Hattie opened her mouth and almost replied to her, but she clamped her mouth shut.

'But, if you must leave, please do not go without

saying goodbye to us all. Please. We care for you, my dear. You have become…family.'

Fat tears streamed down Hattie's cheeks, but she said nothing. She was frozen, locked in her grief as she had been as a child. She didn't know how to reach out and ask for help. She kept her silence long after the sound of Mrs Chisholm's footsteps disappeared. She hadn't felt such sadness since her mother passed and she didn't know how to weather it without Trudy and Ophelia. She had never faced such grief and hurt without them.

But what would they say when she returned with her tail between her legs, broken and shattered as Trudy had warned? Hattie scoffed and chuckled as she wiped her eyes. They would envelop her in the warmest of hugs. That was what they would do. Chastise her later, perhaps, but never would they berate her when she was down. They would help her grieve and she would recover as she had after every disappointment and setback before.

'It's their loss that they did not choose us.'

Trudy's words echoed in Hattie's ears and she smiled, if only for a moment.

Trudy always said that when the wealthy families came to scrutinise them before passing them over for a younger child with a 'less ambiguous' birth.

'She's right,' Ophelia would agree, playing with her

long curls. 'We are pretty enough. There is nothing we can do about how we came to be in this world. At least we have one another.'

Hattie sniffed. William's rejection was the same, was it not? The icy truth of it pained her more than she wished to admit. He didn't know of her *truly* lowly birth as she had fibbed to him about having a titled regal father who had claimed her before he died. That was a lie crafted to keep her pretend designation as Lady Penelope intact. And even with that he had rejected her. What would he have done when he discovered she was the bastard daughter of a man she did not even know? That she was a product of a mistress and clandestine affair like he abhorred his wife for having.

Perhaps this was the end that was always coming. The one she'd ignored for too long. There was no hiding from her past…at least not for long.

Sisters for ever, tears never.

It echoed through her mind as Hattie wiped her tears. It was what they always said to one another after the families left and they realised their fate as orphans would continue…at least until another visiting weekend. Hattie took a slow steadying breath and then another before pulling back her shoulders and pushing herself up to standing.

'Sisters for ever, tears never,' she said quietly. Then

she took in a breath, released it and said it aloud once more.

She blew her nose in a handkerchief and tucked it back in her dress pocket. She stared down at the dark-brown dress that had somehow helped stir William's memories of her. Would he have remembered if she hadn't been wearing this and been out at the lake?

Did it matter?

He would have remembered, or she would have been plagued with guilt and the need to tell him eventually. She had only hurried along the inevitable. All because she had not wished to soil the hem of one of the beautiful day dresses he'd had made for her.

She sighed, set aside her sadness, and searched her room for her portmanteau and small travelling trunk. She pulled them from beneath the wardrobe and began packing. It took far less time than she expected as she would take nothing except what she arrived with. Well, almost nothing. She gathered up the drawings little Millie had made for her to help her decorate her chambers. Those Hattie would claim as her own. And she would keep the fine ruby heart pendant as a memory of their love. But the fancy dresses, hats and reticules she would leave. Even the crisp pristine gloves she would not take. She would rather leave with her worn, but clean ones than take anything William had purchased for her role as Lady Penelope.

Lady Penelope Denning.

Hattie's fingers skimmed the fine silk and crepe dresses. The luxurious colours, fabrics and cuts were delicious to see together all at once like a fine bouquet of hothouse flowers. Dressing up as Lady Penelope, wearing fine jewels and having herself coiffed to perfection had been glorious. But it was also fanciful make believe and there was nothing real about it.

She'd known it would end, no matter how much she'd hoped it wouldn't. The truth was inescapable, as she well knew. Her hand fell away and she closed the wardrobe, sealing everything that ever was Lady Penelope within it.

'Goodbye, Lady Penelope Denning.'

Lady Penelope Denning would disappear as soon as Hattie stepped into the carriage to leave Blithe Manor behind. In some ways, Hattie would miss her. Her confidence, certainty and slight tilt of her chin.

The carriage.

Blast.

Hattie groaned. She would have to ask for use of the carriage to reach the station to get home to Stow. She had more than enough money for her return, but no way to reach the station. It was an indignity she would have to suffer to return home to Stow. *Best get on with it.* She emerged from her chambers and quietly descended the stairs. The sound of raised voices stopped her cold in her steps before she reached the landing.

'Why would you be in on this scheme as well? I trusted you. I trusted you all.' William's tone was harsh, but rang of another emotion as well: hurt. She almost felt sorry for him.

But not quite. She harboured her own hurt caused by his words.

'Because the Doctor told us it was best for you and your recovery, Your Grace,' Mrs Chisholm answered firmly. 'Lady Buchanan was in agreement. We all were.' If there was a woman who could hold her ground against him, even if he was her employer, it was Mrs Chisholm. Hattie almost smiled.

Before she could talk herself out of it, Hattie continued down the stairs and stood at the doorway of William's study where he stood in front of several of his staff, people Hattie had come to treasure and love because they had accepted her for who she was and it had felt like a home despite it all.

'It was you who created this scheme, Your Grace. You cannot be angry about the outcome of it all,' said Hattie. To her surprise, her voice was clear and carried through the air without a tremble, despite how her heart pounded in her chest.

His body stiffened and he faced her. 'How dare you,' he began, his gaze cutting through her as if she were nothing, a mere whisper of what she knew she'd meant to him but hours ago.

'How dare *you*,' she countered before she even thought about the words. It was as if Penelope Denning was rising in her and refusing to be cut down in such a way. She approached him.

'Your staff is part of your family and so was I, no matter how brief a time it may have been. They did what the Doctor bade them do after your accident: maintain as much consistency and constancy to your world to aid in your recovery. And the world you had created was with me, a façade of a betrothed to keep the reporters at bay. When you woke with no memory, the Doctor did not know of this web of deceit, but asked for me to stay and for us to care for you until your memory returned once we told him of it. Even he agreed to be a part of this charade. What we all did was for you, Your Grace. To care for you. What happened between us was unexpected, but you cannot will it away.'

He took a step closer to her, but she did not move or flinch. The servants held their breath just as she did. 'If that is the case and not more lies, then you have done your part. I am recovered and I know who I am. And I do not *require* a betrothed any longer. Nor an uneducated and deceitful governess. *Leave*. Now.'

Every word pricked like glass shards thrust under

her skin, but she held her emotion and response in check. She gazed past him to the wall, focusing her attention on the early landscape of the estate. She sucked in a breath, set her gaze on those around him and began.

'Thank you, each and every one of you, for your care and friendship during my stay here. I am grateful for it. I will leave as His Grace commands, but I will require a carriage to take me to the stagecoach.'

'Of course, Miss Potts,' Mr Simmons replied. 'I shall tell Eddie to ready the horses.' The small hitch in his voice gave away his emotion. The rest of them gave a slight bow to her, which made her stomach drop.

Mrs Chisholm came forward and pressed a kiss to her cheek. There were no words, but the love in her gaze spoke volumes. Hattie swallowed and forced a smile and a nod. Hattie then lifted her gaze to William and held it without a falter.

Then she gave a deep bow and lowered her head. 'Your Grace,' she said before rising. 'Please give this to Millie, since I cannot say goodbye to her myself.' She extended a bulky sealed note to him that held her small, worn string bracelet with its three lavender glass beads that she had always worn about her wrist. It was Millie's now to keep her safe as it had kept Hattie safe for so many years.

Trudy and Ophelia would have agreed with Hattie's choice to gift it to the girl and would understand her decision to part with it. Her dream for independence for herself hadn't come true, but she had a new wish: Millie's happiness. She hoped if Millie wore it, her hopes and dreams would come true.

It was now what Hattie wanted most in the world.

She was unable to keep the tremor from showing as her hand remained extended towards him. He resisted for a moment, but finally took it from her. The brief brush of his fingertips against hers ignited a fresh wave of hurt and longing. She stiffened, turned and walked back to the hall to wait for the carriage. How long she stood in silence alone in that hall, she did not know, but relief and dread filled her when the carriage came into view outside the front windows, its wheels crunching the gravel on the drive. Eddie came in and gathered her bags.

'Ready, Miss Potts?' he asked.

'As ready as I'll ever be, I suppose,' she replied, fashioning her drab brown hat on her head and repositioning her matching cloak. She stepped outside and entered the open carriage. As he closed the door and sealed her within the warm snug confines of the carriage, she noted he had placed a blanket and wrapped treats from the cook on the seat beside her. The small kindness rekindled the loss she felt and she blinked back tears. As they pulled out of the drive, she reminded herself this was for the best even if her heart said otherwise.

Chapter Twenty-Four

William stripped down to his trousers, casting aside his cravat, shirt and jacket on to the barn floor. He cared little right now about propriety and what was expected of a duke. He was a man right now and a broken one at that. The cool spring air hit his bare torso and goose pimples pebbled his skin. He sucked in a breath through his teeth. Feeling cold was a luxury to the pain, anger and confusion he felt.

He groaned as he spied the barrier between him and the relief he sought. He cursed. Why could nothing be easy today? He lifted and moved aside one large bale of hay after another, so he could reach the heavy black boxing bag hanging from one of the barn beams. He hadn't used it since he was a young man frustrated with the world, which was exactly how he felt now. How many hours had he spent in here each day as a lad just trying to make sense of the world and his future within it?

It was covered in dust from lack of use, but today he would make up for lost time. He slid on the boxing gloves he had pulled from a crate nearby. He smiled, grateful his father had left this area of the barn untouched despite the many years it had been left unused.

William landed one solid blow to the bag. A puff of barn dust from the nearby hay blew in his face and he coughed, but the instant release he felt stirred a familiar feeling in him. He landed another hit and then another. Why had he allowed himself to believe he could have all he wanted? That he was building a life?

He'd been a bloody fool. Just like he'd been with Cecily. He had believed what he wanted to believe despite the truth staring back at him. Miss Potts had lied to him just as Cecily had and only wanted him for his title, his money and the lifestyle of a duchess.

He pounded the bag harder, setting into the familiar light-footed stance he'd learned at university and from his father, who had also enjoyed boxing, despite what others thought of gentlemen taking up such a sport. It had been one of the things they'd had in common, which perhaps was why his father left this area untouched.

'Did you know I would need it one day?' he chuckled, talking aloud to his father. 'I thank you,' he muttered, landing another series of punches to the bag. The repeated pull and push of his muscles were ignited and soon minutes passed. Another flood of memories of his time with Penelope, indeed Hattie, rushed to the front of his mind.

The feel of her touch along his skin and hers beneath his own made him flush as the heated desire surged through him. The moment at the ball when she'd stood at the top of the stairs, he had felt she was his future, no matter how he had tried to deny it. And her love for Millie was real. Had he always cared for her, even when she was merely Hattie Potts, governess?

He clutched the bag and leaned his forehead on the leather, panting from the exertion and confusion. Had she not truly loved him? Had he not truly loved her? Did it even matter any more? He didn't know.

'Your Grace?' a timid voice called from behind him. A familiar female voice. He stilled before turning.

'Yes, Miss Bellows?' he asked, still leaning his gloves against the bag, trying to catch his breath.

She stared at his torso, blushed and averted her eyes as she wrung her hands.

Curses.

He yanked off his gloves, rushed to grab his shirt from the floor and shrugged it on. 'My apologies,' he offered and then faced her as he attempted to right his appearance. It was then he recognised the taut drawn lines on her face and the agonised expression. She wasn't merely uncomfortable with his state of dress. He stilled. 'What is it?'

'It is Millie, Your Grace,' she began, fiddling with the strings of the apron she often wore to protect her clothing. 'I have looked everywhere, but I cannot find her. She has been most distressed about Miss Potts leaving. I thought she was hiding from me in the house, but we have turned it upside down, and…' Her voice trembled. 'I was hoping she might come to you if you called for her. I am so sorry. I did not know what else to do.'

'No, no.' He began grabbing for his cravat and jacket. 'You have done right to find me. Have the household and grounds been searched?'

'Yes, Your Grace. We have all been looking for her for over a half-hour. The groundskeepers have been alerted as well.'

His heart tightened in his chest. Now he was worried, but he would not give in to the fear churning his stomach or the dread creeping along the edges of his skin. The last time Millie had taken to hiding was right after Cecily died.

'I should have realised Miss Potts's departure would unsettle her and been more alert,' he said aloud, mostly to himself. 'Have them do a wider and more expansive search around the lake,' he told her. 'I suspect she is there.' He almost believed his own lie.

His daughter could be anywhere…or far from here. His mind took a wild turn to her running off like a vagabond or being snatched by some reporter bent on a keen story. He was being ridiculous. He reined back in his imagination.

'Yes, Your Grace,' she replied as she headed off in the opposite direction. He jogged off towards the main house, carrying his cravat and jacket in his hand.

When he reached the Manor, burst through the door, and saw the household in a flurry searching for Millie, his concern became alarm. Everyone had ceased their duties to search for her.

Mr Simmons spied him first and came to him. 'The groundsmen have expanded their search and we are turning the house upside down for her, Your Grace.'

'Thank you, Simmons. She could be anywhere. Who was the last to see her?'

'That was me, Your Grace,' Mrs Chisholm added, emerging from the parlour, moving with purpose. 'She was in quite a state. Full of tears and pointing to the drive. I believe she may have seen Miss Potts depart or realised what had happened. Miss Bellows and I soothed her until she fell asleep. When I went to gather some milk and biscuits for her for when she woke, she was gone from her rooms.'

'And no one saw her leave the house?'

She cast her gaze to the floor. 'No, Your Grace. We

have been in a bit of upheaval with all that has happened this morning.'

A loud knock at the front door sent a jolt through him, and he suppressed a curse. The last thing he needed was a visitor, unless it was someone who had found Millie.

They all went to the door. When Simmons opened it and it was only Lady Buchanan, he sighed in disappointment.

'While I am thrilled you have regained your memory, I have a bone to pick with you, Cousin. Hattie came to see me on her way to the stagecoach…' she started, full of bluster, and then her words fell away as she stared at him. 'What has happened?' she asked. 'You look dreadful.'

'Come in,' he urged, waving her inside. 'Millie has disappeared. You can help us look. Perhaps she will emerge to see her favourite aunt.'

He doubted it, but he was game to try. All he wanted was his daughter back.

'Disappeared?' she asked, shrugging off her coat and handing it to Simmons. 'Thank you,' she added as she hurried to meet William's strides as he rushed towards his study.

He paused. 'Has Eddie returned?' he called to Simmons as Daphne fell in step with him, peppering him with questions he could not process. His mind was singularly focused on finding Millie. Nothing else mattered.

Nothing.

'He has not, Your Grace.'

'The moment he returns, I want to see him, Simmons. I need to know where he dropped Miss Potts.'

Daphne stopped cold and clutched his arm, yanking him back from his whirling thoughts. 'That is what I came to speak to you about. Why have you sent her away?'

'Not here,' he said, gesturing to his study. Once within it, he closed the door and let his full frustration loose on Daphne.

'Perhaps the better question is why did you all lie to me? What of that, Cousin? I know you knew. You all knew. Yet I am the bastard for sending her away when I realised I have been duped in such a manner?'

She baulked at him and bristled. 'Yes, you are to blame. She was wonderful. She loved you and Millie. She was your match, William. The one you longed for. Do you not see it?' She approached him and clutched his hand. 'It does not matter if her name was Penelope or Hattie.'

'No union can be made of lies. You should understand that. You were married to a liar.'

She dropped his hold and immediately William regretted his words. They were harsh, cold, and the hurt registered in his cousin's glassy eyes. She blinked back the tears. 'I *do* know,' she replied, unwilling to give in to her emotion. 'I also know how rare true love and companionship is in our world. You are a fool to let standing get in your way, but perhaps you prefer being a fool rather than facing your own mistakes.'

'Daphne…' he pounded his fist on the mantel '…can we not table this for another time well after I have found Millie?'

She sighed and nodded. 'Yes. She is of the greatest importance for now. I am happy to continue railing you about your poor decision regarding Hattie later.'

A man cleared his throat at the doorway and William turned to see Eddie standing with his hands behind his back, a small flush to his cheeks from the outdoors still fresh. He gave a small nod. 'I was told you wished to see me, Your Grace?'

'Yes, yes,' he replied. 'Where did you drop Miss Potts?'

His brow furrowed in confusion. 'At the stagecoach office, Your Grace. She was waiting to purchase a ticket for a stagecoach home to Stow. Did I do wrong by dropping her there?'

'No, Eddie. We are searching for Millie. Is there any chance she stowed herself in the carriage?' He knew he was grasping at straws, but he had to ask.

'No, Your Grace. Miss Potts had sparse luggage

and, even so, I always check the driver box and holds after every trip to ensure nothing is left.' He dropped his gaze and shifted on his feet.

'But?' William prompted.

'Miss Potts left this in the squabs, Your Grace. I believe she meant it to be returned to you.' He stepped forward, pulled a flowered handkerchief from behind his back and extended his hand to William.

William hesitated at the sight of one of Penelope's—Hattie's kerchiefs. The handstitched purple violets, a signature of all she was, made his stomach flip. He braced himself and reached for it. When he opened it in his palm, her familiar sweet, floral scent almost made his knees buckle. The sight of the necklace he had given her when he had proposed, the simple heart-shaped ruby pendant necklace, almost pulled him under. The memory of her beauty that afternoon and how it had been the only thing she wore as they kissed one another and how it had shimmered against her skin sent a flash of heat and awareness through him.

It also made him feel ill.

He missed her desperately, but he could only focus on one loss at a time. He clenched his jaw, stuffed the handkerchief and necklace in his trouser pockets and looked at Eddie. 'When was the next stagecoach leaving for Stow?'

'It was set to depart at quarter past.'

They all turned to the wall clock. It was half past. Could not one thing go right? He shook his head and cursed under his breath. 'Ready a horse for me, Eddie, and send for me once he's saddled.'

'Your Grace,' he replied and rushed from the study.

'What is your plan?' Daphne asked. Her voice was quiet, but resolute.

'While you all continue to search here, I am riding to the station. If she has already left, I will follow the road to Stow and intercept her stagecoach. She may be the only one who can bring Millie back. And as much as I do not wish to leave the search here, I do not think Millie will return if I do not go and plead for Miss Potts's help—without her we may not be able to find Millie.' He had all but banished the woman from here. He felt ashamed of what he had done after all she had done for him, for Millie, for the Manor. His stomach soured.

But there was no way but forward now.

'Is that all?' Daphne asked.

'No. That isn't all, but it is all I can manage right now.'

Daphne smirked at him. 'Then that is enough. I will join Simmons in the search here.'

'And I will meet Eddie in the stables, so I lose no more time than needed. It has been some time since I have ridden so far.'

'And to think what the reporters and locals will say about this, Your Grace,' she teased.

He groaned, knowing she was right, but he couldn't think of any of that now. He needed to find Millie and if begging for the help of the woman he'd just cast out of his house and his heart was the only way to do it, he would.

Even if it cut him to the quick.

Chapter Twenty-Five

Hattie shifted on her feet, restless to get settled into the stagecoach and head out for Stow. It felt as though she had nettles under her skin the longer she waited. She ran her fingers over the beaded ridge of her reticule as she watched the poor driver attempt to stack and restack all the luggage on the top and back of the carriage.

Even though there were only four of them for the journey and all of them were, thankfully, women, there was an excess of luggage. Thank goodness her contribution to the mess was slight, otherwise she had no idea how the poor man would have managed. They were already almost an hour past the designated departure time, but the driver had been reluctant to begin the journey with empty seats, so Hattie had been forced to wait for additional travellers to arrive.

The call to adventure she had answered almost two months ago had manifested into an unexpected romance and now heartache. She missed everyone at Blithe Manor dearly. They had all filled her heart so much it now felt empty without them in it. How would she ever fill that extra space? How would she ever not feel this tight constriction in her chest and the pain of holding back her tears at the loss?

Her eyes welled and she looked down with a smile. She almost laughed. Ophelia would be clutching her hands now, telling her it would somehow all work out and Trudy would be chastising her for her romantic spirit while also counselling Hattie on how she didn't need a man for her happiness.

How she missed her dear friends. She blinked away her tears, took a deep breath and reminded herself that she was going home to them. She was not alone, nor would she ever be. Time would heal her heart. It had faced heartbreak and loss before. She would recover and be stronger than ever.

'Let us be off then, ladies!' the driver called, yanking Hattie from her woolgathering.

She smiled, waited for the others to board, then settled into the seat facing backwards next to another young woman and opposite an elderly woman with her adult daughter. Everyone smiled cordially and nodded to each other. The driver closed the door, hopped up to the driver's box behind her and clicked the reins in time with his tongue to get the horses to begin. They rocked forward and then began to pick up speed as they manoeuvred out of the yard. Soon they were on the road, jostling back and forth. It was a far cry from the smooth ride of William's fancy carriage, but she didn't mind. She was exactly where she was supposed to be…she was headed home.

The stagecoach stop disappeared and soon there was only lush green hillsides and blue sky. The horses settled into a smooth, rhythmic cadence and she sighed. Eventually, Hattie's eyelids became heavy and she allowed herself to be lulled to sleep. It would be a long journey and she might as well rest. Her mind was drifting off and all she could hear was the *clippety-clop, clippety-clop* of hooves along the dirt road. Exhaustion was overtaking her. It had been a long day and it was not even mid-afternoon.

'Stop! Stop!' a voice called off in the distance. The carriage shifted, causing Hattie's head to bump against the window.

'Ouch,' she mumbled, opening her eyes. She glanced around, trying to wake herself enough to determine what was happening.

The woman next to her pointed out the back carriage window. There was a man on horseback shouting at them and riding up to the side of the carriage. 'Reckless young man,' the older woman scoffed and shook her head. 'The young are always in such a hurry,' she added, clucking her tongue.

'Go round!' the driver shouted back, the carriage shifting slightly as he slowed a bit, to let the rider pass.

'Stop!' the man called again as he eased alongside the carriage. When his gaze turned towards them, Hattie gasped.

'William?' she said aloud, her words came out in a confused whisper.

He caught her gaze and the relief she saw as he sighed and slowed his pace was palpable.

'You know this man?' the older woman said.

'I do,' she stammered. 'Something has happened… I do not understand…' she babbled. She knocked on the top of the carriage above her. 'Driver! I know this man. Please stop!'

She heard a curse and then the driver slowed the horses to a stop. 'This will cost you extra, Miss. I have no time for stops.'

'And I will pay it,' William replied, as he dismounted. 'She is needed. Gather her belongings. Now!' His words were fierce and tight. It was unlike him to be so harsh. He pulled the carriage door open.

'Hattie, come with me,' William ordered, his gaze wild, his features taut. She recoiled into the squabs of her seat.

'Not until you tell me what has happened. It was

only a short time ago that you sent me away. Why are you here now?' she argued. 'And why should I go with you anywhere, Your Grace?'

'Your Grace?' the older woman said, eyeing William with suspicion before looking back to Hattie.

'I do not have time to explain myself. You are needed,' he said, his desperation and impatience increasing.

'I will go nowhere with you without an explanation,' she replied, lifting her chin.

'It is Millie. She is gone.'

Everything stilled around her. Buzzing filled her ears. 'When?' she asked.

'After you departed. We cannot find her and I cannot lose…' He paused, holding her gaze. 'And I cannot bear to lose her. Please. Help me find her.' His gaze bore through her, but Hattie was frozen, torn between hurt, longing and uncertainty.

The women across from her were wide-eyed and their mouths gaped open. 'That is the Duke of Wimberley,' one whispered.

His gaze did not falter, but held her own, transfixed, as if there was no one else but the two of them. 'I am sorry, Hattie. Please. Help me. She is all I have.' His voice was husky and full of emotion. He reached out his hand to her.

'Go on, lass,' the older woman said, gripping her arm gently. The touch jolted her out of her indecision.

'Yes, yes,' Hattie said. She slipped her hand into his and her body reacted, sending a tremble through her limbs, making her almost weak in the knees. He steadied her.

'Where are your belongings?' he asked, scanning the carriage.

'Leave them,' she answered. 'Let us find Millie first.'

He closed the carriage door and thrust coin in the driver's hand along with orders of some kind. Hattie took that moment to focus on the ground beneath her feet and the wind in her hair. She closed her eyes to steady herself.

Focus on Millie. Focus on Millie. All else can wait.

'Ready?' he asked. He was somehow already atop his mount. His hand was outstretched. She hadn't thought about *how* they would be getting back to Blithe Manor. The carriage pulled away slowly.

'Yes,' she lied, eyeing the single horse and how they would have to ride together.

'Just put your boot in the stirrup, take my hand and I will pull you up.'

She nibbled her lip.

'Trust me,' he said and then winced. 'Poor choice of words, perhaps, but I promise I will not let you fall.'

She said nothing, but set her boot in the stirrup, gripped his hand and allowed herself to be lifted. She settled in front of him, trying hard to maintain some distance between their bodies. Even still, she could feel the heat off his form and a delicious desire budded up in her against her will.

Curses.

He sighed. 'As much as you must detest me, you must tuck into my body as we ride. It is safer that way,' he explained. 'And less strain on the horse.'

She cringed and closed her eyes. *Focus on Millie.*

She said nothing, but settled back against him. His arm slid around her waist and pulled her gently and more firmly against him. Her body was aflame with want.

He cursed aloud from the contact. 'It will be a long ride,' he murmured. Although she shouldn't have been pleased, she felt some comfort in their shared agony.

They rode in silence for several minutes. The wind and the beginning of a soft mist of rain helped cool her desire and clarify her thoughts.

'When did you last see her, Your Grace?' she asked, trying to sound as formal as possible.

'Before you left with Eddie. Mrs Chisholm said she was most distressed to see you leave. She left Millie's room to get some milk and biscuits after she finally fell asleep. When she returned, Millie had vanished.'

'I am so sorry. I didn't know how it would upset her, but I should have,' Hattie replied. She should have known. She had been Millie once.

'Nor did I. Truth be told, I was in my own grief. Too distracted to think of anything or anyone else. It was my fault. I should have known. This happened before…'

Of course. Hattie knew the answer, but asked the question anyway. 'When your wife died?'

There was a weighty pause before he answered, 'Yes.'

'And when she disappeared then? Where did you find her?'

'She was in her mother's room, cuddled in her closet.' He paused, clearing his throat before beginning again. 'She was snuggled in with her gowns. I think she missed the smell of her.'

Hattie's chest tightened. She pressed her lips together and gathered herself before responding. 'I did something very similar when my mother died. I wrapped myself in her favourite blanket, desperate to have her back.'

His hold around her tightened. Whether it was intentional or instinctive didn't matter. She was grateful for the immediate comfort it brought. It didn't matter that she was still heartbroken and angry about how he'd treated her earlier in the day. It felt as though a lifetime had passed since then.

'I think you had become a mother to her in the time you were with us. I should have realised your departure would bring all that loss back up to the surface.'

'So should I, Your Grace. Let us each forgive ourselves for now and focus on finding her. Agreed?' she offered, pressing her forearm over his and threading her fingers through the hand that held her so firmly about the waist.

'Agreed,' he whispered against her ear. She closed her eyes, leaned into him and they travelled in silence. Soon there was only the wind on her face, the rhythmic rise and fall of their bodies against the saddle as the horse moved, and the pounding of hooves against the dirt. Minutes passed and finally the Manor came into view. They travelled up the drive quickly and Eddie rushed from the stables to receive them.

His smile was genuine and warm. 'My lady, pleased to see you back to help in the search.' His smile flattened as he greeted William. 'Still no sight of her, Your Grace, but we are all looking. Lady Buchanan has also returned with more assistance.' He nodded towards the small search party of gentlemen gathered around her with maps in hand.

Daphne turned and paused. After excusing herself from the gentlemen, she rushed over to greet Hattie and William. 'Thank goodness you are both here. We are about to split up and set out in pairs.'

'Thank you for returning with more help, Cousin,' William said, clutching her hands in his own and kissing her cheek. 'I must check in with Simmons.' He nodded to Hattie and left.

'What can I do?' Hattie asked her. 'Just tell me and I will do it,' she pleaded. All these people and still they could not find Millie? Fear threaded through Hattie's veins and she thought she might scream.

'Where do you believe she has gone?' Daphne asked her. 'You know her in a way we cannot.'

Hattie scanned the grounds, the Manor and stables. Her gaze continued past all of it to the gardens and the lake. She shrugged.

'I would hazard the lake, but William told me they had searched there first, thinking just the same, but she wasn't found.'

'Perhaps she did not wish to be found.' Daphne clutched Hattie's hands. Her eyes watered. 'My hope is that if she sees you or hears you, she will allow herself to be seen.'

'I had not thought of that,' she replied. She kissed Daphne's cheek. 'I will go now. Let us hope you are right.'

'I know I am,' she said with a wink. 'And even

though he won't admit it, he needs you, too,' she added, casting a glance to William who had his back to them.

Hattie couldn't entertain the mere thought of it, so she ignored it, lifted her skirts and tore off in a run towards the lake. Finding Millie safe and sound was all that mattered now. Her heart pounded in her chest and the distance between the drive and the lake seemed far longer than ever before. She called out as she ran. 'Millie!' She travelled further and called again, 'Millie!'

A flock of starlings startled from a bush, sending a dozen dark arrows shooting out into the air, and she skidded to a stop, gasping in surprise. She caught her breath and stood staring out at the lake which had seemed so manageable before. Now she was overwhelmed by all the places Millie could be. There were patches of high grass, trees not far off from the lake's edge, and even the shed where she and William had almost made love. All of it seemed so changed to her. Now it was a place of loss and sadness, not the haven of joy it had been the day before.

Her heart stilled. Perhaps that was exactly how Millie felt, too. The wind ruffled Hattie's hair and the once-blue sky was transforming to the grey clouds of coming rain. They needed to find her before the storm. Unlike Hattie, Millie didn't like the rain, especially thunderstorms. It reminded her of the night she'd lost her mother and the night of her father's accident.

Hattie examined the lake in small sections. The far side was the best place to hide, so she trusted her instincts and started a slow, careful search through the thick grass, mindful of any creatures hiding from the coming rain. One step after another, she continued alone. The darker the skies turned, the more worried she became. 'Millie!' she called. 'Millie!'

Still, there was no answer.

She stood, frustrated and uncertain. Then she heard it. A small, tiny quack. Then another one. It was farther down and a bit from the lake. She followed each quack and paused after each sound to make sure she was still heading towards it as the winds picked up. One rogue raindrop fell and then another. She shivered and hugged her body as the wind whipped her hair along her face.

Quack.

It was close, so Hattie picked up her pace until she reached a large oak. *Quack.* She scurried to the other side of it and spied a big open knot near the base with Millie inside it.

Quack.

'Millie!' Hattie squealed in delight.

'Miss Potts!' she said. Hattie almost didn't believe the words. Millie had spoken.

Millie's eyes widened and she climbed out of the tree, clutching a small duckling in the folds of her skirts. Hattie knelt and opened her arms, enveloping her within them. The tiny duck quacked in alarm. Millie pulled away to calm it. She cooed to it and ran her tiny fingers over its furry head.

'We have been so worried,' Hattie said, pressing a kiss to Millie's head and running a hand along her hair. 'Everyone is searching. I am relieved you are safe.'

'I am sorry,' she murmured and tucked herself under Hattie's arm. 'I—' She paused and looked past Millie.

William stood panting and out of breath, his gaze full of love and relief. 'Millie,' he said, his voice raspy and full of emotion.

'Father!' she cried and rushed to him, the tiny duck jumping from her hand and into Hattie's lap. She held its tiny trembling body against her chest. Joy consumed her. Millie was found *and* she was talking. There was no greater gift the day could have given her.

Except perhaps to be a part of this reunion…this family. For it to be real rather than the make believe it was.

William fell to his knees, gathered up his daughter in his arms and wept. Soon, Hattie gave up all efforts to quell her emotion, wrapped her arms around them both and wept, too. For she knew what she wished for would never be. It had all been a product of her fancy.

Her life was no fairy tale, but at least Millie was found and she had found her long-lost voice, too.

Chapter Twenty-Six

In the light rain, the trio of them hurried back to the estate, barely making it before the sky opened to a full-fledged downpour. Mrs Chisholm and Miss Bellows fussed over them all and soon they were all wrapped in blankets, snuggled in front of a roaring fire with mugs of steaming tea in their hands to warm them. Millie sat between Hattie and William and the ache of knowing it would never be real plagued Hattie. But there was nothing to be lost in enjoying sweet Millie and this moment, no matter how fleeting it was.

Millie yawned and leaned into Hattie. Her mug teetered in her small hands and threatened to spill over the rim. 'Let me take that, sweet girl,' she offered as she took it from her hand.

'I am glad you are back, Miss Potts,' she murmured before she drifted off to sleep.

'So am I,' William said quietly, his gaze searching hers.

She swallowed hard. 'I am glad Millie is found, but I cannot stay.'

'Why? She loves you, and I… I—'

'That is why. We cannot trust one another.' The truth pained her.

'Hattie,' he began, reaching out and touching her shoulder.

Hattie shifted Millie's weight against him, no longer able to hold her emotion. She had to leave. She could not be pulled in again by his charms and promises. They had found Millie and she would explain to her tomorrow that she had to leave and this time for good. But that she would write to her and visit if she could.

She carefully removed the blanket from her and stood.

'We will speak tomorrow and I will explain to Millie as best I can. Goodnight, Your Grace.' She gifted him a small bow and left, ignoring the sweet sound of her given name on his lips as he called out for her to stay one last time.

William sipped his tea and went through his prepared statement for Hattie as best he could. She was reasonable. She would stay.

Or at least he hoped she would.

She was what he had always wanted and she was right. He'd loved her until he'd feared her lies, her rank and lack of social standing. His father would be ashamed of what he'd done. But didn't he also deserve a bit of leniency? He'd lost his memory. He'd been lied to. He'd been confused.

But he'd also been cruel. Like Cecily. He shivered at the comparison despite its accuracy. It was then he heard voices outside.

'I have spoken to Millie, Mrs Chisholm. All I need do is speak to His Grace. Is he about?'

'Yes, Miss Potts. In his study.'

William stacked his correspondence neatly, stood and straightened his cravat and jacket, preparing to offer an apology and his heart to Hattie. Yesterday showed him that she wasn't ever after his money or standing, but cared deeply for his daughter and he hoped she still cared…for him. Daphne was right. They were a match and, as unintended as it might have been, he had fallen for his governess.

She entered the study and the sight of her in her simple navy day dress, one that he had purchased for her role as Lady Penelope Denning, reminded him of the ease they had once had with one another, starting their days together in his study, when he'd believed she was his betrothed. She stood before him and smiled.

How he hoped she would agree to become his betrothed for real now.

'I am off, Your Grace. I spoke with Millie, so she understands. There should be no more running away.'

Her words had tumbled out before he'd even uttered a syllable of his pretty speech.

He stood frozen, his mouth hanging open. He must look like a dolt.

'Your Grace?' she asked, her brow creasing.

'You are leaving?' he asked, still confused. He tried to remember the words he had crafted, but every syllable fled his mind. His thoughts were blank parchment.

'Yes,' she replied with a nod. 'I do not wish to confuse Millie further. You are well and I am destined to be Miss Hattie Potts once more.'

'And you are fine with being Miss Hattie Potts?' he asked.

'Why would I not be?' she asked, pulling back her shoulders. 'I am capable and I deserve a happy life. You have taught me that.'

'I have?' he asked, uncertain where this was headed.

'Yes, Your Grace. I am lovable, beautiful and will be loved by a man that believes in me and loves me as I am, no matter my birth or standing.'

'But that man is me, Hattie. I love you. I know you are beautiful and I believe in all that you are and all you can be.' He sighed and smiled. Some of his pretty speech had come back to him after all. He reached for her hand.

She pulled away, but met his gaze. 'You do not truly

know *me*, Hattie Potts, and I do not trust you after all that has happened.'

He baulked. 'I do not understand. You do not trust me?' He'd lost the thread once more.

She crossed her arms against her chest. 'I am leaving. I do not trust you. It is as simple as that,' Hattie replied.

'You—' he scoffed, hurt and anger rose in him. '*You* don't trust *me*?' he accused, pointing a finger to his chest. 'I was not the one who lied to you.'

'No. You did lie to me,' she countered, closing the space between them. 'You made me believe that you cared for me, but you were like all the rest of them.'

He shook his head confused. 'All of who?'

'Men of means. You make promises, pretend you love a woman and then disappear when it suits. You…' she stammered and then continued. 'You are like that duck. You find a mate and then abandon the mother to care for the product of your coupling without a thought.'

'Duck? What bloody duck? What are you carrying on about…?' He stilled and stared at her. 'Wait… Are you with child?'

She groaned and suppressed the urge to stomp her foot. 'No, I am not with child. We did not even consummate anything between us, if you remember,' she stammered. 'I am hurt and trying to make a point. You betrayed me, William. I believed you cared for me,' she said, clutching her chest. 'You made me believe that you loved me for me, not some title or promise of standing. But you didn't. The moment you realised I was not Lady Penelope, just an orphan, just Miss Hattie Potts with no title or rank, you abandoned me, just like—'

She cut herself off, swallowing the next words. She hadn't meant to go so far.

'Just like what?' he demanded, clutching her shoulders.

She squirmed in his hold, trying to escape, yet desperate to be held, needing comfort. Tears streamed down her cheeks. The anger in his face softened into concern, which made all the fight drain from her.

'Like what?' he said softly.

'Like my father,' she sniffed. 'I never knew him.'

His hands fell away from her arms. 'Why not?'

'Because he didn't want me,' she said louder, wiping at her tears, the anger welling up in her once more. 'I was a bastard. A product of his pleasure. Nothing more. Once my mother became pregnant, he abandoned her and me in the process. Years later she died of a broken heart. Crushed from being thrown away as though she was nothing.'

He cursed, running a hand through his hair. 'That

isn't me, Hattie. I would never abandon you in such a way…' he began.

'No, William,' she hiccupped. 'That's what you don't understand. You are. You already did.'

Chapter Twenty-Seven

'Hattie, are you sure about this?' Ophelia asked, as she and Trudy followed Hattie to the line that would take her to Mr Sneed to purchase her ticket.

'I am positive. It will be a fine adventure and once I am settled, I shall send word for you both to join me. Bath will be beautiful and the family seems lovely. His Grace was kind to send them a reference for me.'

'It was the least he could do,' Trudy muttered under her breath.

Hattie smiled at her loyalty. 'He did not have to, especially after how we parted.'

'Are you sure you've done the right thing in leaving him?' Ophelia asked.

Hattie shrugged. 'He let me go just as I let him go. We merely let go of one another, I suppose.' She ignored the prick in her chest at the lie she told herself. She had thought a thousand times about how things could have been different. If she hadn't told him of her birthright or shoved him away. If she hadn't been so proud. He said he loved her as she was, but she just couldn't believe him. It was far easier to believe his rejection than that he wanted her as she was…as orphan Hattie Potts. But she couldn't deny she missed him. That she wished she had behaved differently at that moment. That she had dared risk trying to make things work between them. That she had given them a chance.

The queue moved forward and Hattie smiled, knowing she had enough in her reticule to pay for her journey this time. Gaining confidence, she stepped forward and set the coins from her reticule on the counter. It did not matter now. She was on to another adventure.

'A ticket to Bath on the next stagecoach, please, Mr Sneed.'

Mr Sneed shuffled through some papers and then glanced back at her.

'No need, Miss Potts,' he answered behind the counter. Without looking at her, he pushed the coins back towards her.

'Is it not enough?' she stammered in lowered tones, her cheeks heating. Surely she hadn't underestimated the expense. She leaned back to glance up at the time bill and cost on the placard above him.

'I only wish to travel by stagecoach,' she said. 'It is enough according to your sign. Is it full?'

'Your transport has already been paid for,' Mr Sneed answered, leaning closer with a wry smile. 'No stage-coach for you, Miss,' he replied with a wink. 'Exciting opportunity awaits you. Just beyond that stagecoach there.' He pointed behind her. She turned as a stage-coach pulled away to see the most glorious sight she'd ever seen.

The large, emblazoned gold crest of William's black carriage came into view and reflected in the morning sunlight. Two chestnut-brown horses were bridled and ready, nibbling on the patchy grass beneath them. Their manes were braided with flowers, purple violets by the look of them, and her heart lurched in her chest. Eddie sat on the box seat with his hat resting beside him as he held the reins loosely in one hand and ate a red apple with the other. He smiled and gave her a wink.

The carriage door opened, and out stepped William Sutherland, Duke of Wimberley. He was dressed in the finest of dark trousers with a matching purple waistcoat and jacket. He carried a single red rose and wrapped box. Millie hopped out behind him and rushed to her. The crowd parted between them and Hattie could scarcely breathe as they walked towards her. Millie crashed into her and wrapped her arms around Hattie's legs. Hattie stooped to hug her.

'Please say yes,' the little girl whispered in her ear.

Before Hattie could ask more, Millie pulled back and ran behind her father.

'William,' Hattie said, breathless as she rose to standing. The sight of him, the surprise, all of it undid her. Her heart hammered in her chest. 'What are you doing here?' she asked.

'I heard you were leaving and I simply could not let you leave without trying again.' The warmth in his gaze and hope in his smile unsettled her. He knelt before her and the crowd gasped. 'Without telling you that I love you and wish to spend the rest of my life getting to know all there is to know about you, Miss Hattie Potts, if you will have me. Will you marry me?'

'But I am not…' she countered.

'Not what?' he asked.

'The usual duchess. I can offer you no lineage or fine manners. If anything, marrying me will ruin you and I cannot have that.' She laid out all her fears. Her words came out as a trembly mess. A tear slid down her cheek.

He rose to stand with her. 'You offer me more than I could have ever asked for. You cared for me when I had lost everything, kept up a lie for my well-being and loved me and my daughter with all your heart. That is more than I could have ever hoped for in a betrothed.'

'Even if it was a fake one?' she laughed.

'Especially since it was a fake one.' He cupped her cheek. 'The question is if you can trust me.'

Her cheeks heated and her gaze dropped. 'That was unfair of me to say before. I have had some time to think about it and I was punishing you for my past. For a decision my father and others made. I can trust you. I do trust you. Can you trust me?'

'With all I am,' he replied, his timbre deep.

'Then I accept. I will be your betrothed, for real this time.'

He smiled and kissed her, letting the reporters get their gossip and the crowd their romance. She laughed and nestled into his side.

The Duke of Wimberley had finally found a wife.

Epilogue

Late August 1814

'Shall I tell you a story?' William began in a low husky rumble matching the mood of the late-summer evening thunderstorm brewing outside. Another flash of lightning cast a shadow through the sheets they had strewn about the furniture in his study to create the fort the three of them hid under in a sea of lush pillows and blankets.

Millie laughed aloud. 'Yes, Father!' she exclaimed clapping her hands together before crawling into Hattie's lap, carefully gliding her small hand over the slight growing bump of the child she carried. *Their child.* He leaned over and pressed a kiss to Millie's head before meeting Hattie's gaze. Her eyes were glistening, the unshed tears matching the tightness in his chest.

This was more than he could have ever dreamed of. Being here with his daughter and new wife, joyful, healthy, and with a new baby on the way. Hattie squeezed his hand and he brought it to his lips and kissed it reverently. He was a grateful man with a grateful and overflowing heart.

'Once upon a time,' he began, pulling Hattie closer to his side, so they were all cuddled together.

Hattie chuckled. 'Ah, you *are* a fan of the Brothers Grimm.'

'I am. It was on my nightstand when I awoke after my accident, so I could not help but read it, and now my mind is full of tales although I have taken a few liberties with this particular story.'

'How so?' Hattie asked.

Millie laughed and tugged on his rolled-up shirt sleeves. 'More, more.'

'Once upon a time there was a duke,' he continued. 'A lonely, rather set-in-his-ways man, who lived alone with his daughter in a far-off manor. He had given up on love and hope, but then one day a beautiful woman arrived. She was a governess for his daughter, but turned out to be far more…'

* * * * *

Whilst you wait for the next instalment in
Jeanine Englert's Regency Fairytales miniseries,
why not check out her
Secrets of Clan Cameron miniseries

A Laird without a Past
The Lady's Proposal for the Laird
A Highlander to Protect Her

And why not pick up her
Falling for a Stewart miniseries

Eloping with the Laird
The Lost Laird from Her Past
Conveniently Wed to the Laird

MILLS & BOON®

Coming next month

THE MAID'S MASQUERADE
Catherine Tinley

Book 1 in **The Heiress Switch** series

'Why will you never speak of your mother, or our betrothal?' he asked, and her heart was sore at the sincerity in his eyes. 'You must know I wish you to be my wife.'

Marguerite could not help it; she allowed her eyes to show the feelings she must never give voice to.

'Sophia!' he cried, moving to kiss her, but she recoiled, his use of Sophia's name feeling like a slap in the face to Marguerite. 'What is it?' He paused, ever the gentleman.

'No. I—I must not! I am so sorry for leading you to believe…for even suggesting that I might… I cannot!'

'But why?' He took her hands. 'Can you not be honest with me?'

She winced. Honesty was the one gift she was not free to give.

'I have come to know and admire you very well these past weeks,' she began carefully, weighing every word. 'But there are things…there are matters which I am not free to discuss, my lord.'

'You should call me Benedict,' he offered, confusion clear in his expression, but she shook her head.

‘It would not be right,’ she said firmly. A servant should never, ever make use of the intimate name of a peer of the realm.

‘You are a puzzle, Miss Van Bergen!’ He ran a hand through his hair. ‘A puzzle, and a damn—a *dashed*—paradox, and I know not what to make of you!’

His anger was clear, and suddenly it occurred to her that his own recovery from her betrayal might be expedited if she gave him a disgust of her. So, hardening her tone and lifting her chin, she shrugged. ‘It is very simple, my lord. I have done what I needed to do in the pursuit of my own interests.’

COMING SOON!

We really hope you enjoyed reading this book.
If you're looking for more romance
be sure to head to the shops when
new books are available on

Thursday 20th November

To see which titles are coming soon, please visit

millsandboon.co.uk/nextmonth